THE NATURAL ORDER

Ursula Bentley was born in England, has travelled extensively in Europe and the United States, and has worked as a stapling-machine operator, cosmetics salesperson, teacher and domestic help – not necessarily in that order. She now lives in Switzerland.

Following the publication of THE NATURAL ORDER, she was selected by the Book Marketing Council as one of the twenty Best of Young British Writers for 1983.

Ursula Bentley

THE NATURAL ORDER

An Arena Book
Published by Arrow Books Limited
17-21 Conway Street, London W1P 6JD

An imprint of the Hutchinson Publishing Group

London Melbourne Sydney Auckland
Johannesburg and agencies throughout the world

First published by Secker & Warburg 1982
Arena edition 1983
© Ursula Bentley 1982

Made and printed in Great Britain
by The Guernsey Press Co Ltd
Guernsey C.I.

ISBN 0 09 930810 X

TO FRANCES AND MAGGIE

READER, I was born in Kingston Hospital (Alight at Norbiton) and brought up in Worcester Park. It follows that well into adolescence my close friends – equally disadvantaged – and I were never without the bitter taste of not having been one of the Brontë sisters. Our temperaments seemed to dictate it: some terrible failure of astral conjunctions must have occurred to put us down in Kingston in the 1950s rather than Yorkshire in the 1840s. In a recent biography of Charlotte Ms Margot Peters has written, "What twentieth-century city dweller would not like to undergo the torments of solitude in a moorland village?" I knew torment all right – but the torment of giving one's address as 53 Forsythe Gardens, the torment of a complete dearth of real torment.

Of the three of us Damaris was the Emily figure, the intellectual giant, so to speak. I think of Emily as wasted with moral intensity, capable alike of breaking glass with the sheer energy of her genius, or tossing off a verse on mortality with one hand and humping wholewheat bread around the kitchen with the other. Damaris is the sort of person who feels pangs of loss when a leaf falls, and who spends long hours seeing the skull beneath the skin. Damaris was musical and had no mother.

Reader, I was Charlotte. That is, several inches shorter than Damaris, my body hardly robust enough to support the Gothic passions that frequently wracked it, given to performing sado-masochistic historical dramas in front of the dressing-table mirror, and yet determined from a young age to venture out into the world and take it full on the sensibilities. Picture me trembling with technicolored tragic imaginings in my boxy bedroom with

1

the candlewick bedspread, the current fantasy of voluptuous cruelty among royal persons slowly giving way to the bay window with the Terylene net curtains, and through it to row upon row of other bay windows and other Terylene curtains.

Anne was Anne. She had no specific creative thrust, rather what one might call a genius for love. At the height of our Brontë-mania we were fond of saying things like, "Anne's entry into a room is a signal for discord to quit it." She had the same effect on people as a dose of Valium or *The Sound of Music*. At the age of nine or ten she had a painting in a local authority exhibition, which to her family promised notoriety in later life, but she was burnt-out at twelve and, quite frankly, the most we hoped for Anne was a husband from the professional classes and translation to Carshalton Beeches or Ripley, where she would be set off to the best advantage.

Another thing we shared with our spiritual predecessors was an allegiance to each other before all manner of folk. Our girls-only school had provided a fertile ground for intimacy and, more specifically, a large, unlit storage room off the gym, where vaulting-horses, landing mats and tennis rackets were kept. All our break-times, summer and winter, were spent in here, under the blind eye of the gym mistress who was hoping we would turn out to be Lesbians, like her, and who thought we were beautiful and different.

No subject was unexplored in those too short hours in the storage room: politics, religion, greenhouse cultivation, ambition, incest, the Beatles, open-cast mining, package tours, the story of the wheel, choux pastry – anything, everything. And because we talked about it, however mundane the subject, there was always a thrill of heightened awareness in the air with the whiff of stale sweat and perished rubber. Sex? Yes, we discussed sex, but once we had finally decided what went where the subject palled. As we grew into adolescence we, at least Anne and I, went out with the odd humanoid from the boys' school, but as we were not satisfied with anything less than Heathcliff and Rochester – and possibly Mr Darcy's income – rolled into one, the affairs were short-lived. The best thing about "dating" was that it provided grist for the mill of our intimacy. Talking about these creatures was always more pleasant than talking to them.

After leaving school we clung to each other more than ever, as we discovered a world where the rarified emotional bond we

2

shared was as passé as liberty-bodices, and raised as many eye-brows. It was hard to believe that even in marriage one could re-create the relaxation of being with someone to whom one could say things almost too private to say to oneself.

Separated geographically, we tended to mope and work. Damaris went to the Northern College of Music in Manchester, from where she wrote that a gross and disordered exterior – meaning Manchester – can conceal much of beauty and value. I ended up doing a General Arts degree at a little-known university in the Midlands. So little-known, in fact, that its very existence was questioned whenever I mentioned it. In a sense Anne was more fortunate. Her gifts being of an intense, but general, nature, life in general seemed to satisfy her, so she took a secretarial course.

After further education came the ordeal of hawking ourselves in the marketplace. Unemployment was rife in the South-East at that time and although Anne was "lucky" enough to get a job in the office of an agricultural machinery firm, I could find nothing.

But it appeared that there was a shortage of Catholic male teachers in the North, and Damaris was hired to teach at The Blessed Ambrose Carstairs Grammar School for Boys in the urban hinterland of Manchester.

I heard the news with mixed feelings. Certainly it was relief to know that Damaris had found employment and could stop living on parsnips, but I was tortured by the idea of her having to teach piano to a few, and notation to many, sweaty adolescents. What blows her private, passionate and sensitive nature would receive in such circumstances I could not know, though my imagination forked over the possibilities relentlessly.

At this time I would often meet Anne after work at the office in Wandsworth and we would go up to town for a plate of egg and chips and a foreign film classic. Damaris wrote to us alternately, knowing that we would show each other the letters.

How naïve it all sounds now! How naïve it actually was.

Night after night we would walk the streets around Leicester Square, arm in arm, speculating on the sheer awfulness of Damaris' existence and endlessly quoting from her descriptions of the school and its contents. I know now that underpinning my sympathy for Damaris, was a feeling of some satisfaction that she was having problems: I was simply jealous because she had got a job first. This became clear with the subtle change of attitude I experienced

3

towards The Blessed Ambrose Carstairs School on hearing that they needed more female staff. The Catholic male teacher seemed to be a vulnerable caste; the junior English master had fallen into the Mersey after a drunken evening of war games with the sixth form, and the search was on for a replacement. It was the middle of term. Damaris suggested to the Headmaster that I would be a suitable choice, if temporary, and in due course she suggested it to me.

I cannot deny that I was seduced by the idea of my own pay-slip, the status of a job in a jobless world, the opportunity to try my intellectual mettle in whatever sordid surroundings. I began to re-interpret Damaris' letters more positively.

Anne was happy for me, but she could not hide her gloom at the prospect of being alone in London while Damaris and I were together in Manchester.

Damaris met me at Piccadilly Station. She stood back from the bobbing cluster of friends and relatives at the ticket barrier and did not wave. I felt as nervous of seeing her again as if she had been a lover and was consequently mortified at my ungainly progress up the platform, a heavy suitcase in either hand, hold-alls and vanity case dangling uncontrolled from everywhere else. There was an awkward moment as we stood finally face to face while I divested myself of enough baggage to embrace her. She seemed taller than ever in her long black cloak with its Sutton Hoo clasp, which lightly nicked my chin as we kissed. She held me at arm's length, trying to decide which of my eyes to peer into, while I sniffed at her aura of Pears Soap and warm wool.

"Good journey? You look splendid, Carlo."

My name is Carol, but Damaris had decided that it bore too many echoes of Worcester Park and none of my real quality.

"So do you. Like the young Tchaikovsky. Where did you get the cloak?"

"Tchaikovsky had a beard. Don't try and deflect my compliments, you know it annoys me. It is liberating to see you again." Once more I was kissed on both cheeks. "Come on, I'll carry these cases. Gott in Himmel! They're heavy. What have you brought – twenty years of the *Readers Digest*?"

"Forty." Once, in Savanarola-like mood, I had led a campaign to find and destroy *Readers Digests*.

"It's not far. We can catch the bus."

4

"Let's take a taxi this once. Muriel gave me ten pounds." Muriel was my stepmother, and the gift had had the air of a freight charge, to my mind. I did not like my stepmother, partly because I could find no objections to her other than relentless good cheer, and a penchant for wearing lurex jumpers at ten o'clock in the morning.

"Taxis are too expensive," said Damaris. "You'll need every penny for the gas meter. Honestly, it's not far."

Damaris was not the sort of person with whom one argued about taxis. She was already impatient with the subject, so I meekly followed her down the long ramp from the station, turning my eyes from the happy faces in taxis that roared down the ramp in a constant stream.

"We're right in the centre of town at the moment," said Damaris over her shoulder and through a thick wadge of red hair that had blown across her mouth, "but I'm afraid I can't say that you'll have seen the worst."

"Where's that?"

"Rusholme. Where we live. I'm used to it now, as I've been there since college, but I'm afraid it will be your first brush with squalor."

"Who cares? I could do with some honest filth in my life."

"Good girl." Damaris strode manfully ahead. I thrilled to her approval. The fact was, one could not be comfortable with Damaris for long if one stepped outside the bounds of her probity.

At the time of my arrival in Manchester, the city's buildings were still charred with two hundred years of industrial soot. When cleaning was undertaken at last, Mancunians were amazed to find that the stones were hewn, not from high-grade obsidian, but from sandstone of a delicate marzipan colour. But to me the transformation robbed the city of much of its identity and power to stir; like a miner after his bath, its connotations were no longer unique. It should have stayed as I saw it on that late October day, black and faintly menacing. Already skyscrapers and shopping plazas covered in lavatory tiles had appeared like blisters in the black skin, but they did not affect the impression that the whole city had been raised in a few weeks at some point in the industrial boom of the last century. The city centre is dominated by pillared monuments to civic pride; beyond stretch the squalid terraced houses of the labouring poor, whose ill-rewarded sweat provided the wealth that raised them. What remained of the gracious suburbs of the same period were in the process of being bulldozed to make way for the head offices of insurance companies, high-rise council slums and halls of residence for trainee hotel managers.

At least this was how Damaris put it to me as we waited for the bus, but the short journey put flesh on her theory. It seemed that there were suburbs such as I would recognize, but I would never see them as the commute to school lay only through the city.

Damaris snorted. "It will be the Childrens' Tower for us," she said. "You'll get up in the morning, go to work, come home and go to bed and never see the sun, never leave the prison."

My heart dropped heavily onto the pavement and clunked into the gutter.

Sitting on the crowded bus, for the most part in silence, I began to apprehend, dimly, the agitation of the working classes as a thrill in the blood, in a way that is unthinkable in Worcester Park.

"You must read Engels on nineteenth-century Manchester," said Damaris. "Everybody should."

"Why? This is twentieth-century Manchester."

"Because the people's sense of injustice and exploitation is alive and well. They may not know it consciously, but it's knitted into the bone. It's in the stones of the buildings, in the names of the streets."

"' – and think it foul scorn that Parma or Spain or any Prince of Europe, should dare to invade the borders of my realm.' You're taking it all very much to heart, aren't you? I didn't know you were interested in politics."

"Not in politics. In people. It comes to the same thing up here. It's partly the school. They're all dedicated socialists there. The human ones, anyway."

"Even the boys?"

"You wouldn't joke about it if you could see some of the conditions they live in. You and I wouldn't do it to an animal. Football hooliganism is no mystery to me now. Most of them are in my class."

"Poor Damaris. How do you cope? I felt your letters weren't telling the whole story. Are they absolute pigs? What do you do with them?"

"Turn the gramophone up. It drowns the noise if things get

6

really bad. I gave up teaching notation and stuff weeks ago, except to the first class. It's not worth it. I just sling some Wagner at them and grit my teeth."

I was dumb, trying to translate this kind of experience into terms of metonymy and metaphor, prose style, punctuation and paragraphs, which would be my lot.

"Don't have children," she added.

The bus stopped opposite the students' union at the University, a grey building with many windows, around which swilled crowds of scruffy young persons. A gang of urchins played on the steps and took turns at assaulting passers-by.

Damaris suddenly sat up and peered through the window at someone in the bus queue. She leaned right across me to get a better look, her eyelashes fluttering against my nose.

"That's funny. What are they doing here? Perhaps they've been to the museum."

"Who?"

Damaris' pale, freckled skin had taken on a slight flush. "Oh, just some boys from school." She sat back as the bus moved off.

"Where? I'd like to see them."

"It doesn't matter. Don't stare." She yanked at my arm to stop me doing so. "You'll see them all soon enough."

We were silent for the rest of the journey. Damaris was in a brown study, and my heart was too full and my stomach too empty for idle chat.

The stop where we got off the bus was opposite a disused cinema, covered in peeling posters. Damaris led the way through a maze of identical streets of two-storeyed terraced red brick houses flush with the pavement. The evening was drawing in. The serried ranks of dismal brick, wisps of filthy urban fog hovering round the street lamps, the weight of the luggage, increasing cold and the prospect before me suddenly brought a gulp of regret for Muriel's Ideal Home sitting-room and the benison of hot water. But I knew that Damaris would be watching for my reaction to the flat, and my anxiety not to disgrace myself in her eyes stiffened me just enough not to cry.

Damaris stopped in front of a lilac door in which someone had kicked a hole near the bottom.

"Is that for the cat?" I said, trying to sound chirpy.

"Previous tenant," she explained. We went in.

7

The tiny house had been partitioned inside, so that anyone entering almost fell up the narrow stairs, even if it was their wish to enter 52A, whose door was at the bottom of the stairs, to the left. At the time of conversion everything had been painted white, providing a blank canvas for smut, snots and graffiti. Upstairs was a small landing, at the front a sitting-room, at the back a bedroom and in between a bathroom and kitchen, both of submarine compactness and painted bile green.

"We can either have a room each or share the bedroom. There's a double bed. It's up to you," said Damaris.

I inspected the sitting-room. A black plastic three-piece suite, gas fire and bulbous-legged table were prominent. There was a double window with white fibreglass curtains patterned with giant purple flora. The bedroom sported a chest of drawers and wardrobe in unpainted plywood, and a double bed covered with a washed-out blue candlewick bedspread, and a yellow plastic laundry basket.

"We'd better leave it as it is for the moment," I said, sensing that change would imply permanence. I could not, as yet, envisage calling this walled area home. "Do you mind sharing to start with?"

"Not a bit. You hate it, don't you?"

"No." I avoided her eye, searching for something I could praise. "It's very – Manchester." Damaris smiled and hugged her cloak around her. "All right, I hate it. But it's ours."

"That's what I hoped you'd say. Isn't it funny, living together at last. There are so many things I don't know about you. Like how often you wash your hair, and what kind of knickers you wear."

"You'll make me self-conscious. I hope you're not going to stare at me when I undress."

"I don't know. Perhaps I will. Would it bother you? You see, that's something else I don't know. Come on, we can't stand on the landing all night. I'll put some music on and we'll make a cup of tea. I've even got some booze – the bloke downstairs gave me a bottle of Cointreau he brought back from Ibiza. I'll put some in the tea. Why don't you unpack?"

She strode off into the sitting-room, and soon the flat, if not the whole street, was filled with the street songs of Carl Orff. It was a concession to my modest musical taste, I knew, and was suitably touched. Frankly I would rather have had the six o'clock news: BBC news readers have the same effect on me as brandy and hot milk. But Damaris had no radio and I would have felt like a traitor tuning in surreptitiously to my own.

I took my case into the bedroom and unpacked some photographs of my father, and of the three of us, Damaris, Anne and me, taken by Anne's brother at a family wedding. The photo captured us in sparkling mood, champagne glasses aloft, picture hats at an alluring tilt, mouths immortally open in feeble protest at the camera. I liked the photo, for we seemed to be raising our glasses to youth, ourselves and the future, none of which were exhausted yet. I expected resistance from Damaris over putting it on display. The past had no interest for her, therefore to capture fragments of it on celluloid and exhibit them under glass earned the same disapproval as doing the same thing to butterflies. But I had always had that photograph, and one of my real mother, with me, and I was feeling vulnerable to rebel homemaking instincts and would put up a fight over it if necessary. No doubt I would also descend to buying scatter cushions and Mucha posters before the mood was spent: meanwhile I put the photos on the chest of drawers, unpacked my books and started taking them through into the sitting-room.

Damaris was busy in the kitchen. The record finished and I turned it over. Steam, thick with the smell of fried peppers, pasta and year-old bacon fat, seeped through the flat in a friendly way.

"Want any help?" I yelled, knowing the answer.

"No."

Damaris favoured a heroic style of cookery, in which the ingredients were dispatched without quarter and with no concessions to pleas for special treatment. Vegetables were cooked in the skin, meat slammed in a naked dish in the oven, everything else burnt in the frying pan. Her meals could hardly be faulted on nutritional grounds but they lacked allure. Aesthetics and food had nothing in common for her. My joyful murmurings when the food appeared were therefore pure hypocrisy.

But there was a dumpy, re-cycled candle on the table, and some specially purchased paper napkins, printed with slightly unseasonable poinsettias, stuffed into chunky Woolworth's tumblers. I dared not comment on these – for Damaris – refinements, but for that very reason was more deeply touched, knowing the effort they represented for someone who when alone ate her food standing up in the kitchen. She put in front of me a plate of macaroni, boiled carrots, fried peppers and onions, deluged with

9

coarsely-grated mousetrap, for protein. The pile of cheese was decorated with a few sagging tufts of parsley. They spoke to me movingly of Damaris' affection and, after the tension of the day, almost unmanned me.

"What's the matter? Do you want to sneeze?"

"No. Cry."

"Oh Christ. Don't. Here, have some wine. It's only dago muck, but it'll dry you out."

"Thanks."

"I suppose you forgot what my cooking is like."

I laughed. "Cheers." We tried the wine. It dissolved a few teeth in passing and brought tears of a different kind to my eyes, but a couple of swigs were enough to take the edge off my nerves.

"Look," said Damaris, "I'm being crass, aren't I? I'm sorry. It's just hard to start talking again right off, isn't it?"

"Yes. It's funny, but I feel a bit shy with you. I suppose that's what you mean. I'm glad you brought it up. We should be quite frank – always."

"We haven't seen each other for so long we don't quite know where to start, that's the trouble. And you're probably nervous about the job."

"I am. You seem so ... settled-in, too. It's a bit intimidating, in a way."

"Well, you can ignore my blustering self-confidence. It's all sham. I had diarrhoea all afternoon I was so excited about seeing you."

"Really?" I looked at her shyly, trying to see her blank solemnity as excitement. She held her glass in both hands, her elbows on the table, her large breasts laid on the edge. The chiaroscuro effect of the candlelight softened the scruffiness of her long, bushy red hair and the unhealthy pallor of her skin into the solid, serene female of a Rubens painting. Damaris' looks were out of place in modern times. In daylight, and skirts and jumpers, she could look like a Henry Moore sculpture brought to life, for she had inherited the piano's legs along with her mother's lovely arms. But in this flickering golden light the strength of her features, informed by unmistakable intelligence and sensitivity, was simply beautiful, the apotheosis of womanly, as opposed to feminine, mystique. We smiled at each other and ploughed into the food.

"Yes, I am nervous," I said. "Your remarks about the school

haven't helped. We're not even sure they'll take me, are we?"

"Don't worry about that. The Head's a pushover. He couldn't organize a bunfight. He was just relieved to have the problem solved. Some of the parents made a bit of a stink about the accident – said the bloke was an alcoholic and should never have been left in charge of their spotty offspring in the first place. All of which is probably true. However, none of the boys has died of their injuries – worse luck – so the fuss has almost died down."

"Had he taken them out drinking?"

"Not out. They used to play these stupid war games in the geography room on Friday nights and he'd supply the beer. Then there was a very hot spell at the end of September and one night they went skinny-dipping in the Mersey. Which is just about an open sewer so they must have been drunk. Anyway, Fallowfield had a heart attack, probably."

"Was he a poof?"

"What?"

"You know – a homosexual?"

"Good Lord, how should I know? Why?"

"I can't imagine a bunch of sweaty sixth-form boys having any charms for a normal person – after 5 o'clock, I mean."

Damaris speared a piece of macaroni thoughtfully. "It's possible. Listen, perhaps I shouldn't give you too black a picture of the inmates. There are one or two who seem almost human – whom one can imagine having a mother and father and their own little bed at night. And there's at least one who is a Joy to Teach. There's hot competition for him in the staff room, I can tell you. The courses he's in are parcelled out like water in the desert."

"Was he at the bus stop this afternoon?"

"What? Who?"

"The Joy to Teach. There was a boy who caught your attention."

"Oh – really? Yes, that was him. And his sidekick. They always have sidekicks, don't they? Those favoured by the gods. To jack up their status with men, I suppose. Ketchup? I don't compete for Shackleton's attention. It's not necessary. The boy's a genius. He knows the time and place for demanding what one can give him."

I had a vision of the boy, Shackleton, enthroned in a soundproof chamber, idly pressing buttons to summon the teacher of his choice. "What a strange way you have of describing him. Like the Child Jesus. I got the impression your attitude to the boys was one of unrelieved contempt."

Damaris assumed her snowy owl look. "How's Anne?" she said.

"Eh? Oh – depressed. I hated leaving her. There are lots of undernourished young men in her office, waiting to snaffle up her free time."

"Don't despair. I have a plan."

"Really? What?"

Her expression softened. "Don't bank on it, but I was rather encouraged by how easy it was to get Brother Bas to hire you. It's on the grapevine that one of the secretaries is leaving next month – nobody's saying why, but it's my opinion she's pregnant. Obviously, coming straight after the drowning débâcle it's got to be kept as quiet as possible – it might look as if there was no one in charge of the place. So if I can discreetly suggest that I have another friend with outstanding secretarial skills I bet he'd have her like a shot. Saves advertising, you see, which could raise questions in the public mind."

"How marvellous! But how likely is it, really?"

"We'll have to see. It would be perfect, wouldn't it? The three of us together. We'd have to get another place, of course, but that's no problem. With three incomes. We might even be able to rent a little cottage, or something. Get nearer the school."

"Oh Damaris – a parsonage, perhaps! I can hardly believe this. Shall we write and tell her?"

"Hold on a bit. It's all speculation at the moment. There may be specifications for the job which Anne doesn't meet."

"That's true." We were in fact rather sensitive about the extent of Anne's marketable skills.

"Anyway, have a good look at the secretary tomorrow and see if you agree with the diagnosis. You're the one with biology 'O' level, after all."

One of the reasons I loved Damaris was for her powers of intuition, and her willingness to use it for our benefit without obliging us to humble ourselves in confession first.

In the early hours of the next morning I lay sleepless in the lumpen bed, prey to the apprehensions about the day ahead which had been dissipated by the jollifications of reunion the night before. Even were I to make a favourable impression on the headmaster – and my experience of working monks was too limited to give me confidence in this area – there followed the prospect of being thrown into a classroom, and single combat, with thirty or more scions of Manchester's slum-clearance programme, boys who spent their leisure time ripping out telephone booths and slashing the cheeks of rival football fans. Raised on suburban platitudes as I was, the existence of such forms of life was known to me, but a head-on collision with large groups of them – not once, but several times, a day – had not been a contingency with which my upbringing had dealt. It was not even as if I were expected to teach them metalwork or botany, something yielding itself to systematic analysis. The inculcation of linguistic skills and literary appreciation was a much more ephemeral task, for to emphasize the factual at the expense of the intuitive was to kill the thing one loved, at least in unformed minds. The suspicion was strong, almost morbid by now, that the boys of The Blessed Ambrose Carstairs Grammar School would be as gentle of fine sentiments beautifully expressed as is the industrial effluent to the blossom that falls upon its frothing stench.

O mothers, educationalists and five-year-olds, that first traumatic day at school from the knee-high level is as nothing compared to the torment endured by the untried secondary-school teacher before their first day in the classroom. As I lay rigid in bed, counting the intervals between the lorries that thundered down the narrow street and wondering when and if I would next swallow food, every instinct cried out for catching the first train back to London. It was tangible proof to me that the deterrent effect of punishment was a pious hope, for the shame and loss of self-respect that would certainly have ensued faded quite away beside the allure of the secure, sane, though tedious, familiarity of home. Had I been alone I have no doubt that flight would have followed. But my tension must have transmitted itself to Damaris, although I lay scarcely breathing for fear of waking her. Slowly she turned her monumental head towards me and looked at me for some moments. Then she felt for my hand and squeezed it.

"Would you rather hear clichés about everyone going through it, or get up and have some tea?"

"Get up and have some tea."

"Come on, then."

So at a quarter past five on that first October morning we got up and put our coats on over our dressing-gowns, made a pot of tea and sat together on the plastic sofa drinking and eating chocolate biscuits and smoking and talking about the inescapable awfulness of the day before me. Damaris knew so well how false cheer undermines whatever dregs are left of real optimism, how much more bracing it is to face hard truths head-on. And then the wartime atmosphere of drinking tea at such an unusual hour and in such circumstances, gave me a precious sense of detachment from what lay ahead, as if that dawn hour were again the store room off the gym at school where we could always retreat into the security of our friendship, a friendship which had proved immune to changes in place and time.

As a result of our huddle I was calmer in my mind, but my stomach was acting independently. It advised me of the rising sun, the imminence of washing in a dribble of hot water from the enamel egg over the basin, and of trying to swallow the hard-boiled variety that Damaris would insist I eat, to fortify me.

"Well," I said, my teeth chattering, "well, well, well."

"You get washed. I'll make breakfast."

The hot-water egg with the little red eye was an irrational brute, one of those minor irritations that help to make a vale of tears of the average bed-sitter. Later it became the cause of many unpleasant scenes. On this morning it only succeeded in burning my hands in the jet of boiling water that ran cold without warning before I had finished. As a result, guilt about what Damaris would use to wash with was added to the basic discomfort of standing stark naked in a cold bathroom, dabbing myself with water too hot to touch. It may not rank with mapping virgin forest, say, as a new experience, but at a time when I was in need of any familiar comfort it was harrowing enough.

Damaris kept me busy with small tasks about the flat in a transparent ploy to keep my mind occupied, aiming a little low. But again, gratitude kept me from protesting.

It was still dark as we left for the bus stop. The fog had thickened overnight. It seemed to be breathed out by the houses. Cars and buses had their headlights on, and the little shops were lit up as their proprietors rolled up shutters and swept dust-sheets from sweet counters. It was the scene of the evening before thrown into reverse, for the shops had been closing then, and the dark confused temporal distinctions. I was reminded of Damaris' remark about the Children's Tower, of how the poor little mites had been forced to and fro to the mill by underground tunnel and had never seen the light of day. The analogy was becoming more relevant by the minute and added to a sense of impending doom. But we were on the bus before I could take action on its promptings.

The Blessed Ambrose Carstairs Grammar School for Boys occupied several acres of scrubland in the northern conurbation of Manchester, equidistant from Rochdale, Oldham and the city itself. Its function was, said Damaris, to act as the main sewer to the said towns for the disposal of the brighter Catholic boy.

"The men all support the idea of comprehensives, of course," said Damaris, as we walked up the asphalt drive to the main entrance.

"Then why are they teaching here?"

"They have families to support," she said, a little crossly I thought.

The buildings were of the glass and concrete school, familiar enough even then, and much of the original glass remained, a record, said Damaris, of which the brothers were extremely proud, as it was unique for a school more than five years old in that area. Nonetheless the façade was freely brightened with cardboard and masking tape. From the entrance hall in the main building wide, glassy corridors led away into the inner reaches of the school. It was still only ten past eight and almost deserted except for a few forlorn-looking small boys who had been dumped off by parents on their way to work and who lolled around the corridors blowing bubblegum at each other.

Two prefects stood talking in the hallway. I braced myself: the first brush with the enemy.

"Good morning, Miss Fotheringay," they chimed in unison.

"Good morning, Pirozynski, good morning, Ryan. This is Miss Slade. She's going to join the English staff."

"How do you do, Miss?" said Ryan. He was a thin-faced boy with an unhealthy complexion and a crop of greasy brown curls which also looked under-nourished. "Mis-layed did you say?"

"Shut up, Ryan," said Damaris, with an angry toss of the head that sent a long strand of hair thwack across my left eye.

"Sorry, Miss." He did not look it.

"It will be nice to have some more ladies around," said Pirozynski ponderously, clasping his hands behind his stocky body.

"I haven't noticed it's made much difference so far," said

15

Damaris. "Hasn't Mr Pollock said anything to you about your hair yet, Ryan?"

"A great deal, Miss. I can't get him off the subject, it's quite embarrassing."

"He's not angling for a lock of it, if that's what you're hinting at. No one in their right mind would approach it from an extension ladder, even."

"It's me sebaceous glands, Miss. I can't help it."

"Glands be blowed," said Damaris. "Try Fairy Liquid."

"Yes, Miss."

"Come on, Carlo." Damaris motioned me towards the stairs.

When the boys were out of hearing, I said, "You're very ..." (I wanted to say "personal", but was not sure that was the right word. I had just not expected bodily hygiene to be a subject upon which Damaris would freely converse with these characters.) "... blunt," I concluded.

"Ryan's a pain in the arse," was her only comment. "I'll take you to the staff room first. There'll probably be someone there. Brother Basil is expecting you at eight-thirty."

"Will you come with me?"

"What? To the interview? No, of course not. Did you think I would?"

"Just a forlorn hope."

"Poor Carlo. You really are frightened." We had come to the door of the staff room. A large notice on a page of exercise book cautioned the visitor to KNOCK and WAIT. Damaris gave me a hug. "Cheer up!"

"It's just I've never been alone with a monk. Do they wear anything under those dressing-gowns?"

"I presume so. It's a religious order, not a highland clan."

She opened the door to a large room that occupied the width of that wing of the building. Windows down either side gave onto the road in front of the school, and the quadrangle behind, with tennis courts and playing fields beyond. Between the windows was a landslide of rubbish roughly spread over tables, chairs and cupboards. A pall of exhaled smoke hung in the sunbeams. A few men sat at desks, partly concealed behind piles of books and boxes, most of them gagging on cheap cigarettes. They raised weary hands or eyebrows in greeting as Damaris came in.

"Is Martin here yet?"

This I knew to be the head of English.

"In the bog, I think. He'll be back in a minute."

"This is Carol Slade, gentlemen. Fallowfield's replacement."

"Not yet!" I protested. None of the men did, and I went round shaking hands and answering simple enquiries about my background.

Presently a large young man in a tweed suit and academic robe rammed through the door at the far end of the room. Damaris repeated the introduction.

"This is Martin," she said. "Now I'll leave you to chat for a few minutes. She's got to go down at eight-thirty, Martin."

"Fine, fine!" beamed the head of English. He held onto my hand for a few moments, kneading the bones. His face was broad and freckled, the eyes humorous, the sandy hair plentiful and unregulated. Here was no wasted aesthete who would cringe at the hostility of the Philistine young. I sensed, and was later proved correct, that he believed in the brute force method of applying literary appreciation. The thought filled me with hope.

"Damaris has told me all about you," he said. "Can you start this morning? 3B is getting a bit restless."

"But I haven't seen the headmaster yet."

"Don't worry about him. I make all the decisions about the department. Have you had any experience, by the way?"

"Teaching? No. I sold ice-cream as a holiday job once. Do you think that will help?"

He laughed. "There's practically no difference. Here, let me give you a timetable sheet. I expect you'll be wanting to know your classes, won't you?"

"There's a lot I'd quite like to know. Like how to teach."

"You'll soon get the hang of it. The English store room is just through that door. All the books are arranged in years. Just take a pile and look as if you mean business. But one directive I would like to emphasize, we've done away with formal grammar and parsing and all that rubbish – in fact I burnt all those. Now, let me see." He settled at his desk with his own timetable book and a clean, squared sheet of paper in front of him. "Now, then, Monday: 3B, 5B, 1C, 4B, Lower 6th Science II, 1C, 4A. Tuesday: 3A, 5B, 4B, 1C, 3A again, 4A, Upper 6th Science I, Wednesday: 2B, 3C, 4B, 5B twice, 1C, 5C. Thursday: 5C, Lower 6th Science I, 2B, 3C, 5B, 4A twice. Friday: 4A, 1C, 5C, twice, 3A, Upper 6th Science II and 2B. There you are. I'll fill in the library periods later. That should keep you busy for a while."

"Perhaps I could help with woodwork in my spare time?"

"Do you think it's a lot? Umm, I suppose it is a bit heavy for a beginner, but it's best to jump in the deep end. Don't worry, you won't drown." He grinned.

"Are they well-disciplined?" I asked in a weak voice.

"As to that, if you have any trouble, send them straight to me and I'll smash their heads together."

"Promise?"

"Promise. Now don't forget to come and have coffee with us at ten to eleven. Damaris usually goes off to the music room with her cronies, but I like our department to get together at least once a day."

"Right. Is there a plan of the school anywhere, or shall I just ask a policeman?"

"Sorry. Yes." He fumbled in his drawer. "Here you are. Now, I'm sorry, I have to go and fix up the tape for recording a programme now. Tony used to do it, but I won't ask you to just at first."

"I don't want to shirk my duties."

"No, no, it's all right. Well, good luck. See you at coffee." He heaved a tape recorder out from under his desk and backed out of the door.

I looked round for Damaris. She caught my eye at once – had been hovering with it on the proceedings, I suspected.

"All right?"

"Wonderful."

"Come on. Let's go down now. And remember to have a look at the secretary. You have to go through their office to get to Brother Basil."

"What am I supposed to be looking for?"

"You remember. To see if she's – you know – *schwanger*."

"Of course." I felt a guilty twinge of having been too pre-occupied to spare a thought for Anne, alone in London, as she thought, indefinitely. It was 8.25. She would just be catching the train from Worcester Park.

Damaris introduced me to the two secretaries. There was no question as to which one I was meant to scrutinize. Mrs Prudhoe was a pleasant, bespectacled woman, but at that stage where a love-child would have been an occasion for public rejoicing – by her, at least. Miss Cromwell was evidently the guilty party.

Miss Cromwell was a corker, slow though I usually am to

appreciate looks of her type. Miss Cromwell was tall, with a broad pair of shoulders on her, above which she held her head high. Her hair was long, dark and straight, parted in the middle over a face of flamboyantly well-made features, among which the huge blue eyes dominated, eyes fringed with a perfect set of her very own lashes. Her mouth was red and sensuous, never completely at rest, of the type frequently called generous, under the suspicion that it was freely and often donated to others. Her figure, as far as I could tell, went in and out in all the right places. Miss Cromwell, however, had a Derby accent as broad as her body was beautiful, and surprised me with the modest manner of her greeting.

"He's hovering," she said in a stage whisper, pointing to Brother Basil's door. "Better get in quick, 'e 'ates interviews."

Damaris knocked, a voice called "Come in", almost anticipating her. Not for the last time that morning she introduced me and left.

Brother Basil advanced and shook hands. I could have sworn he was on stilts and instinctively looked down for signs of tell-tale stumps, but saw only a set of hairy toes protruding from leather sandals. I caught a whiff of freeze-dried BO as he took my hand and then retreated behind the desk.

"So, you're Miss Slater." He shuffled papers on the desk.

"No, Slade." Brother Basil's nervousness calmed me. I looked with cool interest at his fleshy face, dense whorled glasses and halo of dry, sandy hair.

"Ah! Slade. There is a very ancient Catholic family called Slade, in Burnley I believe. Any relation?"

"I don't think so. We're all Methodists."

"Ah – but Methodism is a relatively recent development, Miss Slade." He smiled, plainly relishing my ignorance of Catholic pedigrees in the locality.

"I see."

"Miss Fotheringay isn't a Methodist is she? She doesn't look like one, somehow."

"I don't think so. Her grandmother was a Calvinist of some sort."

"Really? Oh dear, oh dear, poor old Calvin." He swung round in his swivel chair to face the window and fiddled with his leather girdle. "Not that it matters here, of course. We've always had non-Catholic teachers. But the North has always been a strong

Catholic area. You've heard of the Pilgrimage of Grace, no doubt?"

"Yes." I had not, but nor did I want to. "And wasn't Guy Fawkes born in York?"

"I believe he was, I believe he was." Brother Basil laughed delightedly, then became very sober. "A lot of Polish boys. You'll find a lot of Polish boys here. They're the backbone of the Church round here. In my opinion." He nodded thoughtfully, then swung round to face me. "So you want to teach English, do you? Good. Yes."

"I'm afraid I have no experience."

"That's not so important. Attitude is the important thing. We all have to start somewhere. You are keen to teach I suppose?"

"Desperately."

"Yes, well, there you are then. Where are you living?"

"With Miss Fotheringay, in Rusholme."

"Ah – Rusholme. Poor Mrs Gaskell. How do you get here? On the bus?"

"Yes."

"You must speak to Mr Miller. He's from round there. He might be able to give you a lift."

"Miss Fotheringay didn't mention it. Perhaps it's better to be independent. Giving lifts is like lending money – it always ends in tears, doesn't it?"

"Perhaps it does, perhaps it does. You know best. I like the staff to be punctual, though. It sets a good example. What you do when you get here is up to you. Apart from smoking in the classrooms, of course."

"It never occurred to me."

"No, that's right. I must talk to Miss Fotheringay about the Christmas concert. Do you sing?"

"Not in public."

"Ah! Well, if you'll excuse me, Miss Slade, I have to go and get the football results for assembly. Now don't forget, if you have any problems at all, don't hesitate to come and see me."

"Thank you."

"You'll be hearing from the Education Committee in due course." He rose and shook my hand again. "Are you United or City, by the way?"

"Sorry?"

"Football. Are you United or City?"

"Er ... City."

"Oh dear! Poor Miss Slade. You're in for a rough time. Well, good morning."

Damaris was waiting for me in the secretaries' office. "All right?"

"Depends what you mean. I'm signed-on."

"Welcome to the cloak of authority." She beamed. Mrs Prudhoe and Miss Cromwell looked up from their typewriters and beamed. Perhaps they knew something I did not. "We'd better go down to assembly now."

"If you don't mind, I'd rather look over the textbooks and decide what to use. I've got to teach straight afterwards, haven't I?"

"Perhaps that would be a good idea. Can you find your own way to the staffroom? I have to play the piano."

"Yes, I think so."

I made my way back up the stairs to the staffroom against a stream of teachers coming down for assembly. My colleagues, as they now were. They made way for me with deferential curiosity. Martin stopped me.

"Do you know where 3B classroom is? I'll take you along and introduce you if you like."

"Would you? Thanks."

Alone in the staffroom, I stared out of the window that gave on to the playground and football fields. I noticed two large boys and one small one lurking under a corner of the loggia that ran down one side of the building. They were snickering and passing a cigarette round. One of the bigger boys noticed me standing at the window and they all turned, boldly, to stare at me. Instinctively I turned away.

It was a mistake. I should have stayed.

Having made the decision to retreat, however, I made for the store room, stubbing out smouldering cigarettes as I went.

It was easy enough to follow the arrangement of books: *Animal Farm* and illustrated poetry books with titles like *Soundings* and *Voices in the Street* on the left, running the gamut of literary complexity up to battered Merchants of Venice and James Joyce on the right. I had two classes before break, 3B and 5B. No doubt they would already have work in progress, but I had to be prepared. For 3B I chose a volume of comprehension exercises composed by Philip Matchings, M.A. Oxon., Head of English at a well-known public school near Hastings, and for 5B a poetry anthology with a meaty section on war poems, which I assumed would be acceptable to boys. Wilfred Owen, Archibald McLeish, Robert Graves, the odd Siegfried Sassoon. All that close-up confrontation with the bloodiness of battle which turns the stomach and yet confronts the reader with the reality and inevitable betterness of love and pity. Perhaps I might be able to draw on the boys' experience on the football terraces to initiate a meaningful discussion on the anomalies in human nature. Failing that, Graves was always good for half an hour's scansion practice. I just ran over "Dead Boche" to make sure I could do it myself.

Martin came to find me before I had finished. The school was now thudding with activity and I could see boys streaming like a lava flow out of the assembly hall and into classrooms.

"There you are," said Martin. "I thought you'd be at assembly." He had evidently suffered a small disappointment.

"Sorry. Was I supposed to go? I just felt desperate to prepare myself somehow."

"Doesn't matter. What have you got there? Umm, this for 3B? Yes, that should keep them quiet for a bit. Not nervous, are you?"

"Yes."

"You won't have any trouble. And if you do, I'm in Upper 6th B. Punishment is swift and painful."

"I haven't believed in corporal punishment up to now." I also had an idea that committed socialists did not either, but perhaps Martin did not allow his political beliefs to interfere with professional ethics.

"We'll see how long that lasts. Come on."

Martin carried the books and I trotted at his elbow as we threaded our way through the swarming corridors. I had not apprehended the scale of Catholic boyhood until that moment. Martin seemed to enjoy leading me protectively through the crush, the object of blatant curiosity on all sides, his Angel to my Tobias. After what seemed indeed a journey of Biblical proportions we arrived at our destination, a classroom on the top floor of a corridor in the most remote wing of the school. The door stood open onto a scene of boyish pandemonium. As we entered a missile flew from one side of the class to the other. Then sudden silence as Martin was observed, broken by the scurrying of bodies to their desks.

"Who threw that book?" he asked, his jaws lightly grinding together. A moment's silence. Then a hand was slowly raised at the back of the class.

"Riccio, isn't it?"

"Yes, sir."

"Stand up, you bastard." The boy got to his feet, in no special hurry. He seemed to be going through the motions of a familiar routine. He was long, thin and sallow and the sleeves of his blazer were too short. He attempted a look of shifty defiance. "Do you throw books across the room at home, Riccio?"

"No, Sir."

"Then why do you think you can do it here?"

"Don't know, Sir."

"Whom were you trying to hit?"

"Swarzenski, Sir."

"So, you think books are for hitting people with, do you? It's true you're not likely to apprehend the contents any other way. Very well. Pick up the book and wait outside."

The boy reluctantly did as he was told. I stood, quivering with fright, a few paces behind Martin. His anger was genuine and terrible to me, the more so as the Wrath of God act came as a shock after his genial behaviour up till then. And I had not previously envisaged respect for the written word taking quite such violent expression. Martin allowed a dramatic pause after the door had closed behind Riccio. Then he said, "If I catch anyone else treating a book like that, that boy will carry the scars for the rest of his life. Is that understood?"

I felt eager to assure him that it would not be me, but the boys recognized a rhetorical question when they heard one, and kept their eyes down.

His tone brightened. "Now, I've brought your new English teacher along. Miss Slade." Thirty-three pairs of eyes were trained on me. I smiled. No one smiled back, so I was left stranded with the damn thing on my face. "Miss Slade is from London. She's new to the school, of course, and I expect you to give her all the co-operation and respect you had for Mr Fallowfield. It's not easy to take over in the middle of term and I shall be taking a special interest in seeing how well, or how badly, you behave under the circumstances. I've told Miss Slade to send any trouble-makers direct to me.

"All right, Miss Slade, I'll leave them to you. Riccio will be back in a minute."

"Thank you, Mr Lewis."

The boys straggled to their feet as he left the room. "Sit down," I said.

"We usually say the prayer first, Miss," said a well-groomed boy in the first row.

"The prayer? I'm afraid I don't know it. Can you start, please?"

"Yes, Miss. In the name of the Father and of the Son and of the Holy Ghost, Amen. Oh my God, I offer Thee this lesson –"

As the boys crossed themselves, Martin's muffled voice could be heard in the corridor. It was followed by the sound of the impact of a large textbook on Riccio's behind and his yelps of agony.

"– for Thy greater honour and glory. Accept it as an earnest of our –"

Howls.

"– love. Blessed Virgin Mary, save us. Blessed Ambrose Carstairs, pray for us. In the name of the Father and of the Son and of the Holy Ghost, Amen."

"All right, thank you. Sit down." Most of them had already done so, and were exchanging indignation over Martin's treatment of Riccio.

"That's enough talking," I said. The noise level rose.

Riccio came back into the classroom. He had evidently been crying, and still gulped and snuffled in an attempt to control himself. He approached me, but looking at the floor.

"I'm sorry I'm late, Miss."

"That's all right. Go and sit down." My eyes must have betrayed my horror at the sight of what amounted to my first battered child. I felt outraged at having been exposed to such brutality. Not that my sympathies were especially with Riccio; even before being reduced to a pulp he had struck me as a repulsive type. But my feelings towards Martin had suffered a sea-change. Besides being distasteful, the incident had something ostentatious about it: I sensed that he had been pleased to have the opportunity of demonstrating his authority. The hostility now rippling through the class suggested that he had also buggered my chances of capturing the hearts of 3B. For them, I would probably always be the bitch who got Riccio creamed.

There was nothing I could do about that at the moment, however. Of greater note was restoring order. Most of the class was commiserating with Riccio, and quite a few were threatening colourful fates for Martin. Above the row I heard someone say, "Shut up. She'll snitch on ya."

"Don't care if she does."

"That's enough talking," I repeated.

A chihuahua of a boy in the first row looked up from doodling on his book cover. "You'll have to shout louder than that, Miss."

"I should knock a few of their heads together, Miss," added the dapper boy beside him.

"That should not be necessary." However, I felt slightly comforted at having established some sort of rapport with these two. They looked at me with friendly, laconic sympathy.

"Why don't you take the names, Miss?"

"All right." I reached for the plan with the legend 3B inscribed at the top, under the name of the school and the crest of the local authority.

"Now I'm going to take your names, so pipe down," I shrieked. There was a slight lowering of the noise level. "All right, you at the back with the boiled sweet stuck to your collar, what's your name?"

There was laughter as he indignantly felt for the sweet and raised a threatening fist at a boy across the room.

"Cod," he said, still disgruntled.

"Cod? Is that your Christian name or your surname?" Again there was laughter. I was cheered by their willingness to be amused.

"Boiled Cod, Miss," someone suggested.

"You shut your face, Rattray, or I'll break your head open," responded Cod.

"Kindly address your remarks to me. Your full name, surname first."

"Cod, Arthur."

"Thank you. Next?"

"de Maria, Paolo."

"Baxter, Elvis."

"Gottfried, Richard."

The roll-call took some time, accompanied as it was by continual back-chat, spontaneous humour, occasional threats of physical violence and sporadic attempts by me to conduct the exercise in silence. At the end I was exhausted. Surely I did not have to teach them as well? I got my two friends in the front row to distribute the books.

"While the books are being given out, would one of you please tell me what you did with Mr Fallowfield."

This time the outburst of laughter all but threw me against the blackboard. Even Dapper and the Chihuahua paused in their duties to laugh.

"You name it, Miss," called Riccio, by now, unfortunately, restored to high spirits.

"Lay off it, she's blushing," cautioned a kindly soul.

"I don't know what you're talking about. Er – Paton, can you please summarize your curriculum under Mr Fallowfield."

Even as I spoke the words, the inappropriateness struck me with great force. I was horrified to feel wracked with the desire to laugh myself. Despite my feigned ignorance, I knew well enough that the *double entendres* referred to the fact that the late Mr Fallowfield had been a homosexual. In my position I could not, of course, be party to such jokes, but the boys felt no such restraint.

When the hysteria had died down a little, Paton rose to his feet.

"He used to play with us, Miss," he said, encouraged by the others.

"A play you mean? Which one? What was it called?"

"No – I mean games, Miss."

"Oh, shut up and sit down. If you're all going to be so puerile about it I can find out from Mr Lewis."

"He don't know half of it, Miss. Him and Mr Fallowfield were daggers drawn."

"I said sit down. And all of you turn to page 43." To my surprise some of them actually did. "I'll read you the passage first, and then you can go over it again yourselves before we go on to the questions. Pay special attention to the sentence structure and the function of the imagery."

"What's imagery, Miss?"

"Oh Lord. Just pay attention, then."

I began: "'Unfortunately for our curiosity the wind-driven sands bury the bones of the dead beyond chance of recovery and we can only surmise what may have gone on within these earth-spanning gardens during the pluvial periods when the deserts were brought to bloom. All we know is that at the end of the third ice phase men retreated from the re-born deserts, and farther north, from Europe into Asia, a short, heavy-muscled, beetle-browed man hunted the huge arctic mammals – the mammoth and the woolly rhinoceros. They did so in fact throughout much of the third and last of the interglacial periods which endured for something like fifty thousand years. These Neanderthal men made more elaborate flint weapons and tools than ever before, faced bitter winds and cold, wet winters, co-operated effectively in trapping and chasing their lumbering prey.

26

" 'By modern standards the Neanderthals were anything but handsome. They had retreating foreheads, but their brains were as large as human brains are supposed to be, while in the spring the Neanderthal youth dallied as much as their rather grim circumstances permitted.' "

"What does 'dallied' mean, Miss?" asked Gottfried.

"Put up your hand before you ask a question."

"Is that what it means, Miss?"

"Of course not. We'll get to all that after you've read it through again to yourselves. Now get on with it."

Moans filled the air. During the exchange with Gottfried, Dapper and the Chihuahua had read the passage and while the others had their heads down these two sat looking me over. I feigned fascination with the passing clouds, growing increasingly flustered as their little eyes feasted on every detail of my person with primordial glee. As the others finished reading the chatter started slowly building up again. After a few minutes the noise was deafening.

"Quiet!" I shouted.

No response.

"Quiet!"

"What did you say, Miss?"

"The next person to speak after I count five will go straight to Mr Lewis. One, two –"

"– three, four –" They all chimed in.

"– five!"

There was silence of a sort, mouths buttoned suppressing giggles.

"Right. Now close your books." I took up my own copy. Unfortunately I had lost the page. While I fumbled for it, a quiet voice started, "– six, seven, eight –"

"Baxter, what is the subject of the passage? Which anthropological group?"

"The staff, Miss."

"Leave the room, Baxter."

"Yes, Miss."

I waited until the door closed behind him. The novelty of this ruse had a momentary sobering effect.

"Riccio?"

"Neanderthal Man, Miss."

"Yes. Good. Neanderthal Man. Does anyone know what that word means? And what kind of adjective is it?"

"It means thick and hairy, Miss, like Mrs Prudhoe's legs."

Again I almost burst a blood vessel repressing my own laughter. The energy was translated into ostensible rage. "I will ask Mrs Prudhoe if she agrees with that definition, Riccio. Or perhaps it would be better to ask Mr Lewis?"

"Sorry, Miss."

"Anyone else? Well why does it have a capital letter, for heaven's sake? All right, we'll come back to that later. What phrases does the author use to describe the probable land of origin of Neander-thal Man? Christoff?"

"Umm – earth-spinning gardens, Miss."

"Earth-spinning? Have you ever seen a garden spin?"

"Yeah, every Saturday night."

"That's as maybe, but the word is spanning. Earth-spanning gardens. Now that is an example of figurative language, because the author uses an image which is familiar to us to convey the quality of what he is describing, rather than being strictly literal. That is, it's not an exact description but creates a picture." Several of the boys yawned loudly. The chatter resumed. I raised my voice. "What would be a literal description of these areas? Macey?"

"What Miss? I can't hear you."

"What would be a –" The bell rang. Lingering restraint was abandoned, desk lids thrown up, Mars bars ripped open, scuffles resumed where they had left off.

"Good morning, 3B," I shrieked above the din.

"Good morning, Miss," said Dapper.

Although I walked out of the classroom under my own steam, I had all the sensations of having been ejected, wooshed out on the rising tide of noise and chaos. I noticed that my hands were trembling and were making damp stains on the copy of *Comprehension for Middle Forms* that I clutched to my bosom like a shield. The corridors swarmed with boys and teachers changing rooms, but my feet carried me blindly through them, though I had no idea where I was supposed to be going. I wanted to go home. I felt harrowed. Why had I exposed myself to such punishment? I, who had never so much as lifted a used napkin from a Wimpy Bar? A surge of outraged innocence shook me to the core. I may even have muttered out loud. But there was no escaping the rest of the day at least, even if I returned. I felt, unreasonably, that Damaris should have come to see how I had got on. I needed to express outrage before it turned inward into what remained of my self-respect. But no Damaris appeared. The crowds began to thin out, reminding me that classes were re-forming.

I consulted my time-table. 5B was waiting for me somewhere in this inferno, no doubt twittering with anticipation. At least they had exams to prepare, usually a sobering exercise. And it could not be that 3B's behaviour was the norm. I stopped to try and locate myself on the map of the school that Martin had given me.

"Can I help you, Miss?"

I looked up. His head slightly tilted to one side to assist gravity in keeping a flank of silky brown hair out of his eyes, the boy I had caught sight of at the bus stop stood looking down at me with an expression of courteous enquiry. To my intense annoyance I felt myself blushing. Despite his willowy, almost girlish good looks, his expression, his casual stance and his ability to wear the school uniform as though it sported a Gucci label established him as claiming, if not deserving, equality. More, there was even an air of patronage about him. It was this that surprised and confused me. I had taken so much abuse already that morning that I was sensitive to its most subtle forms.

"I don't know. Are you a pupil here?"

"Officially. Are you looking for something?"

"5B. But first I have to get to the staffroom to pick up some books." Why did I explain myself like that? There was no need to justify the trip.

"If you come with me I'll show you. I'm going that way."

"Thank you."

The boy walked ahead. I followed, a little behind.

"Can you go more slowly?" I said. "I'm out of condition."

He looked round and laughed. "Sorry. My girlfriends always say the same thing."

A casual remark, but loaded with offence. Coupling me in any sense with his girlfriends, as though I had only my sex to distinguish me, was bad enough. But the *double entendre*, if indeed it had been intended and I could swear it had, was outrageous. And yet I could not fault the deference of his manner.

When we arrived at the staffroom door he said, "Shall I wait for you and take you to 5B?"

"It's all right, thank you. I think I can find it. You have a class yourself, don't you?"

"No. It's study."

"Oh. Then I should go and study."

"Okay. Goodbye." He walked back the way we had come.

My indignation rose degrees further. His offer to wait for me carried overtones of an assignation. I half expected him to suggest we go for a milk shake after school.

I bumped into Damaris at the door of the staffroom. "I think I've just met your boy genius, the impudent little sod," I said, anxious to unload my indignation onto someone, as it had been plainly lost on him.

"Shackleton? Where?"

"He just showed me the way here."

"Where's he gone?"

To my amazement Damaris pushed past me to look up and down the corridor.

"How should I know? Did you want him for something?"

"No." She avoided my eye. "Well, we have to discuss the Christmas concert. He's playing the piano."

"There's plenty of time, surely?"

"Oh, yes."

"Aren't you going to ask me how I got on?"

"Sorry. I came to look for you. How was it?"

"Hell."

"Were they noisy? I did warn you."

"It didn't help."

My throat was suddenly burning with tears. The half-hour spent flirting with death in 3B was bad enough, but Damaris, instead of shoring me up with sympathy, had thrown me over for a glimpse of her poofy protégé when I most needed to know that I was uppermost in her thoughts. And there was something in her manner, barely noticeable at first, but obvious now, that showed she could not resist playing the old hand to my greenhorn. I resented it bitterly. She had only been at the school two months longer than I, she could not have forgotten so soon what it was like to be new. In short, there was an Atmosphere. We stood looking at each other for a moment, both at a loss to know how to cope with what was, for us, a new experience.

"I'll take you to your next class," she said.

"Doesn't matter. I can find it."

"Are you sure?" She cast another quick glance down the corridor. I knew that she wanted to find out where Shackleton was, and that after I had gone she would amble casually past the likely rooms as though by chance. Her hostility clearly masked embarrassment that she had given herself away. It was a discovery that would require a great deal of digesting, but in the meantime, restored my own self-respect somewhat.

"See you at break, then."

"I thought you had it in the music room?"

"Yes, usually. But not today. I'll have to introduce you to everyone."

"Just as you like. I'd better get a move on."

"Okay." She blew me a kiss and smiled apologetically, then went off down the corridor with her long, mannish stride.

This suspicion, that Damaris had an adolescent crush on one of the boys, thrilled me with horror and delight. It was the more fascinating since Damaris had never shown any attraction to the opposite sex that I knew of, although she had inspired heady passion in several young men, and at least one very old one. Her unfashionably muscular frame and blunt manner had helped in the assumption that she was not prone to weakness of the flesh. I had thought of her as Amazonian, fierce and sexless, or as a meaty Vestal Virgin, destined to tend only the fires of her genius. The emergence of her feet of clay cheered me up enormously. I would not mind the loneliness of being kept at a distance from her, since it was coupled with such tantalizing knowledge.

My thoughts running busily on these lines, I hardly noticed 5B, let alone what I did with them. My lack of concern must have provoked a positive response, for I do remember that the lesson went remarkably fast and without recourse to violence.

At breaktime there was nothing anyone could tell me about boys, teaching or theory of education. By lunch I was offering advice to heads of department. I felt tried and tested, tempered and toughened.

School dinner lay ahead, however. Martin took me down to the hall, where I was horrified to discover that a system of democratic dining reigned, whereby the staff were expected to pepper themselves among the boys with a view to raising the tone, lowering the noise and teaching the little buggers not to wipe their noses on the roast potatoes. When the suggestion had first been made, it seems, all objections had been drowned in cries of "élitist swine!" from the ruling Left, half of whom now brought sandwiches to eat in the staffroom. The Right, somewhat relishing their righteousness, had compromised by eating in the dining-room, but at separate tables, thus maintaining an equal-but-different status which satisfied the authorities. Places were assigned, and I was able to be separated from Damaris, whom I now saw, with some amusement, to be sitting at a table close to Shackleton's, for the sixth-formers were allowed to sit where they liked, so that they would feel grown-up.

At my table were Brother William (history), Mr Marple (chemistry), and Mr Dacre (maths and cross-country running). I warmed to Brother William at once. He seemed to have those qualities the Lord probably had in mind when he said, "They will know that I live through you." An air of heavenly peace pulsated lightly all round him. He had a large egg-shaped head, completely bald, so that the sun glinted off it like a halo, small oriental eyes and an enigmatic smile which suggested that his secret knowledge was sufficient to ward off the evils of this world.

Mr Dacre looked as though he had been caught direct in their flight path. His features were decent enough – Mount Rushmore style – but his expression brought to mind paintings of desert fathers tormented by demons with pitchforks, jarring their teeth on the unyielding piety of the victim. Beneath a dull grey sports jacket his compact, muscular body was tense.

Mr Marple was pale and bird-like, and tried to compensate for his lack of natural authority by cultivating Mr Dacre's mean expression.

"Aren't we fortunate to have a lady at the table, gentlemen?" cooed Brother William. "No more arguments about who'll be mother."

"Better an unmarried brother than an unmarried mother, Brother."

Brother William rocked breathily with laughter – why, I was not sure – but Mr Dacre looked disgusted, and Mr Marple went bright pink.

Well, how was I supposed to know how to talk to the Lord's anointed?

I helped myself to liver and potatoes in embarrassed silence. The liver was a welcome distraction. It was riddled with little white tubes that had to be pulled out by hand, and smelt like a fresh turd.

"Isn't it curious the way we eat liver as a matter of course," I said, "although all sorts of disgusting things go on in it. And yet if somebody offered me a frog's leg I'd pass out."

"That's because the smaller the animal is, the more sentimental the British get about it," said Mr Dacre, spearing his liver edgily.

"If frogs were the same size as cows you'd eat it all right. Phoney sentimentality, that's all. Look at the fuss that's made about children. Adults hurt just as much, if not more, because they have more experience, more capacity. They just don't look so cute."

The last word was spat out, accompanied by a morsel of liver.

I was thinking of Riccio's rapid recovery after his run-in with Martin, and had to admit that to do the same thing to an adult would cause extensive psychological, if not physical, damage.

"There is something in that," said Brother William. "It's all to do with our tendency to credit animals with human awareness."

"We do that to children too," I said.

He laughed. "Don't you like children, Miss Slade? It's something of a drawback in our profession."

"As I've only been a professional for three hours, Brother, I can't comment. I wouldn't say I didn't like children. I just don't know them."

"You've come to the wrong place," said Mr Dacre.

"What do you mean?"

"Even if you started out by thinking you like children it would only take a week or so in this place to disillusion you. They're animals, most of them. You'll never survive unless you grasp that. Far less teach."

A flicker of pain passed across Brother William's face. "They do have human souls," he said gently.

"Oh come off it, Brother. You know what I mean. I'm not denying that we're all God's children and all that. What I mean is, the evolutionary state of most of the kids is pretty primitive. Their manners, their thoughts, their aspirations. We have nothing in common. Nothing."

The last pocket of Neanderthal Man? I wondered, and cautiously peered round the dining-hall to check that the inmates were under control. Now that Mr Dacre had mentioned it, there did seem something sub-human about the half-developed bodies and watery eyes of the boys, shifting in their seats as though itching to get back on all fours, grasping at their food with predatory lust. "But if you feel like that, why did you become a teacher?"

Mr Dacre shook more salt vigorously onto his dinner. "Because I'm doing something about it. It doesn't have to stop you being an effective teacher. I think I am."

"Yes, indeed," said Brother William.

"That's right," piped up Mr Marple. "A lot of people worry

about whether they're popular with the boys. But that's not important. I intend to be a good teacher." He flushed as he spoke, the words welling up from deep within his personality.

"And how do you think you'll like it, Miss Slade?" said Brother William.

"I'm not sure yet. It's all so different. From everyday life, I mean. I think it might be quite easy to get so absorbed in school life that it becomes the norm, and the outside world gets distorted and unreal. I wouldn't like that to happen."

"It is a danger, yes. But you know, most people move in very small circles – family, office, factory, hospital, or whatever it is. The world is rather large to be gone at all at once. It's natural to have a home base, as it were."

"I can see that. As long as one does feel at home in it."

"If you have any problems at all I'm sure we'll all be willing to help, won't we, gentlemen?"

"Of course," said Mr Dacre. "I'll take care of any troublemakers for you."

"What's your form?"

"3B."

"Ah! I may take you up on that," I said lightly. To myself I swore the opposite. If I could not squash 3B under the weight of intellectual superiority and personal charm they would remain unsquashed.

A boy threw a tin of brownish matter onto the table and another brought a jug of green custard. The first boy collected the dirty plates, and in doing so sent a piece of liver onto the floor, which smeared my sleeve in passing. Swifter than sound, Mr Dacre's large red hand was clamped on the boy's wrist.

"You dirty little pig," he muttered. "I'll see you in my room after lunch." He released the boy's wrist, leaving white weals.

The boy cast him a terrified glance, picked up the liver and hurried off with the plates.

Again I was trembling with the sudden threat of violence. I felt sickened to have unwittingly triggered it off. The scene in Mr Dacre's room rose before my mind in grisly detail.

Brother William started to dole out the pudding, but I had no stomach for chocolate sponge or conversation and maintained an outraged silence until I could politely leave the table.

Damaris was still eating, but she introduced me to the other teachers at her table. "Mr Yeats, Head of Music – that is, of me."

34

This was a small, curly-haired blond, dressed overall in cherry red. Then there was the P.T. master, known to all as Sammy, and another monk, of truly clerical appearance, called Brother Eamonn. The atmosphere at their table seemed infinitely more gay than ours, helped, no doubt, by Mr Yeats, who took no pains to conceal his leanings.

"Hello, dear, come and sit down. Georgie, go and get Miss a chair," he ordered a passing boy. "How are you getting on with the Butcher? Isn't he horrible? He makes my skin creep."

"Are you talking about Mr Dacre?"

He laughed. "Who else? Brother William? Honestly I don't know how that man's survived up to now. Do you know he's nearly been taken to court three times for assault? I reckon it's only a matter of time, don't you, Brother?"

"Probably. He should get married. A woman's influence might soften him a bit."

"Oh rubbish, Brother. He's a repressed homosexual."

"We all are," sighed Brother Eamonn. He had a soft Irish accent. "we only joined for the uniform, you know."

"Don't tease!"

"Did the A.M.A. bail him out?" said Damaris.

"Naturally. Though even their patience is wearing thin."

"Why doesn't Brother Basil do something about it? He's the headmaster."

"He's terrified of Dacre, same as the boys are. Well, I am."

"Come along to football training," suggested Sammy, a handsome young man who sat at table in his sky-blue track suit, chosen, no doubt, to match his eyes. He looked at Mr Yeats with cautious indulgence. "You need building up."

"Please!" Mr Yeats rolled his eyes. "You wouldn't get me near those changing-rooms on the end of a pitchfork. I don't know how you stay so calm, Sammy."

"Habit. I don't smell it anymore."

Mr Yeats turned to me with an air of freshly-minted curiosity. "Now tell us something about yourself, dear. What's your name?"

"Carol. It's an awful name. Damaris calls me Carlo."

"Ho ho! Are you two lovers, then?"

He had an expression of such genuine glee that we all laughed. "Sorry, I don't think it ever occurred to us, did it, Damaris?"

"No. We're a bit backward."

Mr Yeats sighed. "Pity. It's awful being the only one. Especially with all these hairy rugger types running around making me feel fragile."

"You think too much about it, Terry. You should get your mind onto something else," said Brother Eamonn.

"My mother always said the same thing. Now look at me."

"I think Brother Eamonn is right," I said. "You sound like a repressed heterosexual to me."

"Ooooh! I can see I'm going to hate you. Well —" He stretched. "I've got to go and run the first year choir through 'How Beautiful Are the Feet.' Honestly, now there's an example of how much, much too innocent I am for this kind of work. They were yelling their little tonsils out the other day and I thought there was something funny going on, but there usually is. Then Brother Basil comes in looking pothered and wants to look at the score. Apparently they'd been singing 'How beautiful are the teats' – he'd been listening outside the door. So of course I had to get all butch and outraged and keep them in den. last night. Honestly I wish some people would mind their own business."

"He's always snooping," said Damaris.

"At least I've got Shackleton for half an hour this afternoon."

"When?" said Damaris.

"Ten to three. Want to come?"

"I can't."

"Oh well. I'll see you then. Ta-ta."

I watched Mr Yeats out of the hall. He had left me a little breathless, although I was anxious not to show it. The hall was now almost empty. Damaris was clearing the plates. Dinner-duty boys put the chairs upside-down on the tables. Shackleton and his cronies had left. I felt a wicked urge to tease Damaris about him while we were in company. In private she would be too free for evasion.

"Having Shackleton for something seems to be like getting a drink during prohibition," I said at large.

"Can't say I'm bothered," said Sammy. "I'm only interested in them from the ankles down."

"Yes, don't take too much notice of Mr Yeats," said Brother Eamonn. "Shackleton's talents are only relative. I'm afraid his reputation is more a reflection of the general standard of boy. We've had some rather lean years lately."

"They're all a pain, more or less," said Damaris.

*

That November in Manchester I entered my dark night of the soul. Passing through the city every morning was the descent into hell, returning at night to the flat, re-admission to paradise, freezing and fetid though it was. Seven, sometimes eight, lessons a day, a welter of boyhood trampling through my self-respect, hostile, unwashed, unwilling to be taught, argumentative and sullen by turns, as indifferent to the glories of the English language as the common slug to the peal of cathedral bells, interested in nothing that had not to do with sex or football, totally lacking in school or any other spirit, their one conscious ambition to make inroads into my dwindling faith in the natural goodness of Man. After four weeks of daily battles in the classroom, evenings spent propped up over the sputtering gas fire and the blotchy homework, weekends attempting to recover sleep and *joie-de-vivre* in the cramped interludes between shopping, housework and writing home, I came to the conclusion not, as Mr Dacre had suggested, that the boys were anything as nice as animals, but that the adolescent male is the nearest thing to primordial slime still to be found in its natural state.

3B continued to be the most active thorn in my flesh. The lower and higher forms, being closer to childhood watersheds, that is 11-plus or "O" levels, were never a joy to teach, but proved more malleable. One could fob off the former with dramatizations of *Animal Farm*, and the latter with dummy examination papers. But 3B were at the stage where they were neither child nor youth, but a hideous hybrid of the former's brain and the later's nascent sexuality; downy moustaches, spots and blackheads breaking through the perfect childish skin, voices croaking like the death rattles of tom-cats, their minds merely an up-to-date version of the old-fashioned open drain. Certainly, nothing that I had to say survived there for long. We loathed each other with a bitter loathing, shackled together for three lessons a week in the name of education. The only exceptions were Dapper and the Chihuahua, who continued their initial detachment from the *hoi polloi* and observed the battle between us with quiet relish, supporting now one side, now the other.

Nor had my first experience of 3B told the whole story. One morning I was writing a sentence for analysis on the blackboard. "To whom is the laughing policeman speaking?" A piece of screwed-up paper landed with a thwack by my hand, obviously, from its speed and impact, catapulted. I turned round. The class was in its usual chaos, but marginally quieter than usual from the effort of copying out the sentence. There seemed to be no conspiratorial giggles. But in the third row of desks in the central column I noticed a boy I had not seen before, a boy with large, blank blue eyes in a fleshy face, and narrow, hunched shoulders. He was staring at me with an amused smirk.

"What's your name?"

"Me, Miss?" He looked round elaborately. "Grass, Miss."

"Did you throw that missile, Grass?"

"What missile, Miss?"

"This one." I picked it up and unfolded it. It bore a message. "You've got nice legs." Printed, of course. I blushed, unable as usual to stomach reminders that my sex was a factor in our "relationship".

"You deny that you threw this?"

"Of course, Miss."

"If the person who is responsible doesn't own up at once the whole form will be in detention tomorrow night." One had to give notice, so that the doting parents would not worry.

"We can't, Miss," said Dapper. "We're in den. for Brother William tomorrow."

"Wednesday, then."

"Most of us have got an away match at Rochdale Wednesday, Miss."

"Well are you free on Thursday?"

"Thursday's choir practice, Miss. We'd have to get permission from Mr Yeats."

"Then get it." It did not seem like a good way to win Mr Yeats' heart, but at this rate I would have to book them up for detention before they committed an offence.

By this time the attention of the class, always slow to garner, had been attracted by the discussion.

"What's going on?" said Cod with lowered brow. "I can't come any night, Miss. I've got a paper round."

"Yeah," said Riccio, "it's not fair. We didn't chuck nothing at you, Miss."

"So you saw who did?"

"Yeah, it was Grass, Miss."

Grass gasped. "It was not! Honestly, Miss!"

"Yes it was, Grassy. We're not getting in den. for you."

This sentiment was backed by a chorus of indignant cat-calls.

"All right, that's enough. Come to the staffroom after school tomorrow, Grass."

"That's victimization, Miss. You've got no proof it was me. I get blamed for everything."

He appeared to be fighting tears. "This isn't the Dreyfus affair, Grass. Anyway, I'm sure you've done something you haven't atoned for."

"You can't punish people for what they might have done, Miss."

Unfortunately this was an irrefutable principle of British justice. "Very well, but any more tricks like that and I won't argue about it, you'll go straight to Mr Dacre."

"Have a heart, Miss. He beats us with his squash shoe. I've got weak kidneys."

"It's all right," said Elvis Baxter, "Miss doesn't believe in corporal punishment, do you Miss?"

"I could be persuaded." But it sounded thin, even to me.

It was not long before I repented my leniency in this incident. The arrival of Grass heralded an onslaught of refined aggravation. He had perfected his timing, so that all his exploits were carried out behind my back, or when my attention was distracted, making it impossible to catch him red-handed. Four-letter words appeared on the board, the retort of popping bubble gum orchestrated the entire lesson, desk lids were banged in the middle of Odes to the Skylark, or I would turn round from the board to find that someone had tied the Chihuahua's hands to the desk behind him. Grass was always the picture of innocence. Nobody else owned up and, after the first incident, no one admitted to having seen him in the act. I began seriously to think of installing a rear-view mirror on the board. Had the class been quieter and more orderly it might have been easier to catch him out: as it was, the entry of a passing teacher to enquire why 3B was unsupervised became a regular occurrence, and in this atmosphere it was only too easy for Grass to do his worst. On the surface he was a model of politeness, offered to carry my books, clean the blackboard, beat up any boy of my choice.

As it happened I already had help in that quarter. Cod had developed a protective instinct where I was concerned. If any boy became more than usually disruptive he would rise from his seat, cross the room, pick up the offender by the scruff of the neck, shake him and say, for example, "You shut your fucking hole while Miss is reading her bleeding pome or I'll smash your face in." Then he would turn to me with the air of a plumber who has fixed a leaking gasket, "It's all right now, Miss. You can carry on now." "Thank you, Cod. Please sit down." "Yes, Miss."

I looked for the end of term as a man looks for water in the desert.

I also had my problems with Damaris. The combined strain of living with someone who got up at six in the morning to do yoga and did not see the necessity for peeling vegetables, and my unspoken suspicion that she had a crush on Shackleton, began to open a rift between us. Fortunately I was too busy to be as concerned about it as I felt it deserved. I tried to be philosophical. Previously the longest time we had ever spent together was on holiday touring the Cistercian ruins of Yorkshire. No domestic arrangements disturbed the day, the setting and the circumstances alike made for harmony. Besides, Anne had been with us. I now began to realize why she was necessary, why we could not function so well alone: Anne was the passive element, a kind of earthing device down which excesses were sloughed off. Her very passivity provoked the desire to please, allowing us to credit her with having expectations of us that were in fact our own. It was hard to analyse the soothing effect she had on us: all I knew was, that had she been there, no arguments about buying soap powder in bulk, leaving the immersion on, or the lavatory seat up, would have arisen.

We began increasingly to talk of Anne, and to contrive to have her with us.

But after a few weeks I began to suspect that we had been mistaken about Miss Cromwell's condition. I had kept a hawkish eye on it, but her comely figure did not register small changes graphically, and her naturally high colour – her cheeks were actually stained with tiny red veins – meant that she rarely looked pale. Damaris said she had forgotten who put the idea into her head, so it was impossible to check the rumour at source.

One morning, however, I went to the toilet and found her being sick in the basin. My spirits rose.

"Miss Cromwell, are you all right? Can I help?"

"No, I'm okay." She splashed her face with water and flushed the vomit quickly down the drain, casting an anxious glance at the mirror. "I wondered when it would start."

"What do you mean?"

"Morning sickness. Actually it's elevenses sickness, I suppose. I should never have had those Penguins."

"You don't mean you're –?"

"Up the spout? Hadn't you noticed? I thought everyone would've by now."

"I had no idea. I'm so sorry."

"Don't matter. It's the luck of the draw, isn't it? I should've been more careful. I am usually. It was – unexpected." She grinned. "I'm not on the pill, see. I was, but I put on too much weight."

"I know, that's exactly why I'm not on it. You seem quite resigned. I admire you for that. Does your boyfriend know?"

"Not yet. I haven't decided whether to tell him or not."

"That's a bit risky, isn't it? I mean, if you got married and he found out afterwards he could probably sue you for false pretences, or something."

"Yeah, he definitely could. Especially as the kid's not his."

"Oh. Are you sure?"

"Yeah. Pretty sure. I always took precautions when I was with him."

"So you won't be getting married?"

"No. Doesn't look like it."

"What will you do? Can you marry the father?"

Miss Cromwell grinned again. "Not exactly. We haven't got much in common. I don't hold it against him, though. It was just as much my fault."

"It wasn't – it wasn't Brother Basil, was it?" I said, rather horrified at my own imagination. "After all – bosses and secretaries –"

Miss Cromwell laughed outright. "Brother Basil? Do me a favour. With all the men floating about this place, do you think I'd settle for him?"

"I see." I concluded that it was probably one of the other teachers, a man already enjoying a good Catholic marriage. However, she obviously intended to be discreet, and I did truly admire her cool.

"Actually," she said, "I was sick of work anyhow. I've got an auntie with an 'erb farm in Wiltshire. I think I might go down there, at least until the kid's born. Might stay on, too. I hate the city. It smells something awful, doesn't it? I suppose I notice it more now, though."

"That's a good idea. You intend to keep the child, then?"

"Course. Why not?"

"I think you're very ... mature. I envy you in a way."

"Me? Why?"

"The way you accept things. Your life has a sort of haphazard quality. You get pregnant – you go off somewhere else and start something new. You take chances, I suppose that's what I'm saying. You submit to chance imperatives. I don't think I would. I'm afraid I'd cave in on them. You must have very understanding parents." I was picturing the reaction at 53 Forsythe Gardens, Worcester Park, were I to come home pregnant by a married man. What with my father's helpless self-accusation and Muriel's crocodile tears, I would be in a straitjacket of complexes for the rest of my life.

"I don't know about understanding. I've got eleven brothers and sisters so Mum and Dad don't have much time to get worked up over little things like this."

"Well, I wish you luck. If there's anything I can do, just say. I'm sure I can speak for Damaris as well."

"Thanks. I'm sorry you've come just as I'm going. We could have had some fun."

"Yes."

"Listen, do you mind if I tell you something about your friend? A bit of advice?" She took out a pencil lipstick and began to outline the fulsome lips.

"About Damaris? No, of course not." I was too surprised to object.

"She needs a good screw. I've been watching her. She's on the boil but she won't admit it. I should encourage her to get it off her chest."

"I'm sure you're mistaken." I found that I did mind her giving me advice. And the idea of Damaris having a role in the world of Miss Cromwell's barnyard couplings was extremely offensive. "Damaris isn't like that at all. Not everyone is."

"Okay. You know her better than I do. But as I say, I've been watching her. In my opinion, if she doesn't get herself a boyfriend soon she'll end up in the same fix as me."

"I think your hormones must be influencing your outlook at the moment. I don't think you can have any evidence for saying that." But unfortunately I did. It must somehow have come to Miss Cromwell's notice that Damaris' heart beat high for young Shackleton – Everard Shackleton, to give him his full title. It was infuriating that Damaris should have given herself away, and alarming that we had all been watching each other. I wondered how many other people had been engaged in the same pastime.

Miss Cromwell shrugged. I could tell she was hurt by the implicit distinction between her and Damaris as lower and higher forms of life, but I was not ready to forgive her for judging Damaris with such crude simplicity.

"I'd better get back to work," she said. "Brother Basil's an awful clock-watcher. Honestly – Brother Basil!"

With Christmas approaching preparations were well under way for the concert. It was to be mostly a musical affair, though Brother Eamonn, a colleague on the English staff, was organizing dramatic poetry readings – Eliot's 'Journey of the Magi' and a noisy narrative about Daniel in the Lions' Den. Brother Eamonn managed to take rehearsals at lunchtime, but Damaris claimed that was too rushed and two or three evenings a week would stay after school. Shackleton – revelations – stayed too.

"You don't have to wait for me, Carlo," she said one day as the stampede from the staffroom began and we were being lightly trampled underfoot by fleeing teachers. "I don't mind coming home alone. In fact Terry will probably give me a lift."

"Thy wish was father to that thought, young Harry."

"What?"

"You want me to go home, do you?"

"Of course not." She flushed and shook her mane. "What a nasty thing to say. I just don't like to think of you hanging about for me. They turn the heating off at five, you know."

"That's all right. I can mark and do some preparation. I'd be quite glad to get it done here."

"Just as you like. Good. I'll see you later, then."

The rehearsals were conducted in the hall. From the staffroom, especially if I turned the lights out, I could look down through the plate-glass wall and make out what was happening. Shackleton was playing Gerald Moore. He sat at the piano with his back to me, the view occasionally impeded by one or other of his music teachers leaning over his shoulder for consultations. The knowledge that both of them lusted after him contributed to the bizarre appeal of the scene, conducted as it was to me in silence, as not even the massed first-years singing "See Amid the Winters No" could penetrate two sets of double-glazing. Occasionally Brother Eamonn, playing the fellow *artiste* for the duration, ambled in to remind the boys that Real Authority was within hailing distance. Brother Eamonn did, in fact, have real authority, if it is to be judged by its effects. With his slight build, gold-rimmed glasses, slicked-down hair and compressed, humoress lips he was as sinister as a

Nazi spy-catcher. At least he persuaded the boys that he had ways of making them not talk, although I never heard him raise his voice. He seemed to enjoy talking to Damaris. They and Terry Yeats would stand behind Shackleton's discreet back, chatting while the boys sang. They made a curious trio, Damaris assuming the proportions of a civic monument beside the slim, black-clad priest and wasp-waisted, blond-haired Mr Yeats.

I had suggested to Damaris that since she was so intimate with Brother Eamonn she might plant in his mind the idea that Anne should replace Miss Cromwell at the typewriter. Unbelievably, Brother Basil thought that Damaris and I were doing a splendid job. Brother Eamonn intimidated Brother Basil, so I assumed it would be an easy job once Damaris had done her part. She seemed reluctant.

"I don't like using my friendships in that way," she protested loftily when I brought the matter up, shortly after the conversation with Miss Cromwell in the toilet. "It smacks of payola."

"Not if no money passes hands. You don't actually have to suggest the swop. Just mention you have a secretary friend unemployed. Don't you ever discuss female unemployment in the home counties?"

"Frankly, no. There is no discreet way of introducing the subject. What am I supposed to say – '*Vis-à-vis* Schopenhauer's influence on Nietzsche I've got a friend who can take over from Miss Cromwell'? I think you're being a bit obtuse, Carlo."

"I think you are. Not to mention downright chicken. It's not as if Anne were a liability. She's quite up to it."

"I'd rather go straight to Brother Basil."

"Yes, well why don't you? You got him to hire me."

"That's partly the reason. It would be awkward to do it again so soon. He might think I'm planning a *coup d'état*."

"Then why did you mention it in the first place? It was your idea. I'm beginning to think you don't want her to come up."

"That's not true." She looked at me with pain and came over from the stove to sit opposite me at the kitchen table – fold-out Formica flap, to be precise. "Why can't you accept that I have genuine scruples?"

"Scruples generally are genuine. It doesn't mean they should always take precedence over personal loyalty."

Damaris looked down at her feet, which were built, like the rest of her on a heroic scale. I waited for her to protest. In vain.

I was becoming rather tired of our conversations disappearing without trace into the depths of her private thought.

"Well?" I prompted. "Do you want me to do it?"

"No." She sighed and rested her head on her hand. At this juncture it had become my habit to start the washing-up or something else symbolic of actively turning away from the lowered portcullis, of avoiding frontal attack. I had never known it difficult to speak my mind to her. I assumed the reason was, that when we did not live together we would save up whole days of thoughts, acts and words to share when we did meet. Now we knew exactly how the other passed the time, the need for concealment had arisen, at least on her side. She looked tired. Even her lightly freckled lips looked drained and pale. The life of the school was sufficient to explain her exhaustion, and to provide excuses to let the matter slide, but I realized that if these barriers of silence were not demolished our life — my life — would be barren indeed. I did not again expect to acquire friendships such as ours had been, nor could I face watching ours become a museum echoing with past assumptions, in which I was forced to live for lack of somewhere else to go.

"Damaris," I said, feeling as though I were jumping out of an aeroplane, "what's the matter with you? It's all gone wrong, hasn't it? I can't talk to you."

Damaris looked up. "Carlo! You're crying! What have I done? What's the matter?"

"I don't — hic — know. I'm lonely. Why don't you want — hic — Anne to come up here?" I wanted to say "You don't love me anymore", which is what I was thinking, but shrank from the furthest reaches of absurdity.

Damaris came swiftly round the table and pinioned me against her torso. "I'm sorry. Don't cry. I don't know what's the matter with me. I suppose I feel the same as you, that if I let go, even a little, it would all come out. Please stop crying, it's killing me."

"What would come out? What do you mean?"

"Oh — just everything. Self-loathing, life-loathing. Just everything."

"Terminal lacrimae rerums?"

"Something like that."

"I wish you'd said. I've felt so cut off. It's that school that's killing me. It's just total humiliation, day after day."

"I know. I thought talking about it might only increase the pain.

But you're right. I was only being cowardly. I'll talk to Brother Eamonn tomorrow. He usually comes to rehearsals, he knows it leaves Terry and me more free to concentrate on the musical aspects."

This gratuitous prattle about rehearsals, and by implication Shackleton, cast a tiny shade, no bigger than a man's imagination, on the emotional glow around us. Consciousness of the wretched youth must have been fluttering continually in her mind like a trapped insect, ever ready to escape into speech.

"Damaris," I said, keeping my eyes averted, my arm still around her, "are you sure there isn't anything you want to tell me? Anything to do with the school?"

"No. Like what?"

"You're not involved with anybody? Nothing's upsetting you? I'd be hurt to think you wouldn't tell me. You know you can trust me absolutely, don't you?"

"Of course. But I don't know what you mean. Are you afraid I'm having an affair with Terry Yeats or something? Really that is silly, Carlo."

"No, that's not what I meant. Why should I mind if you had an affair? I'd be happy for you if it were successful."

"Then stop worrying. Nobody can help me with my problems. They don't concern anyone else." She stroked my hair. "You weren't getting jealous, were you?"

"No. Of what, anyway? We're not lovers. I was just trying to think why you were getting so withdrawn. Love is the usual explanation."

Damaris laughed. "It's just as well you brought this up, Carlo, so that I can set your mind at rest." I looked up at her. She seemed totally sincere. Either I had been mistaken about her infatuation with Shackleton or she had not admitted it. "I'm odd in that way. I'm not really interested in men at all. I thought you knew that."

"So did I." She was looking at me in a peculiar way, with a slightly insane grin on her face.

"Do you need convincing?" she said, and pressing me closer to herself she bent down and kissed me on the mouth, which, as it happens, hung open.

I thought I should faint, and not with pleasure. The physical sensation was minimal; her mouth was soft and dry and sexless – it was like kissing a sponge cake. But what did appall me was the realization in its wake. Miss Cromwell had spoken no more than

46

the truth: Damaris was on the boil. But as she was unwilling or unable to acknowledge for whom, her attentions had focused on the nearest object: me. She could not kiss Shackleton, so she kissed me. In itself innocent enough. I shied from thinking of all the other things she could not do to Shackleton. Instead I remembered all the cases of young women whose sexual frustration had turned fatally inward: the girls who had mutilated themselves in order to accuse the beloved of rape, Freud's Anna O, Mother Jeanne of the Angels, Catherine of Siena, for all I knew Joan of Arc. The historical precedents popped up like jack-rabbits. And I shared a bed with Damaris. What demented practices might she get round to in due course? Would I have to sit up half the night to make sure she was still asleep? There was no way I could have my own room in that flat.

Fortunately she seemed satisfied with a single kiss on this occasion. She patted me on the shoulder. "Want some coffee?"

"Thanks." I smiled, to draw a veil over my thoughts.

So much for trying to re-establish intimacy. Ostensibly it had been done, but in fact that kiss had sent me hurtling back into space.

Damaris had become an alien creature, to be watched in fear.

Had I not had Anne to look forward to, my sense of isolation would have driven me to admit defeat and return to the healing waters of the home counties. To myself I had decided that, if she were not coming, I would not return to the school after Christmas.

My secret fear of Damaris drew me closer to some of the other teachers, whose overtures of friendship I had up to then rejected. Martin, my head of department, was anxious to involve me in politics, and our arguments on the subject seemed to provide a suitable launching-pad for friendship.

The majority of the staff belonged to a union, the Lefties to the N.U.T., the conservatives to the A.M.A. Hostilities between the two were kept at the back of the stove except during elections. When Labour won, the Lefties would dress the staffroom overall and have a party to celebrate and Mr Dacre would beat a record number of boys as compensation: if the Conservatives triumphed a hostile silence would prevail in the staffroom for days, and mutterings would be heard about segregating the coffee club along political lines. The Conservative teachers were afraid of the Lefties, of the violence of their rectitude. The Lefties were certainly more

47

passionate, more involved. All the resentment they felt at not having had the chance to be rebellious peasants was directed at their right-wing colleagues in time of crisis. Many of them lived in council houses, shoulder to shoulder with the working man, but spent most of the time out of them because of the noise of children and televisions turned up to pathological levels by people who had long been used to a constant background noise. The two groups did have something in common however: they were all pious Catholics, despised ninety per cent of the boys in their charge and all homosexuals.

At this time the animosity between the two groups had been activated by the threat of a strike by the N.U.T., who outnumbered the A.M.A. two to one at The Blessed Ambrose. There was much excitement as to whether the non-unionized brothers and the A.M.A. between them might break the strike. The object was to close the school. Sammy the P.T. had a friend at Granada Television who had promised to come up and cover the action, or lack of it, if the school were forced to close. The thought of peak viewing coverage brought the potential strikers to fever pitch. Unfortunately, if they were to persuade the potential strike-breakers to support them, they were obliged to be conciliatory, to sweet-talk people like Mr Dacre.

It was in this area of activity that Martin sought to interest me.

"Dacre sits at your table at dinner, doesn't he?" he said, settling me down with a mug of gritty coffee in the radicals' corner of the staffroom. "I've heard he's getting quite sweet on you."

"From whom?"

"The boys."

"God help me."

"But it could be very useful. You could persuade him to take a lead. All the other red-necks follow him."

"How? What am I supposed to say?"

"You'll think of something. We don't expect them to come out in sympathy, just not substitute for any of us, that's all."

"Why not? Why should the kids suffer? That's not fair."

"They won't suffer, they'll have a ball. And anyway it's for the long-term good of the entire educational system. If salaries aren't improved the profession will be seriously undermanned in a few years."

"Not with the training colleges churning out teachers by the truck-load and all sensible women on the pill. It's unemployment you should be worrying about, not salaries."

"They're separate questions. The system needs those teachers – the ratios are the worst in Europe. It's diabolical that the government should try and save money by economizing on staff. That's what's really unfair on the kids. How do you expect troglodytes like Rattray –" he referred to an illiterate, but experienced, car thief in 2C "– to learn anything in a class of thirty-eight?"

"But if they spend more money on teachers' salaries they'll have to put taxes up and you know what that will do to the Pound in your Pocket – particularly the pockets of the underprivileged, whom you're always getting steamed up about."

"Not if they cut down on defence spending. Look, this country contributes a completely disproportionate amount to NATO, which is little more than a fascist club, anyway. Do you know how much they spent on defence last year?"

"Go on, tell me."

He whipped out *The British Economy in Figures*, a slim booklet he kept in his wallet. "It's more every year."

I took it from him. "They spent more on the health service, too. That's just inflation."

He snatched it back, his face dark with frustration. "I'm not saying they didn't. The health service is just window-dressing. It's irrelevant to the main question."

"Well, I doubt if Mr Dacre will be moved by statistics. Can't you think of more altruistic arguments?"

"He's a fascist swine. I'd like to put him up against a wall and shoot him."

"You'll have to wait for the Revolution for that."

"Are you going to work on him or aren't you?"

Martin's ultimatums made me nervous. The gym shoes he used for administering justice were only inches away in his cupboard.

"I'm sorry, I just can't get worked up about politics. I always vote Liberal myself."

"Huh! The Liberal Party's a joke. It ought to be disbanded."

"Why? Millions of people vote for them."

"That's the trouble. It's undemocratic. Having third parties cripples the parliamentary system."

"What about Keir Hardie? Labour was third party when it started."

"That was a different situation. In those days the majority

of working people weren't represented at all. The Liberals just represent people who have good intentions but aren't prepared to give up their privileges to back them up."

"Yes, that describes most people. Are you implying that self-sacrifice is the hallmark of the working class?"

He sighed violently. "It's no good expecting a woman to have a political conscience. I can see I'm wasting my time."

I certainly felt as though I were wasting mine. I had wanted to discuss visual aids and whether Peter Porter was too subtle for 2B. But I was stung by his snide reference to my womanly, and by implication, defective, understanding. "I hardly think the world in its present state is an argument for male dominance," I said, with some dignity.

He looked crestfallen. "That's so true. I'm sorry. I shouldn't have said that."

"It's all right."

"More coffee?"

"Thanks."

In fact I welcomed his abuse, for the more violent Martin became in argument the more conciliatory he was in remorse. My womanly deficiencies were much more susceptible to this side of him, particularly as I felt so much in need of productive human contact. As I got to know him better, I even came to condone, or at least suspend judgment on, his use of corporal punishment. He went about it with a jovial impartiality that put him in a good mood for weeks. And his victims never seemed to bear a grudge, some of them almost adored him. Whereas I, with my humanitarian scruples, encountered nothing but hostility. To oblige Martin, I agreed to broach the subject of the strike with Mr Dacre.

Our table was solidly A.M.A., Mr Marple and Brother William being against disruptive industrial action on principle, the former because it conflicted with his ambitions to be a Good Teacher, the latter because any kind of conflict was painful to him. The task of tackling Mr Dacre had been made more daunting by Martin's suggestion that he was developing an interest in me. It was becoming a matter of wonder to me that people ever managed to fall in love with each other: my experience suggested that the majority of love affairs were one-sided.

"I intend to do my job," said Mr Dacre, on being questioned as to his attitude to the impending strike. "That's what I'm paid for."

"Of course. But will you do more? If Brother Basil asks for volunteers to fill in for the strikers?"

"The question probably won't arise. My timetable is practically full as it is."

"Mine too," said Mr Marple. "But I would if asked. I'm against the strike. If you become a teacher, or a nurse, or a policeman you do it with your eyes open. It's no good complaining once you're in."

"But what happens if what you see from the outside doesn't match the reality on the inside? And anyway people can't just get out and start something else after years of training and experience. The government knows how hard that is, that's the factor they exploit, and the nobility of people like yourself, Mr Marple. Honestly this country might just as well be communist if you have to choose between money or job satisfaction. How long do you think a society that fails to reward merit can remain stable?" I passed Mr Marple his rhubarb crumble with an accusatory flourish.

"I think you exaggerate the difficulty of getting out," said Mr Dacre. "A lot of the men here could easily get a job in industry, except that they don't want to be *that* close to the working class."

"Well, all right, theory apart, how would you advise me to act? Brother Basil is bound to ask me to help out because I don't belong to a union at all." I tried to look anxious for his advice.

Mr Dacre frowned. "The best thing to do is prevaricate. Don't actually refuse, so it can't be held against you, but say you've got a programme to record, or take detention or something."

"Is that what you'll do?"

"Probably. Why not? After all, we'll all get more pay if the strike is effective."

I relayed this conversation to Martin, who was ecstatic, and told all the other Lefties I was "all right".

From time to time, while waiting in the staffroom for Damaris to finish her rehearsals, my attention would wander. Looking around at the darkened bulk of the school, the empty classrooms with their upturned chairs, the silent gym, art rooms and laboratories variously tidied against the onslaughts of the following day, the urge sometimes took me to wander myself, ghost-like, around the deserted building. At such times it seemed to have a soul akin to my own, a place relishing its nocturnal solitude, but vibrating in every fibre with the hostile energy of its daytime inhabitants. It was an urge I felt advised to resist at first: the lights from the brothers' house winked reminders that the school was only nominally abandoned. For all I knew it was patrolled at regular intervals. Besides which I was scared.

But once the notion was implanted it became an obsession. I soon became bored with spying on rehearsals and felt my character challenged by the idea. What was there to be afraid of?

So, one Thursday, having finally made up my mind two days before, I turned the lights out in the staffroom and set off down the darkened corridors.

My route lay through the sixth-form wing and the library. All the doors stood open and sufficient light filtered through to the corridor from the street lamps. These rooms were among the most familiar to me, being so close to the staffroom. By virtue of being the oldest part of the school, they had a comfortably battered appearance. The desks had been moved from rows into two semi-circles, one inside the other, so that they bore faint echoes of the United Nations. I went into Upper Sixth Arts and stood behind the teacher's desk. My only contact with the sixth-formers was through the Scientists, preparing them for an exam to prove they could read and write. It occurred to me that Shackleton must use this room. I went over to the noticeboard, which was on the wall at right angles to the window and in full light from the street. There were newspaper articles about Vietnam and the re-organization of local government, lists of classes, fliers advertising local productions of *The Winter's Tale* and other classics, messages inviting those eager, or even willing, to go to the *York Mystery Cycle* to sign below, brochures about careers in the police force and Inland Revenue and a vacancy in the Catholic Enquiry Centre. I shuffled lightly through them all. Tucked away under a chart for a round-robin inter-sixth-form table-tennis championship was a short, type-written note: "Will the swine who pinched my I Ching sticks during 1st fifteen practice on Wednesday the 15th kindly return them or I will personally see to it that the summer dragon flies up his nostrils. Shack."

I smiled. This must be the demi-god Shackleton for whom Damaris pined, this the Mozart come back to life, the genius who walked to a distant drum. How delightfully juvenile he sounded from that note. I was tempted to add "–up" to the signature, but was afraid it was the beginning of a slippery slope that might lead in time to writing on lavatory walls.

Upper Sixth Arts had no other points of interest, so I moved on into the science wing, by this time almost enjoying myself. The labs were on the top floor. I went there first. A tap was dripping in Biology, which I turned off. In Chemistry I paused before a chart of the elements. It reminded me of the vast realms of knowledge of this type which I had never entered. On the whole I felt thankful that I had not. It seemed to me that by relentlessly probing into the nature of matter, mankind was aiming in the wrong direction.

There was a noise from below. A chair scraped. A window closed with a bang. I froze, my heart thumping. Silence. Could I have imagined it? But I had not been listening for noise, it must have forced itself on my attention. Possibly it was one of the brothers doing the rounds. If that were so he would presumably put the light on. That could easily be ascertained by going to the window in the corridor and looking down for light reflected outside. I crept out of the lab. and over to the window. All was still dark. This wing was hidden from the hall, from where light might reach, by the sixth-form block. Again I jumped at the sound of a slight noise from below, obviously coming from the classroom under the lab.

An opportunity for heroism had me by the throat, strangling breath. My instinct was to run, but I was not sure if the doors at this end of the block were open. Probably not. In that case I would have to go downstairs, virtually past the classroom in question. I doubted if I could do it without being heard by the intruder. And tugging at my instinctive cowardice was the thrill of catching a criminal in the act. More than likely it was one of the boys. I had heard many stories of vandalism against the school: twelve months before some boys had broken in to the art room, smashed up the furniture and daubed the room overall with skulls and crossbones, rampant penises and football slogans – all touchingly symbolic of the role of school in the social and psychological development of the disturbed child, so I was told. It was not only for the good of the school that such characters should be caught and treated: it was for their own good too.

However, it was a bold vandal who walked alone. I was undoubtedly outnumbered. But if I could at least catch a glimpse of one of them, to help the police with their investigations ...

Without really knowing what I intended to do, but walking as if sucked along by a vacuum cleaner, I glided downstairs, my mouth open, breathing shortly, my heart banging about inside my ribcage like a thing possessed. I turned at the bottom of the stairs and tiptoed over to the door of the classroom. There was now complete silence. Either they were waiting behind the door, sawn-off drainpipe in hand, or they had left. I could not imagine a bunch of vandals pausing for meditation. I waited. Still no sound. My own need for action had become urgent. I closed my hand on the handle of the door and pushed it open a crack. Still no sound. In a swift movement I put my hand round the door and switched on the lights.

"Grass! What the Hell are you doing here?"

Sitting at a desk in the middle of the room, staring at me, was the animus of 3B. There was a book open on the desk, and he held a torch in his hand. He had started when the lights came on, but recovered his sang-froid in seconds. "I might ask you the same question, Miss. What are *you* doing here?"

"That's none of your damn business and well you know it." He looked unimpressed. "As a matter of fact I was in the staffroom and heard a noise."

"There are no lights on in the staffroom, Miss."

"I was saving energy. Anyway, stop playing Maigret with me. It's you who has the explaining to do. I'll have to report this to Brother Basil, so you might as well own up and tell me what you were doing."

"Why do you have to? I'm not doing anything wrong. Just reading me book."

Again his exasperating pose of innocence confounded me. "Well you've no business being on the premises after hours. How did you get in?"

"Through the window. The catch is loose. I didn't damage nothing."

It was true. There were no broken windows. "But what are you doing here? Why aren't you at home with your parents? Or out vandalizing the youth club with your friends?"

"I don't have any."

"Which? Parents or friends?"

He shrugged and looked away. I went over and sat on a chair in the row next to him. "Look, Grass, I'm tired. Partly thanks to your atrocious behaviour in class today. Now will you stop being so mysterious and tell me in words of one syllable what you think you're doing? You never know, I might buy it." He continued to stare at the window. "All right, I'll just have to fetch Brother Basil." I got up.

"No! Don't do that, Miss, please!"

"Then what do you suggest?"

"How about coming down to the Happy Cow for a coffee? I'll treat you."

"What?" I stared at him. He had his hands neatly folded over his book, his big eyes faced me, frank and fearless. I began to laugh, helplessly lost, and sank onto the chair with my head on my hand. He went back to staring at the window.

At last I recovered myself. "I'm sorry, Grass. I'm not really laughing at you. Just the situation. And I told you, I'm tired." I assumed an American accent. "You'd better talk, kid."

After a pause, Grass shrugged. "I come here a lot in the evenings."

"A lot? How often?"

"Once or twice a week."

"To do what?"

"Read."

"Why don't you read in the library?"

"They kick you out at seven anyway."

"What are you reading?"

"*Angelique and the Sultan*. It's awfully good, Miss."

"You don't say? Now why don't you take it home and read?" He shrugged. "Is there anything wrong at home?"

"Depends on your point of view."

A thought struck me. "Grass, you do go home sometimes, don't you?" I had been reading Melville's "The Dead Letter Office", the story of an unfortunate who spent the night at the office because he had nowhere else to go.

"Yeah. To sleep, of course."

"Are both your parents at home?"

"No. Just me Dad."

"Does he drink or something?"

"Sometimes."

"Well, does he want you out of the house?"

"No, I want to get out."

"Because he has women in? Is that it?"

"Far from it." He snorted. "You're in the right area, but you haven't got your finger on it."

"Don't be vulgar, Grass. I'm just trying to help. You're not telling me he brings boyfriends home?"

"No."

"Well, what is the problem, then?"

"I don't think you'd want to know, Miss. You'd be embarrassed."

"Grass, it's awfully sweet of you to want to spare my feelings, but I am grown-up. I doubt if you could shock me. Besides, it can't be as bad for me to hear as it is for you to put up with, whatever it is."

I wondered if it was in fact proper for me to encourage him to share the ghastly secrets of his domestic life: I was not sure if I was conducting an academic enquiry or downright snooping. But the ease with which I suddenly found myself conversing with Grass as though he were a genuine human being, seduced me into further enquiry. I had never actually talked to one of the boys on his own before: it made me realize how theatrical the classroom situation was. Grass, taken out of the proscenium arch that invisibly separates teacher and taught, was not grotesque at all; in fact he was somewhat pathetic, and almost touchable.

"You'll call me a liar."

"I won't."

He turned to look me straight in the eyes. "All right. It's like this. He's as queer as a coot, all right. He keeps wanting me to give him a blow job and when I don't he beats me up – or tries to. That's what it boils down to any road. I won't go into details, like I said, you'd be embarrassed." He spoke without emotion, as if explaining which bus route he took to school.

My stomach lurched through a complete circle, and I could feel the blood rush to my face and plummet back down my legs with sickening force. I was totally unprepared for tales of sexual deviation. I had imagined some more garden variety problem, of the kind one hears about all the time – the Demon Drink, parental fights, simple overcrowding. The houses of most of the boys were small and the families large. My imagination had been working strictly along these lines. But what Grass had told me took my breath away. It was gross, ugly, debased, quite lacking in the tough-romantic quality of the problems I had envisaged. Rejection was instinctive.

56

"Grass, what a terrible thing to say! It's a terrible thing to accuse anyone of, but your own father –"

"See? I said you'd call me a liar."

I covered my face with my hand. The appalling fact was that I had no instinct at all for knowing if he was telling the truth or not. If he was, my sympathy and indignation were potentially boundless: if not, I was being taken to the cleaners by the roots of my hair. The latter was the possibility that haunted me. "Look," I said, "please try to understand my point of view, Grass. Let's be frank. Your behaviour and attitude, they don't exactly inspire confidence. If I can't believe you right away, it's mostly your own fault ... well, partly."

"I suppose you want proof?"

"That would be difficult. I'm not going to go to your father and ask him, am I?"

"Let me ask you a question, then. Do you think I'd come back and sit in this fucking cold school all by meself at night if I had a nice cosy little home with a nice cosy little mum and dad in it?"

I was startled by his vicious tone. His voice was trembling and there were tears in his eyes. But, agonizingly, he could still be faking. I knew him too well. "That's true, Grass. But then why aren't you with your friends? I'm sorry, but I thought boys in your position always spent the evening drinking under age, or playing football in corporation flowerbeds."

"I've told you. I don't have any friends."

"Why not?"

He shrugged. "They're stupid, the kids round here. I don't want to end up in Borstal and p'raps get screwed by the whole bloody staff."

"Oh Grass!" His look of disgruntlement finally convinced me that he must be telling the truth. I shook my head. "So you come in here and read historical fiction in the freezing cold. What's to become of you? Haven't you any relations who'd take you in?"

"Why should they? I'm properly cared for, ain't I? Fed and clothed and all that, and me Dad's always home in the evenings, except Tuesday and Friday."

"But if he hits you, you must have bruises –" My voice faltered before my imagination.

"Still don't believe me, do you?" He sighed and began to take off his jacket.

"No, no, I believe you. There's no need for that. But if you

57

have evidence, you could be taken into care. I know it's second best, but you could be comfortable. No one would assault you."

Grass assumed an air of great weariness. "Ah, but it makes life interesting."

"Grass, don't try and be sophisticated. It doesn't fool anybody. How soon can you leave home? Do you have any plans?"

"Yeah. I wanna go to California and grow oranges."

"Oh dear. That's a rather romantic notion, Grass."

"But haven't you seen the photos in our Geog. books, Miss? Acres and acres of oranges, and mountains with snow on them behind."

"I'm afraid the textbooks around here are rather out of date. Fruit farming in California is big business nowdays. You couldn't buy yourself a little farm and pick the fruit yourself, you know. You're thirty years too late."

He shrugged again. I suspected that Grass knew as much about modern fruit farming as I did, that he had picked on this clichéd vignette of a golden future in order to characterize, by contrast, his wretched present. His dissembling was as pathetic as if he were really living for an impossible dream, and I felt cruel for having exposed it.

"There are other possibilities, though. New Zealand is supposed to be beautiful. How do you feel about sheep?"

"Dunno. I just want to get out of this rain-sodden, pissing dump. I hate it."

"I understand that, Grass. But you know, just changing the scenery isn't necessarily going to make you any happier. One of these days you're going to have to forgive your father, or you'll never be free."

"I don't get it. Why should I ever forgive the old goat? I hate him."

"All right. You can't do it now. But what I mean is, the fact that you haven't any friends. Do you hate everybody? That's so self-destructive."

He thought for a moment. "I suppose I don't hate you, Miss."

"Thank you. But my opportunities for helping you are somewhat limited. How old are you?"

"Fourteen. This year."

"Thirteen. All right. You're quite mature for your age, though. In some ways. You should get yourself a girlfriend."

"You think a good fuck would set me straight with the world?"

58

"Please don't be so vulgar, Grass. It shows your age."

"Sorry, Miss."

"Anyhow, with your experience you should know better than to take advantage of young girls in that way."

"Yeah. You've got a point there."

"What I meant was, for companionship with someone your own age. You're an attractive boy, I'm sure there are lots of young girls who'd be interested."

"I'll think about it."

"Okay. I'd better go now. Miss Fotheringay will be waiting for me."

"You haven't got time for that coffee then?"

"I'm sorry. Another time."

"You won't tell Brother Basil?"

"No. But we'll have to do something for you. Perhaps a foster home."

He glowered. "No. I don't want any more snoopers coming round trying to sort me out. If you tell anyone else I'll kill you."

"All right, all right." I felt the sincerity of the threat. Shame for his father must still be stronger than resentment of him. "You'd better go now, though. I'll let you out the front door."

"Don't bother. I'll go the way I came, if you turn the light out."

"Good night, then."

"Good night, Miss."

I turned the light out and watched him climb through the window. When he had gone I went over to make sure it was shut. He had already disappeared.

I walked slowly over to the hall, in reflective mood. How obtuse I had been not to suspect some trouble at home behind Grass's aggressive behaviour. What disturbed me even more than the relationship with his father was the loneliness of his existence. The unnatural situation at home must have made him shun the friendship of boys from normal homes; or perhaps it was the other way round and his nonchalance was a defence. How different from the comfortable warmth and companionship that I had shared with Damaris and Anne at the same age. Grass must get up and go to bed, perform his ritual tasks of disruption and defiance in total mental isolation. Pathetic, too, that he was one of the few boys who took a pride in his appearance. Having no mother, he must wash his shirts and press his trousers himself,

59

thinking God knows what under the perverted eye of his father. I felt a little guilty for having pried, but glad too. I hoped Grass had been as fortified by our conversation as I had. It was my first real contact with any of the inmates: it made me feel humble and proud and human to a degree that was almost thrilling.

The hall was dark and empty. I cursed. Damaris must have gone looking for me and thought I had decided not to wait. I went up to the staffroom to fetch my things. Outside the book store I heard voices. One of them belonged to Damaris. Relieved, I barged in.

Standing in the open doorway between the book store and the corridor were Damaris and Shackleton. She had her hand on his arm in a gesture of urgent supplication. I switched on the light and both of them blinked into it.

"Damaris, what are you doing? I thought you must have gone. You evidently thought I had." I could not keep the contempt out of my voice. Damaris' obsession with Shackleton, compared with the real sorrows of this world, as just movingly evinced by Grass, suddenly seemed trivial and indefensible.

"I was having a private conversation. Do you mind? What are you, my nanny or something?"

"For God's sake, let's talk about it later." I indicated Shackleton, who lolled against the door, looking at me with amusement from under his flank of wavy hair.

Damaris rolled her eyes. "Christ. All right, I'm coming. Excuse me, Shackleton," she said over her shoulder. "I'll see you in the morning."

"Okay. Good night. Good night, Miss Slade." He left.

Damaris brushed past me into the staff room. I followed, fuming.

"'Excuse me, Shackleton'! What the fuck do you mean, 'Excuse me, Shackleton'? How dare you speak to him like that in front of me, as if I were a nagging kid? God, what an unspeakable fool you're making of yourself." I was shaking with rage. I had thought nothing would have made me break my silence on the subject of Shackleton, but had underestimated how pain cries out for vengeance.

Damaris was ready for a fight. She stood before me, arms akimbo like a fishwife, deliberately throwing her height into the fray. "Oh I am, am I? Look at yourself for once. Why are you suddenly playing the schoolmarm down to the brass buttons? And it doesn't

60

fool me, anyhow, but I've got too much on my plate to deal with your jealousy at the moment."

"Jealousy? Is that what you told him?" I was remembering his amused expression. I shook my head. "Poor cow. You think I'm jealous just because I try to tell you how ... how dangerous it is to be found in a darkened closet with a lovely sixth-former."

"Well, of course we didn't want the brothers beetling over to put the lights out. Anyway, it was his idea. We'd just been to the library to check up something about Franz Schmidt."

"Also in the dark?"

"Will you shut up! It's lit up like a gin-palace from the street lamps. And the reason we stopped in the book room is because the staffroom is out of bounds to the boys, if you must know. I'm quite well aware of proprieties in these matters thank you."

"They've obviously changed since I was at school."

"For Christ's – Why do you persist in talking as if there were something fishy going on? That's what you want to think, obviously. It's just your filthy imagination."

"Oh really? Listen, Damaris, it's not just me. I'm sorry, but everyone knows you've got a crush on that boy. You seem to be the last to find out. That's too bad, but it's about time."

"*I* have a crush on Shackleton? Are you mad? *I* have a – Oh, no, this is neurotic, Carlo, really. This is what I mean – you're twisting the facts to feed your jealousy. You're the only one who could possibly think that. Just because I was talking to him alone? I can't help it if he happens to be the opposite sex – they all are. I'm not interested in sex, damn it, you know that."

"Your relationship is purely professional – platonic. You only have his future career at heart."

"Damn right. I suppose you're wondering what we were talking about. Well, he's talking of joining the Navy. Yes, *your* jaw's dropping – you can imagine how Terry and I feel. That boy has music in every bone of his body – he must do music. He's going through some sort of macho phase at the moment, I think that's the trouble. I'm afraid Terry doesn't help – in fact I think that's where Shackleton's got the idea it's a pansy profession."

"Well, of course, there's only one way to prove to the little darling that he's every inch a man. I'm sure you wouldn't mind making such a sacrifice for the sake of Art." I was jaded by her assumption of the importance of saving Shackleton's talents for Mankind. Brother William had said they were only relative. I now doubted whether Damaris herself had enough talent to judge.

"Just what do you mean?" she said, the skin between her freckles pale as an egg.

"Go to bed with him. Go to bed with somebody. Get it out of your system before someone like Brother Basil finds you in a broom cupboard with Shackleton and is less willing than I am to believe you're discussing his career in the Navy."

"Oh!" Damaris took a step back, took aim, and struck me, accurately, on the cheek. Even as she lifted her hand I could not believe what was coming.

I staggered back. "Cretin!" I gasped, fighting paralysis of the larynx. "Is that your last word?" I picked up a book and lobbed it at her. It missed, and crashed against the window, fortunately without breaking it.

"Carlo, stop it! I understand, really I do." She was creeping round the room towards the door and spoke with deliberate calmness, as if I were a psychopath. "I'm sorry I hit you, but you've got to come to your senses about this. You're just embittered because we haven't been all-in-all to each other as you expected – because I've got involved with the school more than you. I understand, honestly. I'll make it up to you."

I was reeling with disbelief. "Don't talk to me as if we were a couple of bloody dykes! That's got nothing to do with it. You're the one who doesn't know what's going on, going around hitting people who are just trying to stop you making a fool of yourself – how dare you hit me!" I hurled another book at her. It hit the door just as Brother William came through it.

He stood looking from one to the other, I at the far end of the room, clutching my cheek with my left hand, another missile in my right, tears streaming down my face: Damaris just to his right behind the door, crouching. She got up.

"Is there anything wrong, ladies?" said Brother William. "I heard shouting."

"No, Brother," said Damaris, smoothing her hair. "We were having a slight argument. You know what women are like."

"Can't say I do, really. But still, I think it would be a good idea to go home now. It's quite late."

"Yes. Sorry, Brother. I hope we didn't give you a fright."

"No, no. I was just fetching something from the library and curiosity got the better of me. Now hurry up and get home. You live on the other side of the city, don't you? Such a long way. Have you

62

anyone to make it nice and warm for you when you get in?"

"No. I'm afraid it's impossible to make it nice and warm whatever we do."

"Oh dear, that's too bad. Warmth and sleep are so important in the winter. No wonder tempers get frayed, hmm? Well, good night, ladies."

"Good night, Brother."

We went home, made ham sandwiches and coffee and went to bed, in silence.

The next morning I stayed in bed and told Damaris to say I had sinusitis.

"Why?"

"Well, how do you suggest I explain this?" I touched my Victoria plum-coloured cheek.

"I'm sorry about that. You could put some make-up over it."

"Go to Hell."

The truth was, my morale was so battered it could not support a day of eight classes, lunch with Brother William and Mr Dacre and enforced good cheer with one and all.

I stayed in bed until half past ten, huddled under the covers, staring at the tatty curtains. When I got up, the post had come. There was a letter from Anne, addressed to both of us. I made a cup of tea and went back to bed to read it.

"Dear Damaris and Carlo: I had to write straight away when I got the news. Thank you so much, dears! Of course, I can't seem too cheerful at home as Mummy and Daddy are a bit depressed about it – only chick (female) leaving the nest – you can imagine how it is. If you two weren't there already I think they might have tried to stop me, but then I wouldn't be coming anyway! Roger, my latest, was upset too. Did I tell you about him? He's a very nice young man I met at upholstery class. He's a junior undertaker so he's quite a realistic person, as you can imagine. But he's starting to talk about putting his money in bricks and mortar, which of course means a house i.e. nest, for us, so it's as well I'll be leaving. I'm sure he'll find someone else pretty fast, what with the house and having such a steady job. Will I be wanted to start before Christmas? I don't mind, in fact I can't wait. I've bought all new lingerie for some reason!"

There was another two pages of news and views, which I skipped through. So Damaris had fixed it with Brother Basil after all, but forgotten to tell me. Too obsessed with her sea-going prodigy, no doubt. Renewed anger at Damaris struggled with elation at the prospect of having Anne with us. The latter won. Suddenly I could not face the weekend alone in the flat with Damaris. It could not be got through without further scenes. Hurriedly I dressed, packed an overnight case and, leaving Anne's letter on the unmade bed, left to catch the London train.

I intended to tell Anne everything, to warn her that the *ménage à trois* might not last long. But when I saw her that evening in dear old Worcester Park I could not bring myself to say anything about it. Anne is unspeakably lovely, serene and soothing. Under the influence of her simple nature I reflected that with her there, the atmosphere would be different anyway. It might never be necessary to tell Anne that Damaris and I had come to blows. After five weeks! In the familiar surroundings of home, where every object was witness to a happier past, it was difficult to understand what could have triggered such passionate disruption.

On Saturday evening Anne, her boyfriend Roger, myself and a friend of Roger's – not in the undertaking business, but a graduate management trainee for Marks and Spencer – went out together. We ate at a Chinese restaurant in the West End, followed by a party in Barnes. The graduate trainee was a personable young man with a droopy blond moustache and he wanted to sleep with me at the party. I was tempted, but neither of us was provided with prophylactics and I thought Anne might be mildly shocked, and even wonder what kind of place Manchester must be. The young man and I had a terribly reasonable discussion about it and parted on friendly terms.

The compounded effect of so much that was familiar and unremarkable was to persuade me that I had over-reacted to Damaris' behaviour as a result of the general strain of school life. If we were to live together amicably it would have to be under a new dispensation. If she wanted to make a fool of herself I should not interfere. I would gradually sever my mooring lines to her and head off in other directions, go to evening classes and learn Russian, perhaps, or take up fencing.

When I got back on Sunday evening she seemed relieved, but not pleased, to see me. We talked stiffly about Anne, who was to come up the following week, to get familiar with the job before Miss Cromwell left.

At breaktime on Monday, Martin sought me out. "There's a bit of a problem," he said. "Could I have a look at your time-table?"

"Of course."

He studied it, comparing it with another, not his own. "Umm. I think that would be all right. Listen, the trouble is, Brother Eamonn has got shingles. He'll probably be off for a few weeks. I was wondering if you'd mind taking over his sixth-form class? It's important that they carry on because of the exams. They'll be doing mocks when they get back after Christmas. You'd like a bash at A-level work, wouldn't you?"

"Well – I – what about my regular classes?"

"We'll just have to cover those as best we can. It doesn't matter for the lower forms, they can always read. But the sixth need proper lessons. I've got a lot of exam classes myself so I can't really help. Do you mind?"

"No. But I must know what they've been doing, in detail."

"That's no problem. Brother Eamonn has written it all down. I'll show you." He did. Never one to let the grass grow under our feet, Martin suggested that I should start that afternoon, but I protested that I must at least do some preparatory reading of the text – Blake, unfortunately, a divine I detested. The first sally into Upper Sixth Arts was therefore to be on the Wednesday.

"Why are you reading Blake?" queried Damaris that night as we sat up in bed. Our verbal communication had begun to trickle through again.

"I'm taking Brother Eamonn's lot for A-level."

She picked up her book again, *The Stage History of Parsifal*. But her heart was clearly not in it, for in a moment she said, "Are you sure that's a good idea?"

"It wasn't my idea."

"But you could decline."

"Why? It will be more demanding than what I've been doing so far."

"That's what I mean. Are you sure you're up to it?"

"What?" Damaris was staring ahead of her, frowning behind the heavy tortoiseshell glasses she wore for close work. "What do you mean? That I'm not as smart as the sixth form? Thanks, pal."

"No, I don't mean that. But you have no experience teaching A-level, have you? It won't be like 3B."

"Thank God. How is one supposed to get experience, then? By reading about it?"

"After thorough preparation."

"Thanks for your encouragement. I never even thought about whether I was up to it until now. Of course I am. I've got a degree in the blasted subject, haven't I?"

"But doing and teaching are different things. I'm not doubting your potential, but your actual readiness."

"To what purpose? I don't have any choice."

Damaris continued to stare at the wall, and then resumed reading without further comment.

I was puzzled and hurt by this exchange, by the fact that Damaris had only come out of her shell for the purpose of undermining my self-confidence. I had never doubted my ability in the subject; it was only discipline that had unnerved me. Why she should so unkindly try to tell me that I had reached my level of incompetence with 3B I could not imagine.

The reason was clear when I walked into Upper Sixth Arts for the first lesson. Shackleton was sitting nearest to the teacher's table, which had been moved up so that it abutted onto the semi-circle of desks. His presence was surprising, irritating, complicating. No wonder Damaris had not wanted me to take the class. She must have wanted to be the only female in the school with whom he had dealings.

Feeling annoyed, I greeted them rather ungraciously. All except one, whom I recognized from the first day as Ryan, had straggled to their feet. He presumably thought himself sufficiently concealed behind the others to escape notice, as a cat stalking a bird will crouch hopefully behind a blade of grass.

"Are you being liberated, Ryan, or is it your varicose veins?"

He snorted breathily. The others had sat down again. "Sorry, Miss."

"Don't let it bother you. I quite agree that distinction on the grounds of sex is undesirable. I don't expect special courtesy. You stay seated when Brother Basil comes in too, no doubt?"

Ryan did not reply, merely blushed between his spots. The others were looking at him sardonically, glad that his nerve had

66

proved a hoist to his own petard, thus justifying their conformity. Shackleton looked disinterested, and pushed his biro up and down on the desk. He sat at half-mast, slouched in the chair with his long legs stretched in front of him, the flank of hair half concealing the face, but to no purpose as his very pose was sardonic.

I said the prayer and sat down. They were looking at each other. "What's the matter? I didn't sing the national anthem by mistake, did I?"

"No, Miss," said a kindly fat boy with thick spectacles, "but in the sixth we don't usually say the prayer any more."

"So that you'll feel more grown-up?" I sighed. "Don't you feel positively constricted by props for your egos? I mean, having your own kettle in the commonroom, a choice of shirt styles – don't you sometimes long for the dependency of childhood?" They met my earnest gaze with incomprehension. Shackleton was grinning. "Ah well, obviously not. Now then. Blake. 'The Marriage of Heaven and' – what the hell!" I had crossed my legs with some vigour, stubbing my toe on Shackleton's calf as I did so. He yelped. "Oh, sorry. I didn't see your legs there, Shackleton. Now, I gather from Brother Eamonn that you should have read 'The Marriage of Heaven and Hell' already. That being so, I assume that you can summarize the drift of the argument?" There was no response. All eyes were intently fixed on the printed page. "Er – Taylor? Hardturm? No? Well, the general structure then. What does it consist of, actually?" Again silence. Heads lowered. Things were not going according to plan. I looked at Shackleton. He re-arranged himself into a carefully casual pose.

"It opens with a prophetic vision of the condition of the just man turned out into- the wilderness," he said, without ceasing to push his biro up and down through lethargic fingers. "This is followed by a statement of the argument that the traditional conceptions of good and evil should be reversed and a refutation of the body and soul being separate and that Heaven is inferior to Hell because it's the graveyard of desire and creative energy. Then he gives a list of Hellish proverbs, expanding the idea. Er – then there are accounts of meetings with prophets like Isaiah, and angels, who show him visions of Heaven and Hell according to received theology, and Blake shows them his own version. It ends up with the Devil explaining that J.C. was okay because he had more creative energy than traditional morality. In between he gets at Swedenborg."

There was a pause, during which we all slowly came to out of a hypnotic trance.

"Quite," I laughed. "Well, shall we all go home now? Perhaps you would like to tell us something about Swedenborg?"

"I'm sorry. I didn't have time to look it up."

"Fortunately, I did. Anyone else?" The others were busily poising their biros for note-taking. "No? Swedenborg was a mystic, a self-proclaimed prophet of impending divine revelation, a former engineer who opened a clinic – I mean, a church – in London. He and Blake shared certain ideas about building a new Jerusalem in the London area, but Blake decided he was too traditional on the subject of good and evil. Blake's ideas on the subject were unorthodox to say the least. From 'The Marriage', can we say what they were, do you think?" Again there was heroic silence. "Er – Baxter?"

"Well, he thought they were all mixed-up."

"Is that how you're going to answer the exam question, Baxter? 'Blake thought good and evil were all mixed up?' Come, come, can we be a little more succinct?"

I was beginning to sweat. Trying to get them to answer a question was like trying to retrieve something from a manhole slightly deeper than the arm is long. I looked again, no doubt desperately, at Shackleton. He shifted in his seat, kicking my foot in the process.

"Oh, sorry." He looked down, sceptically.

I rubbed my instep. "That's all right. Just give us a few thoughts about Blake's morality by way of compensation."

"As far as I understand it, he thought of good and evil as being different aspects of the same dimension, not opposed, but sort of moving in opposite directions from the same source."

"That's one way of looking at it, yes. Let's just say for the moment that he equated evil, so-called, with energy, and good with passivity – a notion that should appeal to young persons like yourselves, I would have thought."

"Does it alter with age?" asked Shackleton with an innocent air.

"With experience, yes." The question had struck a sensitive target. I had wondered myself if I were not overdoing the greybeard bit. "I think we had better postpone the discussion of morality until you're more familiar with the work. Let's take a look at the opening stanzas, shall we?"

"Yes, let's," said Shackleton.

I ground my teeth. A few of the other boys were grinning at Shackleton's impudence. I wished I had been wearing an academic gown that I could have adjusted authoritatively. It was his assumption of equality that grated, as if it were indeed only a chronological accident that separated us, an accident that had no ramifications of status, experience or responsibility. But it would only have been demeaning to seem rattled. He would be squashed in time, but not before I had thought of a method conversant with my dignity.

"The Argument. As Shackleton has already told us, this is the voice of the prophet speaking. It's gnomic, that is, the meaning is cloaked in riddles, but much of it is easily decoded. Is there any term which springs to mind that we could use to designate the language of the work? Hardturm?"

Hardturm, a freckled red-head prone to blushing, wriggled. "There's a lot of ... um ... alliteration in it."

"How true. However, alliteration is closer to phonetics than what I have in mind. Anyone else? I've said already that the meaning is obscured. By what? I mean, he could have said, 'There's trouble brewing', right? What kind of transference of meaning does he use instead?" A few of them looked up to seek inspiration in the wainscotting. "Baxter?" I was determined not to resort to Shackleton again. But none of the others had a word to say. "It begins with M," I added heavily.

"Metaphor!" said Ryan.

"Well done. Yes, metaphor is a general term applied to deliberate comparison, which poets and others use to convey ideas or scenes in a forceful and illuminating manner – a fusion of idea and image which gives the thing described a new reality. Of course, transference of meaning can be analysed more minutely – into categories like synecdoche and metonymy, but the poet's bread and butter, so to speak, is metaphor. Well, well, there we are, 'bread and butter'. Of course poets don't eat metaphor for breakfast, but the phrase conveys so much more than saying 'It is an indispensable tool of their trade.' Didn't you do all this for O-Level?" My foot made contact with Shackleton's legs again, as he suddenly sat up. "For God's sake, Shackleton, there are plenty of schools for children who can't control their limbs, but this isn't one of them!"

A faint blush, like a drop of cochineal in a bowl of milk, suffused Shackleton's features. It was a gratifying sight.

"Now, then, the first two lines, for example, 'Rintran roars and shakes his fires in the burdened air/Hungry clouds swag on the deep.' Why 'Hungry'? What quality is he getting at there?"

"Perhaps their tummies were rumbling," said Crawford, the fat boy.

"Well, yes, I suppose if there were thunder, the primitive mind might interpret that as the clouds' tummies rumbling."

"Or farting," said Shackleton.

"That normally transpires on a full stomach, doesn't it? And if that is the kind of remark you consider helpful, Shackleton, I suggest you make it in the lavatory where it belongs."

The supercilious smile locked into place and, again, the hint of a blush. I was trembling. For a moment we glowered at one another. Then, in an instant, the nonchalant air was back.

"Sorry, Miss."

"I should think so. May we hear some sensible comment on the use of 'hungry' now?"

"Umm – he's implying that the clouds look pretty predatory, I think, menacing – as if they could consume the deep."

"Yes, possibly. Void, too, perhaps, as we've said. Anyway, you can certainly see metaphor at work here – setting off ripples of implication and connotation. Now, in 'the deep' we have an example of synechdoche, that is, a part of the whole – I presume I don't need to say which is which."

"Could you explain that term a bit more, Miss?" said Shackleton.

I looked at him for signs of disguised condescension, but his expression was as guileless as a Gordon Fraser greetings card.

The lesson proceeded without incident.

Far though I was from Damaris' hero-worship of Shackleton, that lesson convinced me that his talents would be wasted at sea. In order to show my superior objectivity where he was concerned, I determined to say as much to Damaris. For once she was anxious to know how I had coped and was hanging around in the staff-room chatting to Terry Yeats when I came back from the class. I could tell from her broad smile that she was keen to normalize the atmosphere, at least for as long as it took to pump me for information about my rapport with Shackleton. Once more I was confounded by the virulence of her infatuation, by its power to twist and deform normal behaviour patterns, like railway lines in an earthquake. That look she gave me, of trembling expectation at the prospect of news of the love object: I had seen nothing like it since Anne had had a brief crush at the age of twelve on a boy she saw on the bus on Tuesday nights. For a few months she had started preparations for the next brief encounter on the Thursday before, had even shampooed her pubic hair, and if the boy so much as glanced at her when alighting she would be prone with achievement for days. I had marvelled then at Anne's dementia, but in a young adolescent it was excusable: in a grown woman, frightening.

"So," said Terry Yeats as I entered, "you've been playing with our Shackleton, have you? I hope you enjoyed yourself. How was it?"

"I think his reputation is exaggerated, but you're right: I don't see his future in a nautical setting. I don't know what his writing is like yet, but anyway he's obviously university material. He's the only one in that group whom I would recommend to read literature."

"Literature?" exclaimed Damaris. "What rubbish. He's a musician. There's no doubt about that at all. He's not interested in literature."

"Yes he is. He's very well read as far as I can tell – far above the call of duty. A lot of kids his age can bash out a tune, but acute critical perception is much more rare. Besides, an academic or journalistic career is more secure. There's too much competition in music these days – you've said that yourself, Damaris."

"For the average, yes. Even for the very good. But Shackleton is exceptional. It would be a crime if he went into anything else. Apart from the loss to the world, he wouldn't be happy – he'd live a life of regret and bitterness, I know he would."

"For God's sake, we're not dealing with the young Mozart. If he were that good he wouldn't be here. Yehudi Menuhin would have snapped him up for his prodigy farm. Aren't I right, Terry?"

We were standing around his desk. He was grinning, and admiring his dapper left foot in its Russell and Bromley co-respondent shoe. "Did you know," he said coyly, "that Mr Rice thinks he's going to art school? Shack's going to be the first from this school. The only point in question is which one. Apparently Shackleton is going to take over where Lowry left off."

"What!" shrieked Damaris and I in unison.

"You never said," accused Damaris.

"Well I didn't take it seriously. I don't know if he can paint, though that's not so important these days. But with you two girls fighting over the body, I suppose it's not impossible that Ricey may be similarly affected."

I drew myself up. "I am not fighting over the body, I'm merely stating an opinion. It's no skin off my nose what the boy does for a living, but I think it's irresponsible of you two to encourage him to go in for music when he could do just as well in literature and have hopes of a mortgage and a family car to boot. He's not as ambitious as you think, I'm sure – as you'd like him to be, rather. I think he's really quite bourgeois. He'd be much more comfortable as an academic."

"*Scheiss!*" said Damaris. "I'd rather he went into the navy."

"Consider the judgment of Solomon," said Martin, who had come in and sat down at his desk next to Terry's during the conversation. "Shackleton's true spiritual mentor is the one who will yield first."

"Why don't you try the Gordian knot approach?" said Mr Dacre from across the room. He was marking books with a speed and decision more fit for killing chickens, and we had not been aware that he was eavesdropping. "You lot are always going on about that bloody little pansy. Haven't you got anything else to talk about?"

Terry blushed to the roots of his blond fuzz. "Bastard. Look at him. I bet he's having a hard-on just thinking what he'd like to do to Shack if he could get his hands on him."

"Umm," ruminated Martin. "'Thou rascal beadle, hold thy bloody hand'."

Damaris had turned only her head to stare Mr Dacre out, as if to convey that any further exertion would be casting pearls before swine. His neck began to twitch under her gaze.

"What would you like us to talk about, Mr Dacre? Changes in local government?" I spoke lightly. Not that I had not been incensed by his remark, but because it seemed to me that he hurled his remarks at us from across a vast distance, seeing us as an alien prospect of ease in personal relationships which he could never reach.

He glanced at me, and his look accused me of betraying his nascent respect for me by ranging myself with Shackleton's fans. Another reason for extending a slim olive branch. I felt wrongly labelled; I eschewed identification with Shackleton's Angels. "It would make a change to hear something of educational significance under discussion round here. The general level of conversation is just about at the level of the corner pub."

"Then why don't you give us a lead, Mr Dacre?" said Terry. "You know the old maxim, 'Those who can, do.'" He smiled, from the lips only.

"I've got better things to do," said Mr Dacre.

Damaris had turned away from him. "Manufacturing perverts," she muttered, in a tone of thrilling distaste.

But Mr Dacre's chance to lead an improving discussion was forestalled by the bell for the next lesson.

That evening, however, we were both still reverberating from the incident and the need to talk about it proved stronger than our proud reluctance to resume talking to each other. Shackleton's name was avoided, but, carefully draped in allusions, he was constantly referred to. I had never before known one person to be such a bottomless pit of conversational topics.

But there was another factor working to bring us together: Anne was arriving in two days.

On the Friday I had the A-level group again, in the morning. This time they stood up to a man as I entered. Shackleton was subdued, helpful, and sat up straight with his feet tucked under the chair. We discussed Blake's cosmic schema, compared and contrasted it with historical and present day theories of diabolism. There was only one awkward moment. *Vis-à-vis* influences on Blake's thinking, Shackleton asked – I think innocently – whether I considered that Paracelsus was a charlatan. The answer required careful thought, because I knew nothing whatever about Paracelsus. Shackleton obviously did. In fact I had an *idée fixe* that Paracelsus was a famous sixteenth-century pastrycook. Shackleton's large hazel eyes were trained trustingly on mine.

"I only wondered," he prompted, "because he seems to have had such a high opinion of himself and yet he must have known from clinical tests that the essences weren't effective."

"Well," I said, with a knowing smile, "if you're going to call Paracelsus a charlatan, you might as well call Aristotle one, too."

"That's true. I suppose Blake was mainly attracted by the archaeus theory. And the numerology, of course."

"I think that's very likely. As we know, he was rather prone to standing received theories on their heads."

"Who was Paracelsus?" asked Ryan.

My smile became fixed. "Shackleton, perhaps you would like to explain?"

He did so, to no more attentive ears than mine.

Nevertheless, despite such nasty moments, I always left the class feeling braced. After a few weeks I was obliged to admit that the vibrations which produced this effect emanated only from Shackleton. The others were good for the occasional wisecrack, and could be persuaded to part with opinions once they had got used to me, but otherwise they seemed content to make notes and gather up the pearls of wisdom that Shackleton and I left lying about. Once he was absent, and the difference was painful. They had become so accustomed to playing a passive role that it was impossible to get them re-activated in an emergency. After this experience I determined not to let Shackleton dominate the proceedings, and to force the participation of the others. But my resolution was as chaff before the wind. It proved to be so much less effort to co-operate with the natural dispensation of talent. The other boys did not seem to mind.

"I hear you've got Brother Eamonn's lot eating out of your hand," Martin said to me one day, a couple of weeks after I had started with them. "Enjoying it, are you?"

"Yes, I think I am. What have you heard?"

"Oh, I was chatting with one of the lads yesterday. He said your classes were the only bright spots in the week."

I glowed. "Really? Who was that?"

"It wouldn't be fair to tell you. Are you teaching them something too?"

"Time will tell. At least I'm not un-teaching them." Martin's expression was tinged with suspicion. It occurred to me that he might even be a little jealous. He took pride in the enthusiasm of his own classes: perhaps it was hard for him to accept that I could produce the same result with no experience. "When will Brother Eamonn be back?"

"I'm not sure. Why? Is it getting too much for you?"

"No, no. I was only thinking that he could probably make good any damage."

"From what I hear you'll be called back by popular demand."

"I'm sure you're exaggerating."

Nonetheless, I was tempted to believe it. I had already acknowledged that I dreaded giving up the class and being cast back into the pit of 2As and 3Bs. It had made all the difference to my outlook, a salve to my pride, physically a quiet interlude, an expansive walk in a life spent, emotionally, underground. Most of the lower classes continued as normal, but mentally I only lived for the twice-weekly sessions with the sixth form. Consequently discipline was worse than ever, alienating me still further from the screaming hordes.

Grass, however, continued to force himself on my attention. He seemed to be trying harder than ever to be objectionable. After our nocturnal tryst, I had expected a change in his behaviour. We had established a rapport, I thought: he was assured of my understanding. I tried to treat him differently in class, to be patient, to encourage him to be co-operative rather than disruptive. But my efforts seemed to have the opposite effect. The harder I tried to be nice to him, the worse he became. During one class – we were reading *Great Expectations* – he occupied himself with lassoing the boy in front of him, Dapper, as it happened. At first I requested him to stop, with a smile: then I told him: the third time I shouted. It was particularly annoying because reading sessions were the only occasions when the attention of 3B could be guaranteed. They still took a childish delight in the unfolding narrative and although some of them insisted on putting their feet up on the window ledge, or blowing bubblegum, I did not protest, being unwilling to do anything that might threaten their rare enjoyment of the written word.

"Grass! How many times do I have to tell you? If you don't stop that I'll have to send you to Mr Dacre."

"Oh you wouldn't, Miss."

"Yes, I would."

"No, you wouldn't."

"Yes, I – Now look, I'm warning you. Why are you being so annoying? I thought you liked to read."

"Dickens is boring."

"Everyone else seems to be enjoying it."

"Yeah," said Baxter. "Knock it off, Grassy."

"Shut your face," said Grass.

"That's enough, Grass," I said. "Now, I'm warning you."

We resumed reading. A few minutes later he was at it again.

I put the book down with an angry sigh. Grass and I stared at each other. There was no doubt that his defiance was personal. He was indeed daring me to send him to be beaten by Mr Dacre, confident that I did not have the heart. It was a straight fight between my pride and my better nature. I let the latter win.

"Give me that belt, Grass."

He rolled it up, having first unwound it from around Dapper's neck, and threw it at my desk. It hit me on the arm. There was a gasp from the class.

"Leave the room," I said, when I had got my breath back. "I shall take you to Mr Dacre myself, after class. You'd better be waiting."

When the bell went for the end of the lesson, and the day, I told the Chihuahua to send Grass in. I had calmed down sufficiently to realize that he had hurt my feelings much more than my arm, as if he were determined to let me know that his heart was too hard for me to touch, and, as usual, my thirst for vengeance was on the wane.

Grass sauntered in and lolled against the blackboard while I collected my books together.

"Listen," I said, "I don't know what's the matter with you these days, but it can't go on. I must say I'm disappointed in you, Grass. Your behaviour is retrogressing at a rate of knots. I've tried to be reasonable now I know that you have problems, but my responsibility is to the whole class. I simply cannot let you go on disrupting lessons time and time again."

"That's always the excuse."

"What do you mean?" He shrugged. "You're forcing my hand, Grass. You refuse to take any notice of what I say, so I'll have to take you to someone whose word you do respect."

"Don't you distinguish between respect and fear, Miss? Anyway, Dacre doesn't scare me."

"Mr Dacre. And I don't care any longer whether it's respect or fear. It's the ultimate effect I'm interested in. Come on." I moved towards the door, angry and offended.

Grass caught my arm. He looked scared now. "Please, don't, Miss. I'll behave, I promise."

"I'd like to believe you, Grass, but how can I?"

"I dunno. Please give us another chance, Miss. He's a beast, Dacre – I mean, Mr Dacre. He half kills you."

"All right. But don't provoke me."

"I'll try."

"You'd better succeed." His face had brightened. "How are things at home?"

"Just the same. The old man's away. At an international model railways exhibition. Can you believe it?"

"So you're all alone?"

"Yeah. I can take care of meself. It's great. I wish he'd have a car crash."

I shook my head. "I'm sure he loves you in spite of everything."

"He can stuff it. I got into the second fifteen, you know."

"Did you? Congratulations."

"Yeah. Well, I'd better be off. Expect you're tired now. Can you make yourself a cup of tea in the staffroom?"

"Only with bags. We drink coffee."

"Never mind, it's almost the end of term. Only another week."

"I know. Are you coming to the concert?"

"Jesus, do I have to?"

"Of course not. I just wondered if you would bring your father."

"Well if I did, I wouldn't. You must be joking, Miss."

"Hardly. Well, I'd better go. Have a nice weekend."

"Thanks, Miss. Same to you."

For once, the prospect for a nice weekend seemed favourable. Damaris and I were to meet Anne at the station that evening.

It was raining. The roads bubbled and cackled with rain, and a light steam rose from the tarmac through the pelting slugs of water. Damaris had agreed that we would take a taxi home in view of the weather, but then she was always more indulgent with Anne than with me.

The Friday night frenzy at the station whipped up our nervous anticipation. We had arrived much too early, so went to have a cup of railway coffee. We did not talk much, because we were too excited, but occasionally we grinned at each other. Anne's unifying charm was working in advance of her arrival. Looking at Damaris now, in her father's old Burberry with food stains down the front, her unkempt, newly-washed hair glistening with pin-points of moisture, I felt the old familiar surge of affection, and shame at having been so quick to reject her. Damaris was different, embarrassingly different at times, a little mysterious even, but stiff with integrity, and large dollops of undifferentiated character. These qualities had always moved me, and still did.

Anne's train was late. We worried at some length about how she would manage to carry her luggage up the platform. When we caught sight of her we could not help laughing. Anne was walking encumbered only by her shoulder bag, beside her a short young man with red hair trying to keep up a cheerful conversation while struggling with her suitcases. She was politely giving him all her attention, despite the temptation she must have felt to look for us among the crowd. She came through the barrier first, while her assistant looked for his ticket.

"Hello, dears!"

"Hello, Anne."

We kissed each other.

"You look just the same. How wonderfully just the same you look."

So did she, only more so.

It was not only the regularity of Anne's features which amazed, but the perfect scale of everything about her, her soft winged eyebrows and dainty ears, the delicate points of her upper lip, the flawless hairline, the blonde hair itself, which curled in neat, becoming fronds around her slim, vulnerable neck. Her oval nails were always painted in shades of pearly pink, her hands ever clean and pale, her clothes, as now after three hours in a second-class carriage, fitting without a wrinkle. The effect, on me at least, was to blush for my scruffiness, and resolve to do better, but somehow one felt that Anne's external harmony was only a reflection of the internal, a natural talent that it would be pointless to try and emulate.

"Now, if you don't mind, girls, I must go and thank that nice man who helped me. He's a journalist on the *Manchester Evening News*, you know."

"We'll take the cases," said Damaris. "They're much too heavy for you."

"Oh thank you."

We were introduced to the little man, who was obviously crestfallen to have Anne removed from his protection. It looked for a moment as though he might argue the point, but we formed a phalanx around Anne, and Damaris' expression did the rest.

In the taxi home we pointed out all the features of interest. Anne was charmed by everything she saw. I had not realized what a dynamic and diverse city Manchester was before having the opportunity to point it out to someone else. The importance of pleasing Anne completely re-cast my impressions of the place. She was not even depressed by the flat.

"It is a bit cosy for three," she admitted, "but we'll just have to pretend we're camping."

"We will be," I said. "We'll have to take turns on the lilo."

"No, I'll take the lilo," said Damaris. "I take up too much room in the bed anyhow."

Secretly I breathed a sigh of relief. Sharing a bed with Damaris was to risk the fate of the Blessed Margaret Clitheroe, crushed to death by rocks in defence of The Faith. Anne's slight figure would be hardly noticeable by comparison.

The evening was the most pleasant I had yet passed in that dreary flat. As was our wont, Damaris and I did most of the talking, telling Anne about the school, the laundry situation, the local shops, trying to make her feel at home – a somewhat gratuitous exercise since Anne was never anything but relaxed. We stayed up late, and went on talking after the lights were out, until Anne's habitual quiet was that of sleep.

It was a pleasure to introduce Anne to the staff, to see their shy gratification and instant anxiety to please. She and Miss Cromwell, who was not normally impressionable, had an immediate rapport.

"I wouldn't have thought your friend was like that," she told me. We were again in the ladies' lavatory, which seemed to be the only venue convenient for an exchange of confidences.

"What do you mean?"

"Well . . . so lady-like, I suppose."

"Thanks."

"I don't mean that you're not, but that's the thing that strikes you with her."

"That's all right. I quite agree with you, actually. One of nature's own."

"Poor old Brother Basil's going to fall for her like a ton of bricks. I bet you anything you like he'll be mysteriously removed from his post after she's been here a couple of months. They do that, you know, if one of them starts heaving for a woman. They send them off to the missions, or something. Rotten, isn't it?"

"Who does?"

"The bishop, of course. They have a sort of inquisition for sniffing those things out."

"Really? How creepy. But still, I should think Brother Basil would be safe with Anne. She might bring out his grandfathering instincts, but that's about all."

"Well, you know her better than I do. She's certainly more together than your other friend."

"You don't understand Damaris," I said, anxious. I wanted to make good the damage done by my temporary disloyalty. "She's a very intense person, she lives on a more spiritual – generally more non-material level than most people. For instance, she can be actually physically moved by an idea, or music. She's quite uninhibited in that way. That's how things come out with her. You'd have to watch her listening to the St Matthew Passion to know what I mean."

Miss Cromwell looked at me, evidently to see if I were joking.

"You can call it what you like," she said.

I was suddenly anxious to see the back of Miss Cromwell.

For the week following Anne's arrival the school was in festive mood. It was the last of the term. The lower forms were permitted to deck their classrooms with streamers and seasonal greenstuff, and the lessons were strongly biased towards poems and stories with a Yuletide theme – tales of Christmas customs in foreign parts, the inevitable Dickens, verbal skills sessions discussing how the holiday could be made happier for the underprivileged.

With so much good will about, even the boys became affected, and for the time being the business of teaching became one of mutual enjoyment.

The Christmas concert was on the Wednesday evening. It was as well that Damaris had been distracted by Anne's arrival, or her nervousness would have been manic. Even so, she had me on edge with her constant fretting.

"It doesn't matter what they sound like," I said. "The parents will think it's wonderful anyway. They'll never know if they miss a few notes."

"But I will. Really, Carlo, do you expect me to lower my standards to those of 1C? I'm not worried about their missing out notes, it's just the timing – I'm sure they're going to come in on the wrong bar, they're always doing that. I'm afraid the Bach's too difficult for them. It was Terry's idea. It wouldn't be so bad if Terry were on the piano, but he insists on showing Shackleton off."

"For very good reasons, I'm sure. I don't suppose Shackleton's in the least worried."

"That's not the point."

On the night of the concert Damaris was occupied with the performance so Anne and I were free to mingle with the assembling audience. The hall was expectantly filled with schoolroom chairs, each bearing a programme sheet, but it seemed it was a bold parent who was prepared to start filling them up. Most of them clustered reverently around the edges, or in the corridor outside, hoping to nail a teacher or two for a chat about the offspring's progress. Sammy the P.T. made his way through the crowd towards us. Unbelievably, he was still in his sky-blue track suit.

"Were you born in that thing, Sammy, or does it peel off and grow again every six weeks or so?"

"It's the most practical thing to wear," he said, as if so much should be obvious. "Aren't you going to introduce me to your friend?"

"Sorry. Anne – Sammy."

"Hello."

"Hello."

"You've come up from London, then?" said Sammy.

"Yes, that's right."

"How do you like it?"

"London?"

"No, no, Manchester."

"It's fine. Really a nice place." Anne nodded her head thoughtfully as she spoke.

"Yes, it is, isn't it?" said Sammy, nodding in his turn.

The conversation did not seem to have much in it for me. And underneath the innocent words I could sense the lethal shockwaves from Sammy's mating instincts – lethal, at any rate, for gooseberries. I left them nodding amiably at each other like a couple of iron donkeys.

As I walked away, Mr Dacre materialized beside me. He was dressed in an unsuitably natty three-piece suit in Prince of Wales check and a club tie. That, and his alien smile, made him almost unrecognizable.

"Would you mind if I sit next to you, Miss Slade – Carol?"

"I'm sorry?" I was sniffing at Mr Dacre in a distracted manner, for my nose was telling me what my head would not accept, that he was wearing Old Spice.

"During the concert, I mean."

"Oh! Well! Fine!" Monosyllabic conversations seemed to be the order of the day, but Mr Dacre's creepy conviviality confused me.

"I'll save you a seat, then."

"Thank you. If you'll excuse me, I was just going to the ladies'."

"All right."

I elbowed my way through wadges of forlorn-looking parents towards the toilets. A short, portly, bespectacled man with a greying moustache and hair sleeked down with plenty of Vitalis paced rather suspiciously up and down outside. He made a pleasant motion of deference as I went in. A woman in a nylon fur coat, presumably his wife, was inside washing her hands.

"Is it all right to use these loos, Miss? I know they're for the teachers really."

"Of course. It wouldn't do to have all the mums peeing on the grass, would it?"

"Oh, Miss, you're a card! You must be Miss Slade." She laughed at some length. Her pleasant, ordinary face suited laughter. "My son's told me all about you."

"Not everything, surely?"

She laughed again. I thought I saw a resemblance to the Chihuahua under the pink make-up. "I must go now. My husband's waiting. Nice to meet you, Miss."

"And you, Mrs . . . er –" But she had already closed the door.

When I came out, the couple were hovering with intent a few yards away. I decided to ease their embarrassment by approaching them myself.

The man held out his hand. "Miss Slade? I hope you don't mind me introducing myself. I'm Robert Shackleton, and this is my wife, Rita."

"How do you do? Sorry, I didn't catch your name."

"Shackleton. Our son's in the upper sixth now – quite a big lad. But perhaps you haven't noticed him. He can be a bit quiet at times."

I stared from one to the other for some minutes, unable to conceal my disbelief. Not that I had ever tried to imagine Shackleton's parents, but had I done so, nothing I could have imagined would have been less appropriate than the truth. They were totally unsuitable – most painfully bereft of any visible distinction. It was all I could do to stop myself laughing aloud.

And my next inexplicable instinct was to hope that Damaris could be protected from the truth.

"No," I said at last, "I know your son, all right. I think everyone does. He's quite outstanding by local standards. You must be very proud of him."

"Most parents are proud of their children I suppose," said Mrs Shackleton. "It doesn't do to make too much fuss of them, does it?"

"He's a good lad. We don't see that much of him these days, actually, do we, Rita?"

"No. When he's at home he's always studying or playing the piano. You think he's getting along all right, then?"

"Good heavens, yes. You don't have a thing to worry about."

"That's what most of his teachers say," said his father. "But, you know, it's hard to take in when you don't actually talk to the lad much. It's hard to communicate with him at times, isn't it, Rita?"

"It's just the age, I think. Most teenagers go through a phase of thinking the world started with them."

"Yes, that's true. Mind you, we're not complaining."

"I wanted my husband to meet you, Miss, because Everard's talked about you. He does enjoy your classes. I wanted to thank you for giving him so much attention."

"That's nothing. It makes a pleasant change to be appreciated, frankly."

"Oh he does that, all right."

"Is Shackleton – I mean, Everard – is he, by any chance, ad –" I was going to say "adopted", but realized just in time, the crushing insult implicit in the question. "– a difficult child at home? Is that what you're saying?"

"No, no, far from it. He's no trouble, is he, Rita?"

"None at all. He's never been a demanding child."

"I see. Well, it's been awfully nice talking to you, but I think the concert's starting now. We'd better go in."

"Right. Nice meeting you, Miss Slade."

We shook hands.

I allowed myself to be claimed and seated by Mr Dacre and sat through the first half hour of the concert in a daze, marvelling at the maverick hand of nature. Not that I could not believe and rejoice that a conjunction of ugly ducklings could produce a swan. The case forced contemplation of the depressing corollary that a mating of swans might produce an ugly duckling – a Muriel, or a Mr Dacre. I glanced at him out of the corner of my eye, at the grim, florid profile that spoke not only of the haphazard nature of reproduction, but of the questionable value of making the effort. Mr Dacre was, in a fashion, human, but in the cosmic order of things, did Shackleton's existence compensate for his? We were sitting near the back of the hall at the end of a row from where I could see both Shackleton's blazered back and the figures of his parents. Their heads were trained modestly towards the stage, only his mother allowing herself an occasional glance at her son, although several of the other parents were watching him openly. It was no surprise that Shackleton did not communicate with his parents. Pleasant enough people, no doubt, but quite lacking the originality and imagination to nurture the talents of a boy like Shackleton. It was to be wondered if their ordinariness were not positively harmful.

During a pause between items, I was tapped on the shoulder. I turned round to find Grass sitting behind me. He was wearing a new black blazer, yellow silk tie and white shirt. I was startled by the improvement in his appearance: he looked all dressed up to go to heaven.

"Evening, Miss."

"Hello, Grass. What made you change your mind?"

"I had to see this next one, Miss. Half 3B are in it, didn't you know?"

"In the speech choir? Good Lord, no I didn't. How did it happen?"

"Brother Bas put the screws on them."

"Shut up, Grass," said Mr Dacre, without turning around.

Grass directed a malicious look at the back of Mr Dacre's head. I shrugged, to indicate my reluctance to take sides.

"See you afterwards, Miss," whispered Grass.

The contingent from 3B distracted me for a few moments. This was the piece about Daniel in the Lion's Den and they had evidently been engaged to lend verisimilitude to the chorus of leonine growls that formed an integral part of the poem. My attention soon wandered to the piano, however. Damaris was the official page-turner for the evening and stayed sitting beside Shackleton during the speech choir's performance. Occasionally she would lean towards him and whisper in his ear. He seemed, wisely, reluctant to respond while a performance was in progress and kept his attention on the stage. I felt all his embarrassment at Damaris' behaviour. Anyone observing them would have ample corroboration of the rumours about her infatuation. I wished I had had a long pole with a hook on it with which I could catch hold of her neck and keep her from veering towards the boy. My only hope was that no one but myself would be interested enough to notice. Anne was safe. She sat with Sammy near the front, so that Damaris was behind her, and mercifully out of sight.

The final jubilation of "Adeste Fideles" could not come too soon for me. Under the pretence of being eager to congratulate Damaris I escaped from Mr Dacre and hurried over to the piano, while the audience filtered out of the hall. Terry Yeats was there before me, pink and effulgent with relief that it was all over. He and Damaris pumped each other by the hand while Shackleton quietly put the music in order.

"Oh those beautiful feet," groaned Terry. "I was sweating like a pig, weren't you, Dammo?"

"Absolutely. Thank God it's over. I could do with a drink. Hello, Carlo."

"Hello. I enjoyed it."

"Good."

"Listen," said Terry, "we could all use a drink. Let's go back to my place, have a bit of a do. We can just catch the off-licence if we don't hang about."

"Good idea," said Damaris. She had another. "Aren't you going to ask – you know – the guest soloist. It's only fair." She motioned her head towards Shackleton, who stood in the loop of the grand piano talking to a couple of friends. I looked around for his parents, but they had gone.

"Of course," said Terry, although it seemed that it was a snap decision. "Hey, Shack, bring your buddies back to my place for a bit of a do. You know where it is, don't you? Have you got a car?"

There was a brief consultation between the three boys. "Yes, we do. Thanks," said Shackleton. He looked genuinely pleased to be asked, which went some way to assuage my sense of mortification that he had been. Hobnobbing with the pupils was a form of democracy that was thoroughly distasteful to me. It was difficult to know whether to refuse on principle to be a party to it, or go along to make sure Damaris did not make a greater fool of herself than she had already.

"Where is your place, Yeats?" said Mr Dacre. He had followed me over. "Don't think I've been there."

"What?" Terry looked horrified, and accusingly at me. But without specifically telling Mr Dacre that he was not invited, there was nothing to be done. "You can follow me," said Terry, ungraciously.

My heart sank. Mr Dacre was obviously determined not to let me out of his sight for a minute. The party was already ruined.

Terry and Damaris went off to round up the inner circle and I found Anne and Sammy. He announced that he would take Anne in his car. That left me with Mr Dacre. I cursed the plethora of private transport.

Mr Dacre went to bring his car round to the front of the school, so that I would be spared the inconvenience of walking to the car park. The entrance halls were still crowded with family and friends and the black-clad figures of the brothers, basking in parental congratulations. The scene depressed me, although it was only a hook on which to hang the depression of being paired off with Mr Dacre for the evening. I went outside and started to walk down the drive.

"Hey, Miss!"

Grass came panting up behind me. "There you are, Miss. I see you've dumped the Butcher. That's good."

"Grass, I'm sick and tired of your referring to Mr Dacre in that way. I'm not one of your buddies."

"Yeah, I'd noticed. Come on, let's go."

"What?"

"Well, you were going home, weren't you? You don't want to do that. You said you'd come for a coffee with me some time – don't you remember? Like now. I was hoping you would, see. That's why I'm all dressed up like the dog's dinner. 'Course, I'd ask you for a drink in the normal way, but I expect you'd get the boot if you was seen drinking with minors and stuff."

"Infants, don't you mean? Don't be so stupid, Grass. I can't possibly go around town with you. Are you actually asking me for a date? How ridiculous. It's past your bedtime."

My tone conveyed all the resentment against unwelcome attention, abandonment by Damaris and Anne, and Grass's own hurtful and insulting behaviour in class. It seemed to me that he was cynically playing on my sympathy for his domestic problems in order to reduce me to compliance with his wishes. His bravado was

86

all part and parcel of his experiences at home, no doubt, but I was feeling too sorry for myself to suppress resentment and give him the benefit of the doubt, as I felt obliged to do in my professional role. I had not looked at him as I spoke, but was keeping an eye open for Mr Dacre's car. After a moment or two I realized that Grass had not replied, but was standing close to me. I smelt a whiff of cheap after-shave and turned to look at him. His expression was one I had last seen him direct at the back of Mr Dacre's head, except that on that occasion there was an element of play-acting, of harmless ritualizing, that was absent now. The boy's eyes were wide with the effort of holding back tears, and his mouth was clenched. His look frightened me. For a sickening moment I thought he might hit me. We stood staring at each other. Then he muttered, "You bitch," and turned away, half-running, half-walking, across the grass, jumped over the low wall into the street and strode up the road, his hands in his pockets.

At once I regretted my sharp words and ran towards the wall. I called after him, but either my voice was drowned by the traffic, or he did not trust himself to turn back.

I was still standing on the wall, staring after Grass, when Mr Dacre's car drew up. He leapt out and handed me down.

"Are you all right? Is anything wrong?"

"What? Oh – you thought I was going to throw myself eighteen inches to my death? No, I was just admiring the view."

"I see." He didn't. "Sorry to keep you waiting. The car park was jammed with damn parents, of course."

"It doesn't matter. I had company."

Terry Yeats lived artistically in a stone cottage in the foothills of the Derbyshire Pennines. It was dark when we arrived, but carriage lamps on either side of the front door and the light from the windows illuminated a small square lawn trimmed with white coral fencing and a stream that gushed through a millwheel at the side of the house. The cottage was one of a cluster on the bank of the stream and they were all situated at the bottom of a gentle hollow, the sides of which were sporadically covered with more stone cottages. It was a scene that might have been designed for the cover of *Coming Events In Britain*. The sound of the rushing stream was the only noise above the banging of car doors and over-enthusiasm from the assembling party-goers inside.

"Why do people live in towns, I wonder?" I said, looking around.

"Because there aren't enough country cottages to go round," said Mr Dacre. "Besides, didn't you notice how long it took us to get here? Yeats is always late for school. Brother Basil ought to have given him his cards months ago, but he's too spineless."

"If that's your opinion of him, it was good of you to accept his hospitality."

"I didn't say I didn't like him."

"Terry's a good teacher. Maybe that's why he's kept on."

"A good teacher? Huh! The boys make mincemeat of him. He has absolutely no discipline. And I suppose you know he's a homosexual? They ought to ban pansies from teaching in boys' schools. It's scandalous. A Catholic school, too."

"Are you suggesting he molests the little ones in the toilets?"

"Well ... no. But it's asking for trouble. Besides, it's not fair on him to be surrounded by temptation."

"I think he would disagree."

"Of course."

"In that case, they should ban women as well. Think what I suffer."

"That's different. You're not likely to be tempted by the boys."

"Ah well, at least he's not Jewish."

"What do you mean?"

"Never mind. Let's go in."

Mr Dacre had driven the whole way at a stately 29 m.p.h., so most of the others were there before us – Damaris and Terry, Sammy and Anne, Martin and what I assumed was his wife, a few other hard-core radicals with their spouses. We were taking our coats off in the narrow hall when Shackleton and his two friends came in.

"Congratulations, Shackleton," I said. "I hardly noticed you. That is the highest compliment one can pay the accompanist, isn't it?"

"If you want to." His expression changed from amiable neutrality to frozen politeness as I spoke.

"Good Lord, you're offended. Are you? That was only a bit of honest raillery, you know. I thought you'd be sick of praise by this stage in the evening."

"Then why bother to say anything?" He smiled, perfunctorily, and flipped his hair out of his eyes. His pose of nonchalance did not disguise his disappointment that I had not been more fulsome, but was nonetheless annoying.

"I won't in future."

Damaris commandeered Shackleton as soon as he went into the living-room. I sat down with Sammy and Anne, on the sofa, hoping that Mr Dacre would take the hint and go and play with the mill-wheel. He went, but only to fetch some wine.

Sammy had Anne proprietorially by the hand. She smiled at me, but I could not tell if she were appealing for help or not. Their relationship seemed already to have passed beyond words. I, however, still felt lost without them, at least in a conversation.

"Did you know," I said, "that ground hornbills have very long eyelashes?" I knew from experience that conversations with Sammy inevitably ended up on the price of radial tyres, so it was wise to give him a long run in.

"What's a ground hornbill?" said Sammy. "That's a bird, isn't it?"

"So I understand. And they plaster their mates up in their nests and feed them through a hole."

"Now is this the male or the female, you're talking about?"

"Guess!"

"The male feeds the female."

"Locks her up."

"I expect they like 'em with a bit of flesh on."

"Do you?"

"Doesn't matter to me what hornbills look like."

"No, I mean do you like female humans with flesh on?"

"A bit. Not too much. I'm a legs man, myself."

"Apparently in some Arab countries the sheikhs make their wives drink asses' milk all day through a tube and they have a man standing over them with a whip in case they try pouring it in the potted date-palm."

"The Arabs have long eyelashes too," pondered Sammy.

"You're right. There must be a connection. Here, let's have a look at your eyelashes, Sammy." He obligingly closed his eyes and Anne and I peered at them.

"Only average," said Anne.

"Yes. I think I'll just go and have a look at Martin's. His lady looks as if she could be rendered down for candles in an emergency."

The eyelashes ploy kept me circulating for quite a time and also provided a perfect excuse for moving on to the next set and away from Mr Dacre, who was shadowing me. I sent him off to fill up my glass whenever I could, draining off unaccustomed quantities of the stuff in the process.

Damaris and Shackleton were doing the same. They sat on the bottom step of the open-plan staircase that led out of the knocked-through living-room. Damaris was flushed and her eyes glazed and her person in a state of some dishevelment. She grinned at me. "What on earth are you doing, going around peering at everyone's eyelashes?" she said, in a mock-arch tone. "Are you sloshed?"

"I'm doing research into the relationship between long eyelashes and a liking for fat birds, as a matter of fact. Anything wrong with that?"

"Nothing. Sounds like the sort of thing you do all the time under another name. What are your eyelashes like, Shack? Let's have a look."

"Byronic," said Shackleton, and closed his eyes.

I was not sufficiently drunk that I could be insensible to Damaris' matey tone in speaking to the youth. Her whole attitude was one of triumphant possession. His easy compliance compounded my disgust.

"I think I've just lost interest," I said.

Shackleton opened his eyes and gave me a cold, sober look. The truth was he had long, elegant eyelashes, like the rest of his anatomy, and my hostility was sharpened by a sudden awareness of his physical beauty that sent my stomach into a brief lurch. It was a disturbing sensation: one should be immune to the physical charms of those outside the socially acceptable limits of age, status and propriety. It was necessary for good government, and seemed to work automatically with, for example, the doctor, the priest, the fathers of one's friends. And in the case of the insolent sixth-former, the need for immunity was reinforced by the law. Shackleton's assumption of parity had annoyed me from the first, but I had not realized before that he had no qualms either about admitting his physical charm into the factors governing his relationship with us. I thought that we had achieved an appropriate level of respect and confidence through our contact in the classroom, but his expression now clearly told me that he was asserting his right to be fawned over by teacher if he so chose and any questioning of that right would be regarded as aggression.

There was a protracted silence, during which we all wished I would push off. Terry had put on a Bo Diddley record and had dragged Anne onto the floor for the first number. They made an amusing spectacle. Terry danced with carefully contrived abandon, his eyes half-closed but nevertheless following the movement of his image in the large mirror behind the sofa. Anne made the minimum deviation from actually standing still, and gave the impression that she was gently rubbing her bottom against an invisible tree. Presently Martin and his wife got up, and soon the room was indisputably full of dancing couples.

Damaris and Shackleton had resumed the conversation that I had interrupted. They were locked into an argument about Maxwell Davies, and were both thrilling to the excitement of conflict. It seemed to me that the subject of it was irrelevant: physical intimacy being taboo, they were indulging in the most intimate form of verbal contact: exchanging insults.

The music began to stir my blood. I looked around for a partner. Shackleton's two friends were propped forlornly against the wall near the door into the kitchen. For some reason they had both been given their wine in stainless steel goblets, which they held close to the chest. Bereft of Shackleton, they seemed bereft of words, and watched the antics of their elders like understudies in their third year with an invariably healthy cast. It seemed like a charitable move to get one of them up for a dance, but I had not got half-way across the room when Mr Dacre's hand removed my glass and substituted his own authoritative mandible.

"May I have this one? You've been avoiding me, haven't you?"

"Of course not. In fact I was wondering where you'd got to. I had no idea you danced, Mr Dacre. You don't look the type, somehow." Not only that, but I would have shed blood rather than find out.

"I wish you'd call me Vernon. Anyone can do this stuff. It's not what I'd call dancing."

"Well, we'll see, won't we?"

There followed the most mortifying hour of my life. Standing up with Mr Dacre was bad enough, but the room was not even large enough to pretend I was dancing with the person behind me, however much I swivelled and contrived movements that involved turning my back on him. Whatever the music, Mr Dacre danced obliquely to the rhythm, with a terrifying earnestness, twisting himself violently this way and that, lashing out at contingent dancers with his fists and Hush Puppied feet. The humiliation was compounded by the presence of so many people I was doomed to meet again, and the smothered giggles of Damaris and Shackleton and his two friends.

At length I pleaded exhaustion.

Being too tired to dance with Mr Dacre I could not politely dance with anyone else, so suggested going home. The party had been thinning out. Anne and Sammy had already gone.

Terry was crestfallen. "Not you too, Carlo. Oh don't be a party pooper, it's only just got going."

"I'm sorry, but we live right on the other side of the city. If Mr Dacre's going to give me a lift and then get home himself –"

"Oh, very well. Hey, Damaris, you're not going as well, are you?"

Damaris and Shackleton had at last separated. He and his friends were draining their wine in valedictory manner.

"I'll have to get a lift with someone," said Damaris. "I came in your car, Terry."

"I'll take you home, don't worry. Don't you let me down too, Dammo."

For a moment Damaris hesitated. "Oh, all right. I don't feel like going home, I must admit."

"Good. Okay you lot, off you go. Don't hang about cluttering up the entrances once you've made your decision."

"You could always get a lift home with Shackleton, Damaris."

"He's drunk."

"Is that why you're trying to light the filter end of that ciggie?"

She glowered at me and put it in the right way with a stabbing movement. "Don't wait up for me," she said.

In the car with Mr Dacre, I felt like a juvenile delinquent being delivered to his parents by the arresting officer in case he got into any more trouble on the way home. I huddled into the front seat, rebellious, sullen, my drawbridge hoisted. I was in no mood to speculate on the sad truths behind the man's grizzly exterior. He was probably still a young man, thirty-four or five, but his potential as a sexual partner was totally obscured by the ageless mask of the bully.

"You're very quiet," he observed.

"I'm tired."

"I was like that in my first year of teaching. It's a physical activity, that's what people don't realize."

"Quite."

We drove on in silence. Then he said in a mock-bantering tone, "You don't like me, do you, Carol?"

"Not very much, no."

He snorted. "It's probably a stupid question, but why not? You don't have to tell me."

"I'd be glad to. I think it's because you're totally lacking in warmth. And seem to enjoy beating the boys."

"If their parents took the trouble I wouldn't have to. And it's not true that I enjoy it. It's just that I hate sloppiness and viciousness and decadence. Oh it's an unfashionable view, I know that. But just think about it. Think of some of the prize specimens in the classes you have. Are they going to be let loose on society in the state they're in when they come to this school? Socially, they've just barely crawled out of the slime. The manners of some of them are disgusting: they spit and fart and pick their noses. And the language. The usual obscenities aren't foul enough for them – they invent their own. Nobody else seems to give a damn, but I do. That's my misfortune. And for that I'm called a sadist."

It was clear that this soliloquy had been rehearsed.

"But this isn't a reform school, Mr Dacre – Vernon. We're only required to teach them."

"And how is one supposed to do that without doing something to bloody well make them sit up and pay attention? Some of those slobs leave the school knowing nothing but what they've learnt in my classes because I damn well frighten the hell out of them. They can't just put their feet up and chew gum during my lessons. They're there to work, and they know it."

That reference to putting feet up and chewing gum caused me a guilty flush. It was an accurate description of the posture of most of my pupils.

"Isn't there any other method of discipline available? Corporal punishment seems so barbaric."

"What do you suggest? What do you use?"

"Nothing, really. I give detentions sometimes, but it's sheer slog trying to get them to attend."

"Exactly. And what's your discipline like?"

"You've got me there."

"I thought so."

"But I'm a woman. In fact I thought myself as little more than a girl until recently. If I were a man with natural authority, like you, surely that would be enough?"

"In that school? Never. Just think of some of the characters in 3B – Riccio, Baxter, Grass. Can you seriously imagine them talking out their so-called problems?"

"Grass is a special case. Actually I feel sorry for him."

"O-oh. Has he been telling you about his father's supposed perversions?"

"Why?"

"Because it's a pack of lies. His father's a perfectly respectable bus conductor who wouldn't hurt a fly. The only time he's come near to laying a finger on Grass was when he found out the stories the kid had been spreading about him. I had him in for a chat about it. The poor man was in tears. He's totally ineffectual for an evil-minded slob like Grass, but quite harmless."

"Are you sure? Why would he make up such a terrible story?"

"God knows. Perhaps it happened to a friend of his and he thought it made him sound interesting. He does as he likes at home. His father has no control over him whatever."

I was silent. So it was true that I had been made a complete fool of by Grass. I tried to find some excuse for him, in order to excuse myself, but it was impossible. But my determination to resist Mr Dacre's argument still twitched.

"Perhaps they do learn some maths in your classes, but don't they also learn that might is right? You're just going by their rules. Admittedly a squash shoe has a more judicial air than a broken beer-bottle, but the morality's the same. And don't say it's the only thing they understand. They're in school to deepen their understanding."

"So you think they should go through life handing out violence, but never know what it feels like. Doesn't the juvenile crime rate on the Isle of Man say anything to you?"

I sighed. There was logic in what he said, of course, but it only proved that it was no guide to behaviour. One could find arguments to justify anything, and in this case evidence for the effectiveness of severe punishment could be obtained at every bookstand. It seemed futile to protest if one could not come up with an alternative. But it did seem strange that Mr Dacre was convinced his attitude sprang from an impartial sense of justice; one only had to look at him to see that it was tethered to his gut. Whereas I knew that my North–Oxford–liberal–carrot approach did spring from an impartial conviction that violence was wrong, and that there are no degrees of wrong, however tempting it would be to make exceptions for protozoa like Grass.

"You know," he said, "I could help you sort your problems out. In the classroom, I mean. You send the troublemakers to me,

94

and I guarantee quiet classrooms from then on. They'll respect you for it, you know. They do me. They don't like me, but they do respect me."

"Thanks, but I prefer it the other way round. Anyway, that sort of cold-blooded massacre is quite against my nature."

It was also achingly attractive. By that simple ploy to reduce 3B and others to quiescence, to have done once and for all with the noise and the back-chat, the shouting and pleading and ringing of changes in the hope of hitting on something that worked. The idea glittered like the eye of the serpent, goading me to crush it.

I looked haughtily out of the window after delivering my opinion. Mr Dacre tried to change the subject – rather drastically, I thought – to the demise of branch lines on the railways.

The phone was ringing as I let myself into the flat. Presumably Anne was already in bed – either her own or Sammy's. It was Damaris on the line.

"Hello? Carlo?"

"Yes. Where are you?"

"I'm still at Terry's. He's had too much to drink and we both think he's unfit to drive, so I'm staying here. I didn't want you to worry about me."

"I wasn't."

"I see. Did Anne get home all right?"

"Don't know. Do you want me to go and look?"

"No, no, it doesn't matter. She's safe with Sammy."

"Yes, but is Terry safe with you?"

Damaris rang off without replying.

Anne was in bed, but not asleep. She put the light on and rolled over as I came in.

"Have a nice time?"

"With Mr Dacre? Does a walnut enjoy being crushed?" She laughed. "That was Damaris. She's staying at Terry's."

"Why?"

"He's too drunk to drive home, apparently."

"That's odd."

"Why?"

"Terry's not there tonight. He told me he was setting off for London as soon as everyone had gone."

"Well if he's had too much to drink he's obviously changed his mind. How was Sammy?"

"Everywhere."

"Did he measure you up for a matching tracksuit?"

"Just about. Why do I always attract men with large hands and good intentions?"

"You can have Mr Dacre if you like."

"Sorry."

"If only one could give people to Oxfam. I don't know what he sees in me, really."

But I suspected that he sensed the latent lust for revenge in me. Even I was beginning to see my liberal posturing as a sham. It was providential that it was Mr Dacre who had detected the rot: my dislike of him would give me the strength to resist temptation.

I got into bed and turned the light out and lay with my arms behind my head. It was the first time that Anne and I had been alone at night. Damaris' absence, true to type, bulked large, but its shadow sheltered a welcome cosiness between the two of us. Anne was less dynamic than Damaris, but exactly what is good to come home to. That, and the fact that she always wore a nightie and I pyjamas, made me feel for the moment as it were man and wife with her, at least as regards unspoken intimacy. There was the added bonus of being spared the disagreeable smells.

"Do you think she'll sleep with him?" I said.

"Terry?"

"Yes. To music, probably."

"I wouldn't think so. He's homosexual, isn't he?"

"Yes, but that doesn't mean his balls have dropped off. It's usually a matter of choice rather than incapacity, I think."

"But even so, they wouldn't fit, would they? I keep thinking of that joke about the mouse and the elephant."

"I hope she doesn't damage him. You know, I'm not sure if she's a virgin, are you?"

"No. I told you about that chap Arnold at the Poly."

"I don't mean you, I mean Damaris. I don't know if she's a virgin."

"Oh, neither do I."

We speculated lovingly on the subject until far into the night.

If Damaris had been a virgin the night before and was not in the morning. I never expected to find out, but whatever happened that night had a shattering effect on her. We were prepared to behave in such a casual way that no hint of criticism or obtrusive curiosity would furnish her with an excuse for one of her dramatic interludes. In fact the problem was toning down the cheerfulness to everyday levels. But Damaris returned in no mood to be cheated of a cathartic scene.

We were washing up breakfast when she came in, and all ready with a little ploy for absorbing her quickly back into the domestic routine. Our carefully laconic greetings, however, were cut off when Damaris, after staring at us for a moment from the door of the kitchen, slowly sank to the floor, her head lolling against the wall.

Exclaiming with real concern, we tried to get her to her feet and into the living-room. Her large body, heavy with despondency, sagged and resisted, but finally we got her spread-eagled on the sofa, her arm thrown across her eyes. She was still wearing the black blouse and skirt from the night before, and they and the blotchy pallor of her skin and crumpled hair, suggested that she had slept in her clothes and come straight from her bed. A more moving spectacle of virtue undone would be hard to imagine, and yet I could not understand how sleeping with Terry Yeats could have produced such devastation. Perhaps, after all, it was appendicitis.

"Won't you tell us what's the matter, Damaris?" I urged, soft but firm.

She merely shook her head slowly and let out a little moan. I motioned to Anne to put some music on and prepared myself, Cordelia-like, for a vigil. But at the opening bars of Brahm's sextet, Damaris leapt off the sofa, felled me to the floor in passing, ripped the record off the turntable and snapped it in two. Then she stood for a moment staring at her handiwork and burst into hysterical sobs on the carpet.

I began to feel that she was over-reacting, and toyed with the idea of saying so. In happier times I would have balked at the idea of castigating Damaris for the magnificent dramas she could produce in moments of great intensity. It was a thing that set Damaris apart, and it was that apartness which we loved. But having observed her at close quarters in the adult world, I now saw her drama as self-indulgent and childish, the ravings of a personality unable to adapt to a world where the oblique was the norm.

However, I did not want to cause her any unwitting psychological damage, either. Anne knelt beside her, anxiously stroking her hair as she raved and tried to pluck tufts from the carpet which, being rubber-backed Acrilan, proved rather unyielding. Anne looked at me, in despair. I shrugged.

"Damaris, are you ill?" I demanded.

She shook her head.

"Do you want us to stay?"

She gurgled, in the affirmative, I thought. I suggested to Anne that a cup of tea was traditional and she went off to make it. Meanwhile I settled myself on the sofa with a cigarette and waited for Damaris to calm down.

Slowly the convulsions grew less frequent, the sobs quieter, the shudders less violent. There followed a long series of quivering sighs. Finally she sat up on her knees and smoothed the damp wadges of hair from her face. The face itself was a grotesque re-vamping of the one I knew, irregularly, but hugely, swollen, crumpled red and yellow and purple, blotched with tears, a little blood oozing from the lip where she had snapped her teeth on it. Her nostrils and mouth still pulsated with hysterical activity. The sight reproached me: however regrettable her emotions, there was no doubt that she was genuinely wracked by them.

Anne brought the tea in. We drank in silence.

Finally Damaris said, "I'm sorry. I'd rather not talk about it. I'll be all right."

"Are you sure, Damaris?"

She nodded. "Thank God term's over," was all she said.

Damaris took up a pose of stoical normality thereafter. We all travelled down to London together and, at her suggestion, made no plans to see each other before meeting to go back on January 2nd. We planned to spend the rest of the holiday looking for a cottage to rent.

Somewhat to my surprise, I discovered that I had tired of Christmas, that its jollifications were empty – becoming to Muriel and her we-never-close gregariousness, but not to me. She and my father produced all the standard clichés of happiness at my return, thereby emphasizing my new status as a non-resident alien and aggravating my desire to go "home", as I now thought of Manchester. It no longer seemed remarkable to me that the allegiances of a lifetime could have been so swiftly tampered with. The explanation was all around me. The same one that accounted for the bond that had developed between Damaris, Anne and me.

It was this: we all came from embarrassing homes. Nothing gross, that was the trouble, really. Just small-scale, unspectacular, garden-variety embarrassment. There was Damaris, brought up in a seedy terraced house in South Wimbledon by her whiskery old grandmother who only spoke German and served all their food in a watery grey sauce, and her strange, unemployable father who left his dirty underwear on the sofa in the living-room: Anne's twin, wordless, identikit parents in their spat and polished council flat, fitted throughout with 100% viscose carpet in bilious Autumn Tints and pressed wood furniture on tapered legs: I with my amiable, acceptable father, sole owner of a successful sweet shop, and his sociable bride with her pink face and her Eastex and Spandex and lurex, dressing my father in Bermuda shorts that showed his veins and making him part his hair millimetres above his ear so that what hair he had left after furnishing the family home from Harrod's basement could be plastered over his bald patch.

What would any of us not have given for a bit of downright deprivation, a little honest child-molesting, violence even, real poverty rather than colourless sufficiency, some active thwarting of ambition rather than goals which, on the evidence of our suburban neighbourhoods, were only too easy to attain. In that sense our deprivations were real enough. Our backgrounds were not bleakly tragic, but cosily pathetic. For some reason we had all rejected that pathos, and that was the bond that bound. And rejecting our families as a source of embarrassment, we had tried to create our own. Lately, it seemed to me, we had been fretting to leave that too.

The suspicion was confirmed by the half-hearted manner in which we went about looking for a cottage to rent. With Anne being so quickly snaffled up by Sammy, the future was uncertain. Damaris and I had doubts of equal magnitude about our ability to survive without her. But the flat was definitely too small. If we all wished to use hot water in the morning, the bathing sequence had to start at quarter to six, and volunteers were hard to find. The landing was permanently blocked by racks of washing, the bedroom was under three feet of Damaris' cast-off clothing, the kitchen floor littered with chip-pans and Pyrex dishes too big for the cupboards, the living-room was beginning to look like a set for Polanski's *Repulsion*. To move, or to split up, were the only alternatives.

I had never looked for property before, but two things helped. One was a five-year-old Morris Traveller, in prime condition, which my father and Muriel had given me for Christmas. The other was that house-hunting is a very easily acquired skill. The car had actually been willed to my father by a great aunt, so no burden-some sacrifice was entailed – burdensome to me, that is – but the giving and receiving of it had made a pleasant cameo of family life while it lasted. It was certainly an advantage on the house-hunting circuit to arrive on wheels, thereby suggesting the stability that goes with ownership. Damaris and Anne gradually ceded the direction of the project to me. Anne had to return to work early, being office staff, and Damaris had started to compose an opera on a portable keyboard she had bought secondhand from a friend over Christmas.

Term started without our having found anything suitable. I was bemoaning this fact to Terry Yeats on the first day, when he offered us his. It seemed he was moving back into the city to take up residence with a chef at the Hilton.

"I'm no tortured genius," he sighed. "But if you're looking for a quiet backwater it's fine. I prefer mine a bit more sudsy, I've discovered."

Immediately I rushed off to tell Damaris the good news.

"It's too remote," she said at once. "And there's a pond in the cellar."

"Oh come on, Damaris. I know it's the scene of the crime, and all that, but –"

"Take it if you want," she said, tossing her head and looking tortured, "but without me."

It was tempting, but, on the other hand, I could not deny that there was a pond in the cellar.

Naturally I was curious to see how Damaris and Terry behaved to each other. It seemed to me that there was more embarrassment and coldness on her side than on his. I concluded that he had probably taken advantage of her drunken condition without realiz-ing that she was a virgin. The latter point had moved up from speculation to certainty after her hysterics the following morning. Several times I came across the two of them deep in one-sided conversations, with Terry earnestly pleading with a statuesque, horizon-scanning Damaris. Gradually his persistence did its work and one could see her attitude towards him softening. Within a week their relationship was almost back to normal.

One salutary effect of all this was to take her mind off Shackle-ton. She did not mention him once after the night of Terry's party, and I noticed that she stopped "helping" Terry with Shackleton's lessons.

On the second day of term I went along to the sixth form as usual. I was just sitting down, bandying quips about the awfulness of Christmas with the boys, when Brother Eamonn walked in. At first I thought he must have come to give me a message and we said hello and chatted for a few minutes. Then there was a pause, during which he was presumably expecting me to vacate his seat. As I stayed where I was, he was obliged to say, "I'm really most grateful for your taking over at such short notice, Miss Slade. It can't have been easy, I know, especially as you're new to the school. It was very, very kind. Thank you."

The past tense broke over me like an egg. Brother Eamonn was telling me, in effect, to go. The sun twinkled on his gold-rimmed spectacles as he stood leaning over me. I felt myself blushing as the combined revelation of my obtuseness and redundancy became clear. The undivided attention of the boys fanned my discomfort. I got up.

"It was a pleasure. Martin must have forgotten to tell me you were back. I always miss assembly."

This was a futile attempt to give him the opportunity to deny that he was, and, failing that, to suggest that without Martin's stamp of approval the legality of the thing was in question.

"He's so busy organizing mocks at the moment."

"Yes." The skirt of his gown brushed against my own. "Well – well." I did not know whether to say goodbye to the class. It was not as if we would not see each other around the school. If I did say goodbye, it would perhaps be assuming a special relationship had been established – a feeling they might not share. It would also have dislodged the lump in my throat, so instead I merely smiled and tried to exit with dignity.

The staffroom was empty except for Martin, who was examining some large time-table sheets.

"Hello!" His tone was cheerful. "Brother Eamonn just kicked you out, did he? I'm glad he was able to get back for the first lesson. It neatens things up."

"You might have warned me."

"Sorry. I thought I had. Did you prepare the lesson?"

"I always prepare my lessons."

"Of course. Sorry." He looked genuinely sheepish. I started to feel mean for giving him something else to worry about. "Are you glad or sorry?"

"Neither really."

"I'll try and give you your own sixth-form class next year."

"Thanks." This was meant to rally my spirits, for Martin had not been deceived by my nonchalance. Somehow it failed to do so. A moment's reflection suggested the reason: Shackleton would not be there next year. Of course, I deplored certain aspects of Shackleton's behaviour, but there was no doubt that he was the axis on which my enjoyment of the class spun.

I went at house-hunting like a truffling dog, by way of compensation. Our luck turned when I found a place belonging to a retired railway engineer and his wife. She had been taken into a nursing home for an indefinite period after a stroke, and the husband was going to stay with relatives. It was difficult to make my condolences sound sincere, but I must have managed it because the man was soon talking as though the whole thing were settled. His wife had been a teacher, so perhaps my personal attributes were anyway irrelevant.

I ripped home to the flat as soon as I could decently get away from his touching monologue on the progress of his wife's illness, forced Anne and Damaris into the car and set off again.

"It's perfect," I explained, as we all stood outside in the narrow lane. "We can get to school in half an hour, it's got central heating – think, constant hot water! There aren't many other houses round here – at least not on this side of the village – it'll be lovely and quiet." The evenings were beginning to lengthen. The square stone cottage, the field wall and the ash trees along the road cast dense black shadows on the long, wind-ruffled grass. On the hills behind the cottage sheep safely grazed. "It's a gift," I said. The others were standing bemused and silent. "We can call this home. What's the matter with you?"

"Is there a vegetable garden?" said Anne.

"Of course. There's everything. There's even a greengage bush. You know how you feel about greengages, Anne."

Damaris had taken up a position in front of the gate, leaning her hands on it, not so much looking at the cottage as encountering it. I knew, roughly, what was going through her mind: this had to be more than a change of address for her, it had to be a small metamorphosis, a step towards Destiny, a fearless placing of the hand in that of The Future. I could feel her thrilling to general emotions. In a way, she performed these emotional rites for both of us. Had she not done so, I would have been obliged to indulge more myself, for it was a strange and thrilling thing for us daughters of Southern Region to contract such an intimate relationship with the countryside, life forces, the elements in their sphere, all those things with which we had only made contact through literature and imagination – and made it more passionately for that. One had to prepare for the fact that familiarity might breed contempt for natural beauty. After all, one does not want one's suburban naïvety to show. But then one only has to think of Emily Brontë, Constable, Wordsworth, to know that the thrill can stay, grow even, with the years. These days one hesitates to invest in the durability of anything, and behind Damaris' hesitance to express enthusiasm I sensed a practical ignorance of how to cope with the fact that something good had happened to us which could develop into a permanent feature of our lives.

After a lengthy pause, during which Anne set off on a tour of the grounds, Damaris turned round. There were tears in her eyes.

"Thank you," was all she said, and that with difficulty.

"It's not entirely for you, you know. But still, you'll be able to compose amazing stuff here, I should think."

"I'm beginning to feel amazing already."

We looked at each other and laughed and hugged and laughed and jumped up and down.

"Come on," I said, "pull yourself together. Mr Lawford will think we're queer."

The owner had been watching us from the living-room window. We walked sedately up the garden path and he met us at the door.

It was decided that we would move in within ten days, Pickfords, or equivalent, being willing.

As it turned out we used an equivalent. Damaris wanted to use Pickfords because she had been told they were nationalized: I wanted to use someone else because I had been told they were rubbish. In the end the amount of our belongings only justified a rented van, which Terry kindly drove for us. Disputations and arrangements such as these kept us dizzy with excitement for the intervening two weeks.

For a time after we had moved in the novelty of disposing of our things among the Lawfords' furniture, fitting keys to locks, finding the cheapest source of oil and investigating the local shops and pub absorbed our attention exclusively. It was a happy time, rediscovering the zest which sharing gives to pleasure.

After a month or so the novelty began to wear off. We had no regrets, but the cottage became simply where we lived, a lovable burden which periodically demanded that its grass be cut and its weeds hoed: the bath still had to be cleaned, though one could see spring lambs from the bathroom window; the hot water and the petrol had to be paid for. Inevitably the old debates and demarcation disputes arose. ("Well it was your idea," Damaris would say, hinting that all the extra expense should therefore be borne by me.) Anne never took part in our arguments. Whenever Damaris and I started she would go and do something in the garden. Consequently the garden flourished.

Along with the backwash of domestic bickering came the distaste for teaching, boys, marking homework and the constant parrying of Mr Dacre's obsession. Devoid though I was of other props for my ego at this point, I could take no comfort in his esteem, or its dimensions. The fact that I had lunch at his table became for me a monumental mushroom under which I ran about, for the expectation of his company ruined the morning, lunch was ruined anyway, and he then had a natural link to attaching himself to me for the rest of the break, or until I made some active excuse to get away. Usually this was marking or preparing lessons, but then I felt obliged to get on with it, and feared to offend him by talking to other members of staff instead of working. Had he been better company, it would have been better endured, but Mr Dacre's conversation was limited to pocket biographies of foul brats he had had in his charge, his sister in Scunthorpe, the chances of the Conservatives in the next election and the future of education. No one, least of all Damaris, understood my growing rage. She suggested I take sandwiches and eat them in the staffroom.

"But I need a hot dinner!" I cried.

"Well, ask Brother David to put you on another table."

"I can't. It would look so obvious."

"But if you despise and dislike the man, why should you worry about offending him?"

It was difficult to say. I knew myself to be trapped by Worcester Park-ness in this respect, but the knowledge only fuelled my sense of impotence.

Impotence, in fact, seemed to inform every area of my life. Dislike for teaching, and for boys in particular, made all my efforts in the classroom vain. Mindful of my pay-slip I would prepare all my lessons to give the classes opportunity for progress in language skills, but it was a sterile exercise. My lack of enthusiasm conveyed itself to the boys, made them restless and troublesome, which in turn increased my hostility towards them, the job and life in general. And now that I no longer had the sixth-form class, I was obliged to walk past their classroom on my way to 2A. Often a couple of them – sometimes Shackleton – would be hanging around the door on the lookout for Brother Eamonn as I walked past. We would exchange cheerful greetings, the occasional quip, and I would hurry on, anxious lest my desire to linger should show.

Whether through a kindly sixth sense, or on some quite neutral impulse, Shackleton would sometimes stop me and ask a question quite irrelevant to either of us – like whether I had seen a particular film – and rather touchingly contrive to keep me talking.

I began to look out for him.

After a while I knew disappointment when he was not there. It was only a short step to looking out for him at other times of the day and in other places. Then at all times and in all places. Perhaps it was that I let my mind centre on him as an absorbing distraction from the unpleasantness of my other concerns. But it was done before I had realized what was happening, or had a chance to stop it.

Suddenly I was living in Shackleton's school, Shackleton's city, Shackleton's world. The truth struck me one morning when, in a hurry as usual, I was trying to decide what to wear. Normally I gave the matter little thought. But, imperceptibly, I had begun to mix and match – not with care, but at least with passing observation. My taste in clothes had been negatively influenced by Damaris' flamboyant artiness. I disliked the idea of "expressing" oneself through clothes and, imagining that I espoused balance, proportion and unpretentiousness, had tried to end up somewhere between Damaris' flapping disorder and Anne's buttoned-down neatness. Now I rummaged among the resulting collection of dreary compromises with desperation. At the far end of the wardrobe I found a garment, neither blouse nor jacket, that I had bought at a jumble sale in Kingston with the intention of using the material for a cushion cover. It was velvet, printed in muted shades of violet and orange and green, with full sleeves gathered at the wrist and a pre-natal fullness in front, the whole slung on a yoke around a boat neck, the sleeves themselves gathered at a seam a couple of inches down from the shoulder. It had an unmistakable Renaissance air, reminiscent of portraits by Titian of

Young Men, courtesans and merchants' wives. It felt caressing, liberating. "He'll notice that," I muttered. "He'll like it."

I was looking at myself in the mirror on the back of the wardrobe door as I spoke. It assisted the impression that another had spoken, that this other creature inhabited my body and, more particularly, mind, and spoke in my place. Late though I already was I backed away from the mirror and sat down on the unmade bed, staring out of the window at the top of the rowan tree that grew beside the front gate. A kind of flabbergasted joy possessed me, such as one might feel on meeting someone one had thought was dead. I had spoken his name – or at least his pronoun – and it was the abracadabra that opened up onto the full realization of what had happened to me. I had been on the lookout for him, I had had his image on my mind, I had probably picked up every opportunity to talk about him. Had anyone noticed? I could not but think at once of Damaris, and of how I had ridiculed the same state in her. But, of course, her obsession with Shackleton had been of a different order, a wild, romantic, proselytizing nonsense, merely an emotional perversion of ordinary sexual frustration. I do not know what Damaris saw when she had looked at Shackleton – an amalgam of tender genius and steely musical intelligence, most likely: it was not difficult to see him as the natural successor to Chopin, Mendelssohn and other beautiful, consumptive musicians. But what I saw was the boy himself, flesh, blood, soul and – yes, divinity, a kind of divinity. As the thought came to me I clapped a hand to my mouth and rocked with astonished laughter. And yet it was not laughter, only a cathartic noise.

Anne put her head round the door. We each had our own room now. "It's twenty to nine, Carlo. We're going to be late."

"Yes, I'm coming."

"Are you all right?"

"Yes!" I knew that I must seem strange to her, transformed, possibly, sitting on the bed half-dressed, grinning at her in a way that must have told her I was already grinning before she came in. My newly discovered passion spilled over into tenderness for her. But it would not have been fair to tell her, to try her affection with the absurdity and hopelessness of it. At that moment these aspects did not worry me as long as it was kept secret: it was too new, too different, too outrageous and fascinating to depress.

Nature's way, no doubt, of giving the spirits a brief holiday before the descent into the pit.

It is astonishing how any details relevant to the love object can pull before one's eyes facts, places, aspects of life that would otherwise go unremarked. Well, well, so his mother comes from Liverpool. How tough-minded of her, Liverpool has such character – the crime rate must be the highest in the country – how much more stimulating to come from Liverpool than from London. One's ear is tuned to references to Liverpool on the media, the street, in magazines and newspapers. One longs to visit it. His father is a mechanical engineer. Yes, well, it's not true what they say about engineers. They're not all unlettered beer-drinkers. Engineering is the track on which modern society runs. What could be better or more defensible in human terms than a profession which harnesses technology to the service of man? Oh? And what about all those things you said about spotty troglodytes who did engineering because they couldn't get in to laundry school? Yes, well, that was before ... before I woke up into the wonderful world of blind prejudice.

However, the very strength of the obsession dictated a like caution, a watching of word and manner that would preserve my public indifference to him. It was not easy. Suddenly everyone seemed to be talking about Shackleton, partly because the struggle for his soul was in full swing. U.C.C.A. dates were coming up.

Damaris, surprisingly, held aloof from the fracas. It was basically a three-cornered affair between Terry Yeats, Martin (acting for Brother Eamonn) in the English corner, and Mr Rice, the Head of Art. Mr Rice would occasionally come into the staffroom during this time. Up till then he had lived and breathed exclusively in the art and pottery rooms. On the first occasion I did not even know who he was, though he was covered in clues. A short man with a fringe of dry brown hair around a bald patch, thick glasses kept on his nose by a large mole, droopy moustache and florid complexion. He seemed to be wearing somebody else's trousers, because they were hunched up almost to the armpits and secured around the waist with a luggage strap. He was lightly dusted with reddish powder and had Burnt Sienna and other umbral stains on his hands and clothes.

He and Terry were standing in the middle of the staff room shouting at each other. If the conversation had started off as a friendly chat about Shackleton's options, by the time I got there it had deteriorated into a slanging match, with colourful slurs on the other's professional characteristics. Terry had gone purple in the face and seemed to be hyperventilating like a cat. Eventually Mr Rice threw up his hands and stormed out of the room.

On later occasions there was less violence, but it was clear that a struggle to the death was in progress.

"Why can't they leave the little pansy to make up his own mind what he wants to do?" spat Mr Dacre at lunch one day. "Do they think he's just waiting for them to produce a Victor Ludorum to claim his hand?"

"He honestly doesn't know which way to go," said Brother William. "I have him for religion. Of course there's no debate about that, but he has admitted to me that he's confused about his future."

"Some use being so intelligent," twittered Mr Marple, "when it can't help you to make the most important decision of your life. I always wanted to be a teacher. I didn't have to think twice about it."

"Neither does a grub think twice about becoming a fly," I said, on the defensive, as it were. "It's the ultimate choice that matters, surely?"

"Yes, that's what I'm saying."

"But be honest, Brother," said Mr Dacre, physically bracing himself to the necessity of challenging an annointed priest, "if Shackleton had shown any sign of wanting to join the Order, the brothers would have had plenty to say."

"That's right," I said. "Brother Basil would be in there with his skirt hitched up taking on all comers."

"I think not," said Brother William, smiling. "One cannot lead souls to the service of God by the scruff of their necks. If Shackleton had had a vocation he would struggle against it as we all did, but in the end he would go quietly."

"'But as I rav'd and grew more fierce and wilde/At every word –'"

"'Methought I heard one calling, 'Childe'/And I reply'd, 'My Lord',"" capped Brother William.

We laughed at our cleverness. "But Shackleton isn't struggling. He's dithering."

"What about V.S.O.?" suggested Mr Dacre. "That might put some stuffing into him."

"They don't let people use V.S.O. for stuffing themselves. You have to have a definite prospect afterwards."

"Well, I'll pray for him to make the right decision," said Brother William.

"Do Protestant prayers count if they're for a Catholic?" I asked.

"Yes, but at a reduced rate of exchange," said Brother William, rocking with laughter. He really was in a good mood. I wondered if the joviality at our table had been noticed by anyone, to wit, Shackleton, and looked round as it were casually in his direction.

Our eyes met. He had been watching me.

I turned back to the table, my heart bumping. "Little people have big ears," I said, hoping to suggest that my agitation was the result of the conversation having been overheard rather than over-looked.

"Not to worry," said Brother William, "I'm always trying to hear what's being said at that table and I never have any luck."

We were now well into the Easter term. The general stirring in the blood had had its effect on the radical members of staff and the question of a strike was again raised. The union's dispute with the government had been stalemated for some time and it now really seemed as though we would see some action.

When the date for the first day's down-tools was fixed, Martin and his comrades became somewhat more subdued than I had ex-pected. His mien lacked anything of triumph, in fact he even seemed a little nervous. I attributed this to the awkwardness he now felt at having to inconvenience the entire school in the interests of monetary advantage, a goal of which he was usually loud in contempt. The contortions necessary to convince himself and the brothers that there was absolutely nothing personal in it, and that they could resume friendly relations as soon as the strike was over, also gave him pain. He was particularly loath to get in-volved in a discussion with me on the subject, which was not easy, as he had something he particularly wanted to say.

On the morning before the first day of the strike, I was in the tiny Resources Centre – a converted broom cupboard – recording a programme from the radio. Yet another odd little tale of children, usually boys, having ethnic experiences in places like Rangoon, or the rain forests of Guatamala. I appreciated the object of trying to inculcate a sense of the oneness of human experience, but occasion-ally longed for a story of boys from Salford ripping out telephone booths – something that my pupils could really identify with.

Martin put his head round the door, an unmistakably conspira-torial look on his face. "Are you alone?" he said.

I looked briefly under a pile of colour supplements. "Yes."

He came in and closed the door. The space was confined, certainly not allowing room for prevarication. Martin was wearing his academic gown, perhaps to bolster his academic integrity under the onslaught the strike was making on it.

"Look," he said, in a lowered tone, "you know it's on tomorrow, don't you?"

"Yes."

"Well, it's like this. We don't want the red-necks to break the strike – or you, either, really. But the point is, if you're asked to take over one of the G.C.E. classes I just thought of suggesting it might be charitable to do it. Do you see what I'm getting at?" He glowered at me, obviously miserable in his role as traitor to the Revolution.

"Yes. You want me to have a fit of altruism if it's the G.C.E. kids, but not the others."

"But you do see the point, don't you? It's a once-in-a-lifetime thing for them. The point will be made anyway. I'd be much happier if I thought you'd do that. Brother Eamonn is going to cover as many classes as he can, but he can't do them all."

"Okay."

"Thanks. And ... you won't let on that I said anything, will you?"

"The secret will die with me."

"One has to keep up morale."

"Okay. You know, you're a real amateur at this business, aren't you?"

He grinned. "I know. I'm pissed off with it all, if you must know. We were going to take the third years to see *Moonfleet* tomorrow. They hate my guts now."

"The third years are very forgiving. And it's for their own good in the long run."

"All right, all right, don't rub it in." He paused with his hand on the door handle. "You know, you'll be a bloody good teacher one day."

"Oh yeah?"

But Martin was mistaken if he thought that my cheerful acceptance of the idea had anything to do with altruism. There was only one thought in my head, and that was that I might be asked to baby-sit Shackleton's class once more. The landscape of my life had become so bleak that the prospect of an hour in the same classroom as he rose out of it flashing bright lights.

It did not seem sufficient to leave things to chance. The G.C.E.

candidates, urgent though their case was, could always sit the exam. again, but I did not know when another opportunity of speaking to Shackleton might be given to me, for he would be gone for ever – as far as I was concerned – after a few brief months. Then I remembered Brother Eamonn took Shackleton's class. Brother Eamonn would not be on strike. I consigned Brother Eamonn to a lurid Catholic fate.

My depression, however, only lasted a minute. Perhaps there were ways of manipulating the situation. The sixth form had other classes, after all, and Thursday was a good day for me as regards free periods. I clearly had to implant ideas into brotherly heads. I found out that Brother William was in charge of re-organizing the timetable. He had probably been chosen as the person least likely to give offence. At lunch-time, therefore, I steered the conversation round to the strike.

"What's going to happen to the sixth-form classes? I have some free periods if I'm needed."

"Thank you, thank you," said Brother William, "but that won't be necessary. They can go to the library if there's no teacher. Are you having prunes?"

My state of mind, as Industrial Action Day dawned, was worse than it would have been if Martin had not said anything. Instead of earnest talk with Shackleton, my free periods would probably be spent parsing passages of *Twelfth Night* with the spotty fifth forms. The gloom spoilt what might have been a day fractionally more enjoyable than usual.

An almost wartime atmosphere prevailed. Those left to man the guns were imbued with a sense of emergency, of managing in a crisis that they clearly enjoyed. Being mostly members of the A.M.A. they also had the thrill of righteousness, of being the group that put the interests of the school before their own.

Anne was spared any part in the business, except having to calm and organize a distraught Brother Basil, but Damaris was actively supporting the strikers. She even announced her intention of joining the Union.

"In time for the next strike?" I suggested.

"That's irrelevant."

"Then why didn't you join it before?"

"You're so cynical, you'll believe what you like anyhow."

3B, cheated of their outing to *Moonfleet*, were in a foul mood.

They were particularly enraged at not getting a free period. A groan, like a bad smell, rose as I entered the classroom.

"Why aren't you on strike, Miss?" grumbled Riccio. "It's not fair."

"The strike has not been organized for the purpose of giving the lower forms a bit of a rest, Riccio. If you think I wouldn't rather be on a demo in Parliament Square than teaching you lot, you're out of your mind, though admittedly it's a short step. Now, get out *Prose and Progress*."

Another groan filled the air, lingering in the fumes of rancid socks and stale fart. I ground my teeth. If only I could have explained to them, that if anyone had been unfairly treated it was I, in being given 3B in the first place, not to mention being virtually cheated of a special lesson with Shackleton. I could not even be bothered to put up a fight against their clamour. Inwardly I had withdrawn in disgust from the struggle, and sat looking solemnly at them, wearing, as I hoped, an almost tragic mask. This strange behaviour seemed to have a subduing effect on 3B. They feared the unknown and the sinister, and my manner must have struck them as both. There was a temporary lull.

"Where's Grass?" I asked.

"Dunno, Miss. 'e was 'ere just now."

"Baxter, kindly look under all the desks. If you find anything, don't touch it."

"Eh?" Baxter looked at me uncertainly. The class exchanged questioning glances. Baxter was encouraged by the others to do as I asked and got down on his hands and knees, and crawled up and down the rows of desks. "He's not here, Miss," he reported.

"Good. Turn to page 28. This is a description of a car accident and when I have read it I wish you to criticize the use of adverbs and condemn the piece as lurid and over-written, is that clear?"

Again there were raisings of eyebrows and muttered comments. This was certainly not my usual style of teaching, but I had had it was trying to "elicit" soupçons of though from 3B, pretending as the fashion then was, that the clever little sods thought it all out for themselves, and all I had to do was gather the disgorged nuggets into a coherent body of information for the use and enjoyment of all.

I read the passage at speed in a threatening monotone. When I looked up, it was to note, with a flicker of satisfaction, that 3B were sitting up straight and giving me their attention.

"Vocab. books," I barked. Desk lids flew up in unison. "Line 3, 'baleful' – sorrowful, pitiful; line 8, 'scrupulous' – extremely careful, detailed, conscientious; line 11, 'meliorate' – make better; line 14, 'ricochet' – rebound from one point to another; line 18 –"

"Hey, hold on a minute, Miss," moaned the Chihuahua, "I can't write so fast."

"– 'coagulate' – congeal, stick together; line 27, 'lacerated' – torn, cut; line 32 'comatose' – unconscious, without brain function; line 35, 'viscous' – sticky, thick; line 41 'moribund' – in a state of living death; line 46, 'incarcerated' – shut in, imprisoned; 'infernal' – hellish; 'conflagration' – fire, blaze."

3B were writing furiously, sweating in an effort to keep up. This was the way to go, I thought grimly: dissect the living language into sterile units of spelling, semantics, syntax and rhetoric and hit them over the head with a small chunk at a time.

"Cod, paraphrase the opening paragraph without the use of any descriptive language."

Cod shuffled and showed alarm. "Er – it's about –"

"I don't want any preamble. Just the facts. Come on, we haven't got all day."

Cod faltered and looked at me almost pleading. "What?"

I sighed. "Hardturm, you do it."

But before he could open his mouth, Grass came, nay, bounced, into the room.

"Oh, hello, Miss. I thought you'd be on strike. Sorry, I just had to go to the bog – me balls were killing me."

Grass accompanied his statement with a gesture.

Immediately the tension in the class broke into ribald, relieved laughter. Grass, not being subject to the mysterious influence of my change of mood, had injected the familiar rebellious boisterousness into the atmosphere.

My gorge rose to it. "How dare you," I said, very low. "You've had it this time, Grass."

"What do you mean, Miss? I can't lie to you, Miss."

"Don't play the injured innocent with me. You've tried that once too often. You were deliberately insulting and offensive. You've had all the chances I'm giving you."

"What? What do you mean, Miss?"

Grass had begun to notice that I had not been reduced to shrill indecision for once. He sensed, as he was meant to, that I was going to make a present of him to Mr Dacre.

At that moment the door opened and Shackleton came in. It was like a shot of neat alcohol. I drew a sharp breath and steadied myself against the freak tide of sensation. He was looking serious, and as he came into the room ran his hand through his wavy hair in a self-conscious gesture. I could not stop myself from smiling at him, or from noticing how his blazer fitted his slim body with elegant ease. Speculation on exploring the contours of that body divested of its school uniform was only halted by absence of leisure to do so.

"I'm sorry to disturb you, Miss Slade, but Brother William said, would you please go to Miss Fotheringay. She needs to go home at once."

"Oh dear, is she ill?"

"Sort of, yes."

"I'll come at once." It was probably the curse. Damaris always had a bad time of it, but sometimes she was totally paralysed with pain. "What about the class?"

"That's all right. I'll supervise."

"Of course." Shackleton, needless to say, was Head Prefect, and the braided blazer entitled the wearer to chastise juniors. Not that he did: I knew him to be against corporal punishment. But 3B did not, and I guessed that they would not give him any trouble. In many ways they had more respect for Shackleton's authority than for mine, shored up though mine was by the school governors and the Education Committee. They saw him as having risen from the ranks and so more deserving of respect than someone who was paid to oppress them. Besides, the prefects could not be sued for malpractice and consequently had a free hand in interpreting their duties.

Hurriedly I gathered my things together, glad of something to do with my hands.

"What about me, Miss?" said Grass.

The wretched boy knew perfectly well that the moment of drama had passed, that I would not so far reveal my lack of control over him in front of Shackleton, for whom he intended to behave, by sending him as an after-thought to Mr Dacre.

"Sit down," I said. "I'll speak to you on Thursday." He did so, with a contented smirk. "And you can all start your homework now, which is to be an imaginative re-telling of the story in the first person, without repeating any of the description. I'm sure Shackleton will be kind enough to explain what the first person is for those of you in doubt."

Shackleton moved up to take my place at the desk. I hardly dared look up into those perceptive hazel eyes, but in the end could not resist it and allowed myself a quick glance, a flash of a smile and a muttered "thank you". He smiled back. My heart – or was it my entrails? – lurched inside me. There was no mistaking that look. It was not the polite reflex of a courteous pupil, it was the silent language of a personal relationship. Shackleton understood how I felt about being thrown into the bear-pit with 3B, and all the other, lesser torments that made up the warp and woof of my working life. He understood my relief in that moment of getting away for a luxurious few moments of unexpected peace.

Outside the classroom I began to hurry down the corridor, but then stopped and leant against the wall. Opposite was a framed print of van Gogh's sunflowers, askew. I needed a breathing space to quiet the clamour that the brief encounter with Shackleton had raised. I felt an intensity that defied definition as pleasure or pain. Its basis was pure physical attraction, or at most physical laced with aesthetic. It was only in this area that I was vulnerable to him. In all other respects – or so I thought – I still kept a cool distance, an ability to criticize and assess the boy objectively. But still, limited as the attraction was, it took a while to recover from it.

Grinning and gasping a little, I stood in the corridor for a few minutes, staring at my feet. Through the closed doors came the muffled sounds of classes in progress, or the thick quietness of supervised reading.

But as my mind cleared, an image of the situation began to formulate in my mind, of a cast sobering indeed.

If I had felt lonely before, what must I feel now? When Damaris had been the victim of Shackleton's charms I could at least still make the effort to get through to her. But the loneliness of so shameful a secret was infinite, and infinitely daunting. The idea of admitting it to Damaris or Anne was laughable, blushable. And there was no one else.

Facing that, I was forced into another bit of self-assessment. Here I was, already 22, in all respects a normal, healthy specimen of my sex, not only never having had a proper emotional attachment to a man, but never having felt the lack of one. I had tended to patronize Damaris for her technical virginity, but in fact we had derived emotional satisfaction exclusively from each other and Anne to an equal degree. And even Anne, who on the face of it had had the most normal sex life, never failed to discuss her boy-friends as a diversion. No transference of priorities had ever taken place.

I wondered if there could be something wrong with me. Why had I stored up the adolescent crushes of a lifetime for such an untimely outburst? Surrounded by men as I was, I should have been gaily playing off the bachelors on the staff against one another, and perhaps joined the Young Liberals for a bit of variety. I had not been without offers. To myself I always justified my refusal on the ground that I hated to see anyone throw their money away; I had a notion that it was morally wrong to go to the pictures with someone unless one was prepared to marry them. Had I no mating instincts at all? Was the odd sexual encounter to be the pattern for the rest of my life?

Standing, Kafkaesque, in the corridor, I made up my mind that it should not be so. This mad, demoralizing lust for the slim-hipped sixth-former had to stop. It was insane, inconvenient, adolescent. I had wisely condemned it in Damaris; I could do so in myself.

Sad, but steely, I went to the staffroom to collect Damaris. She was hunched up in a chair, ashen and tight-lipped.

"Can you walk?" I asked.

She nodded and tried to smile.

"Have a hot bath when you get home," I said, revelling in the sober realities of everyday life.

Damaris leaned heavily on my arm as we walked to the car park.

But on the asphalt under my feet danced images of Shackleton, of Shackleton and me in attitudes of sensual indulgence, and my whole body flushed to the imaginary thrill of Shackleton's flesh against my own.

Such was the pattern of my interior life for the ensuing weeks. The harder I fought to put such thoughts behind me, the more cunning they became in taking me unawares.

In desperation I turned to Jane Austen, Addison and Steele, *New Society*, the six o'clock news, the Society for the Teachers of English, Manchester branch, and other bracing realities, all in an effort to come under the influence of Reason. I engaged my subversive imagination in a head-on struggle, preparing myself for the temptation to indulge, taking immediate steps to distract myself onto some other topic. In some measure I was successful: I developed a facility for latching my mind onto random subjects. But the imagination had powers to adapt and survive beyond my ability to cope with it: my mind developed a facility for sliding off into two levels. Superficially I would be busily thinking received thoughts – of school, Damaris, Biafra, mononucleosis, or whatever was at hand – while at a deeper level the throbbing, shadowy images of Shackleton's body and mine in illicit union tormented me in every waking moment.

All I could effectively do was try to avoid him, or the mention of his name. After all, there only remained the Easter holidays and the summer term and then the agony of his immanent presence would be over. As I reminded myself of this, another voice said, "Yes, and then he'll no longer be a student at this school. Professional propriety will also be at an end." But I shrank from building scenarios that had a foothold in the real world. Shackleton was in some measure attracted to me, I was sure, but that part of my mind that could still recognize facts told me that the chances of his going out with an ex-teacher four years his senior were nil. He could pick and choose where he would: no doubt some tall, blonde Mancunian with filmstar molars and destined for Nursing School, or a career in Marks and Spencers, was the lucky woman, someone quite incapable of appreciating what she held in her arms. I had noticed that in some ways Shackleton's taste was regrettably conventional.

The constant effort of hiding my thoughts only made me jangle the more at any mention of it, blush at it. Fearing that I would do so made it certain, and another contingency to dread.

Everard Shackleton. The name alone was enough to raise expectations. Unthinkable that a boy so called could be fetid and lumpen, greasy-haired, bad-breathed, or cursed with sweaty palms. His name, the boy unseen, presaged something tall and supple, young-tree-like, possibly with raven hair of a silky texture, something that would look melting in a black velvet dinner-jacket and show to advantage eating violets under a palm tree in the foyer of an opera house.

Names are so important for setting up positive expectations. Damaris was lucky in this respect: Damaris – damask – rose – dame – maris – sea – damnation – Darius – amour – day – ame – dare. I was not: Carol – caries – roll (-mop herrings) – arrow – carnal – care – oil – callous – corns – calumny – Arrid – car – cruel. Say "David" and one hears a lyre strum: "Kenneth" and one smells fried eggs. I had always thought it no accident that the achievements of, say, Pepin the Short and Alexander the Great were not comparable. A man called Ferdinand Onions, for example, might do great things, but surely the highest offices in the land would elude him?

But Everard Shackleton – what might one not do with such a name? A name that spoke equally of beauty and virility. The name recommended the bearer. And yet one had not only the name itself, one had the real thing, almost unbelievably a bodying forth of the echoes of his name, in some respects exceeding even the reaches of my, by now, fevered imagination.

My lifeline to normality in these tormented spring days was Anne. Damaris was to be avoided as contaminated with the same disease, albeit cured. Anne had managed to confine Sammy to the weekends, but during the week we were constantly together, the more so since Damaris had become immersed in her opera, now based on a Nordic legend. Most evenings we were too tired to go out, although Anne and I occasionally walked down to the pub at 10 o'clock for a half of bitter and a banter with the locals. After supper Damaris would go up to her room and mess about with her table keyboard and her tatty manuscript paper. Discordant snatches of music were thumped out at uncertain intervals. I longed for her to play something – anything – from start to finish. Anne worked in the garden until it was too dark, and then we would sit by the gas fire while she read and I marked books.

For the sake of taking something in hand which might bear fruit I could eat, I was trying to improve, gently, Anne's taste in literature. She had a distressing appetite for romantic slush, and, indeed, other kinds of slush. Her reading matter ran the gamut from boy-meets-girl in Regency frills to boy-meets-girl in present-day Torremolinos. To do her justice, she always read whatever I suggested of an improving nature, always thoughtfully chosen to satisfy her lust for simple narrative. Dutifully she worked her way through the Brontës, Jane Austen, *Lord of the Flies*, Mrs Gaskell, *War and Peace*, *The Grass is Singing*, *Keep the Aspidistra Flying*, and others, always with the same result. "Did you enjoy that, Anne?" "It's all right, but nothing really happens, does it?"

I was getting pretty desperate. After some discussion with Brother Eamonn, I decided on a last gamble on *Silas Marner*.

If that did not stimulate her appetite for good books, I would admit defeat. What more of fluid narrative, domestic realism, psychological truth and emotional depth one could expect from a book I did not know. Moreover it was all set about with charming scenes of the countryside and the quaintness of a vanished way of life for which I knew Anne to be nostalgic.

She read it in four days, was even seen to laugh a little at times. I congratulated myself on having found, in *Silas Marner*, a door which would open for her onto the realms of literary excellence.

The end was in sight on Thursday evening as we sat grilling our shins around the gas fire – one of several contemporary notes in the cottage. It was not even an honest gas fire, but one of those contraptions with glowing coals fashioned out of fibre glass. The cranking of the mechanism that produced the "firelight" and the occasional sputter of gas were the only sounds.

Damaris had stopped composing for the night and gone to bed. I was tired, but could not miss the pleasure of hearing Anne's reaction to *Silas Marner* while it was still fresh – she had a woeful tendency to lump all read books together in her memory. So I sat in the chair opposite to her, yawning over 2A's putrid impressions of their journeys to school. No less than fourteen of these prose works ended with the phrase, "These are my impressions of my journey to school." In the end I became so exasperated that I scrawled at the bottom of P. Higgins' essay, "No kidding! I thought it was a recipe for pâté en croute!" Poor Higgins was a harmless little boy about three feet tall, two of which were legs, and with teeth that reached part-way to his knees.

At last Anne closed the book and laid it neatly on the occasional table beside her, then stretched and pulled down her jumper. I felt myself to be in a ridiculously excited condition in anticipation of our discussing *Silas Marner* and, as often happens, I tried to focus on a mundane detail in the scene before me in order to syphon off some of the nervous interest. In this case it was a large mole on the outside of Anne's slender thigh which, strangely, only served to accentuate the flawless line of creamy-coloured flesh. I could well imagine the temptation a man would feel to close his hand around that delicate limb just above the knee. Anne's right leg was of equal merit, of course, but the one with the mole had a particular charm. Wishing to disguise my anxiety I continued to mark, but noticed Anne yawning and toying with the book. "How was it?" I asked, casually.

"Very nice. Do you think Godfrey was supposed to be impotent?"

"Perhaps. Probably they never got round to it because relations were strained. George Eliot was a very daring lady for her day, but I don't think she would get hung up on details like that. She was more interested in motive and fatal flaws and whatnot. Did you think Nancy was strong enough as a central character?"

"Oh yes, quite good. Poor thing. They were both so nice, really, weren't they?"

"Yes. George Eliot is very good at doing nice, frustrated women. You should read *The Mill on the Floss* – it's very powerful."

"I think I might try weaving. There's room for a loom in my room."

We laughed at the doleful assonance. " 'Room for a loom'. Now that would make a good title for a novel."

"It sounds more like an article in *Family Circle*. But do you think you'd like to read more George Eliot?"

"Well, I'll see. I won't have much time before the holidays. Perhaps when I go to the camp with Sammy. There can't be much to do in a camp."

"He's not going to give you enough time to read the label on a gin bottle, let alone novels. Do you have to go?"

"No. I'm actually looking forward to it. I've never been to the Lake District."

"But Anne – camping! Of all the asinine activities in this climate – sleeping on the soggy, open ground under soggy canvas and eating soggy sausages for breakfast and soggy chops for dinner, when you've got constant hot water and Heat That Obeys You in your own home. You won't be able to have a hot bath and do your nails halfway up Helvellyn, you know. And supposing you get the curse? What are you going to do with the thing? You can't chuck it into Lake Windermere. You'll come back with double pneumonia, rheumatism and malnutrition and don't expect any sympathy from me – I warned you. Honestly – camping! What do you think you are, a Bedouin? Camping is for juvenile offenders and frogmen – and P.T. masters, of course. I daresay Sammy will make every effort to keep you warm in the only way he knows how. I wouldn't be surprised if you came home pregnant as well. Once he's got you away from civilization and totally dependent on his bivouacking skills he'll pressure you into doing the helpless female bit right up to the hilt."

"Don't you want me to go?"

"I didn't say that."

"Well, why are you so excited about it? I do think you're jealous of Sammy. That's ridiculous, Carlo."

Anne's pencilled brows were contracted a little as she looked at me, and she sat up straight in the armchair, with her elbows lightly touching its arms and her hands joined in her lap, her attitude suggesting a nervous defensiveness.

My outburst had indeed surprised me as well as her, springing like that out of the happy neutrality of the world of books. I sank my head on my hand.

"It's not jealousy. Don't you start saying things like that, too."

"Anyway, Sammy and I won't be alone at all, hardly. There's quite a group of girls and boys going, and other teachers from St Monica's."

"It all sounds most immoral to me. I'm surprised the Church allows it. No, it's nothing to do with Sammy. It's just that it won't be much fun for me here, with Damaris manning the crucible of creative genius all day."

"You could come with us. Why don't you? It can't be as bad as you think. People do it all the time."

"The things that people do all the time are mostly boring or lethal. That's no criterion."

"Then why not go home? Your parents would be glad to see you, wouldn't they?"

"My parent would, yes. But he would be incapable of making my life there more meaningful than it is here."

The real reason, of course, was that I could not tear myself away from the city where Shackleton lived. Who knows? I might run into him in the Central Reference Library.

"I wish you'd said all this before, Carlo. I could have put Sammy off. But now I've promised. He'd be so disappointed."

"He'd probably make you run round the athletics field ten times every night until the end of term as well. Oh, I'm sorry. It's selfish of me to make you feel guilty about going. If you take some electrically heated climbing socks I'm sure you'll have a wonderful time. I hope you do, really."

"Thanks. I'll call you every day."

"For God's sake, don't. You make me sound like a neurotic mother."

"Sorry."

"Me too. Ah well, 'To bed, to bed,' said Sleepyhead."

To bed, and more particularly, to dream.

This conversation brought on another crisis of self-respect. Was I really so besotted by the boy that I would hang around in the city on the off chance of a casual encounter with him? Home to Worcester Park I could not go. I had never cultivated local friends other than Anne and Damaris, and the thought of two and a half weeks of Muriel's jollity and little outings arranged for my benefit made me tired. There was another alternative. Perhaps Damaris and I could go somewhere together, somewhere removed from north and south alike – Norfolk or the Scilly Isles. Besides, pensive walks on lonely beaches was just what our friendship needed at this point.

When I suggested it to her she looked surprised and evasive.

"I thought you'd be going home, Carlo."

"Why?"

She shrugged. "You did at Christmas."

"Were you hoping to be alone up here so as to compose without distractions?"

"All right, there's no need to be sarcastic. What I'm doing may be no good, but at least I'm doing something. I don't want to be shut up in that school for the rest of my life."

"Do you mind answering the question? Do you want to go away somewhere or not?"

"Actually I can't. It's not that I don't want to. I've made other plans."

"You're going away by yourself?"

"Yes."

"Where to?"

"Does it matter?"

"Is it a secret mission?"

"No, of course not. God, isn't there any privacy round here?"

We were in her bedroom. Damaris was just visible through a haze of stale smoke, for she had recently given up yoga in favour of cigarettes and Cyprus sherry. The drifts of manuscript paper round the room were now partly obscured by cast-off clothes, full ashtrays (some split), dirty glasses and coffee mugs. "Look, this place is only rented. You can get your own place if you'd rather."

Damaris said nothing – which she did rather well – got up and went to the window, where she stood blowing smoke at the glass.

"I can see you insist on full confessions as part of my share of the rent. All right. I'm going to Finland."

"Finland? Why?"

"To do some research."

"For the *chef d'oeuvre*?" Damaris said nothing. "Why couldn't you have told me that?"

"Because I knew you'd be sarcastic, as you are being."

"Well what do you expect when you make such a melodrama of everything?"

"I'm writing a melodrama. I like to live my work."

"I see. Thank you for asking me to come with you and hold your notepads."

"Oh go away and leave me alone."

I did, shutting the door on naïve expectations of the joys of the communal life.

Term ended on the Tuesday before Easter. It was hard to fake relief and good spirits. Even Terry was going away, to Corsica. I had hoped at least to see him occasionally.

Martin, always sensitive to my moods when he had time, asked what I was doing over the holiday. I was evasive, trying to give the impression that I had a confusing number of alternatives. I dreaded that he would ask me to make myself at home *chez lui* whenever I felt like it. Contact with close-knit family life was more than I could face.

Mr Dacre was also in probing mood.

"I thought you might like to go for a drive one day, Carol. What about Fountains Abbey?"

"I've been."

"Well then, Rievaulx?"

"Actually I've been to them all."

"Oh. Somewhere else then? Chatsworth? Haddon Hall? Eyam?"

"Why don't you give me a ring in about a week? I'm not sure if I'm going home or not." Places of interest abounded in the North West and I had no doubt he had researched them all. He was also quite capable of suggesting a place which did not exist in order to trick me into proving I just did not want to go.

"All right. What time of day is best for you?"

"Mornings, probably."

"All right." He looked woebegone. In a way I shared his disappointment. Not that my feelings for him had changed, but because I was participating in the perpetration of the small cruelties that accompany the human condition.

Shackleton I saw briefly before I left. He was buoyant, childishly happy at the prospect of holidays. I tried to talk to him about a production of *The Alchemist* that I thought he should see, but he was not in the mood and anxious to be about his business. The meeting depressed me further. I saw myself so clearly through his eyes as merely a figure in the landscape of school life, perhaps of more interest and appeal than most, but still only moving against that background.

Anne was to come back from London on Easter Monday, in time to be carried off to the Lake District on the following day. But my solitude began the moment their train pulled out of the station on the Wednesday before.

I spent the rest of the day in town, shopping for more literary clothes, scanning the crowds as ever for a sight of Shackleton. I could not let it remain only a contingent hope. Several times I retraced my path around the library, John Dalton Street, St Anne's Square and Deansgate, lingering in the vicinity of music and bookshops: to no avail. Rare Records yielded the only surprise – the young man who had lived in the ground-floor flat of our house in Rusholme. His rapture on seeing me was threatening, especially as I could not even remember his name, and it was to avoid being dragged into the Kardomah Coffee House by him that I at last decided to go home.

I had never been alone before, never slept alone in a house or flat. The relative remoteness of the cottage struck me for the first time as a little alarming, although the village proper was only a quarter of a mile down the road.

It was raining when I got home, so I went round checking all the windows. Damaris had left her room in its natural state, the bed unmade, ashtrays, clothes and crockery on every flat surface. Only the manuscript paper had been winkled out. I felt a wicked desire to see it, not that the music would mean anything, but the libretto would doubtless yield a laugh or two. All the drawers in her chest were partially opened. I slipped my hand through the crack and groped around among the crumpled clothes, but found nothing papery. In the bottom drawer my hand came upon a small packet which, being hidden under all the bulky knitwear, promised to be of interest. It was a packet of Orthofoam. I opened it. One of the waxy pink bullets was missing.

For some minutes I knelt there with the thing in my hand, then took one of the bullets from its plastic mould. So pure and pretty they were, they would have been dainty as earrings. The thought of one of them in action, or at least *in situ*, took my breath away.

Sitting on the cold summer floor of Damaris' bedroom, the sordid realities of sex seemed reason enough for eschewing it altogether. No wonder one was provided with instincts more powerful than logic: what human activity could, on the face of it, be more distasteful to the fastidious? Damaris' hysterics after her one night of love seemed quite understandable at that moment. How many women really enjoyed it anyway? How many men, so ready with accusations of frigidity, ever ask themselves whether they are more likely to inspire lust or disgust?

Had Damaris then deliberately carried these things about with her? I did not want to believe it, although I was surprised at my own hypocrisy. Obviously it was responsible of Demaris to be prepared, but the calculated and, I felt, distinctly male, device of being prepared for a casual coupling did not sit easily with my sense of what was becoming in a woman, especially in Damaris, who made a lifestyle out of submission to spontaneous emotion.

I put the bullet back and replaced the box in the drawer, then left the room exactly as I had found it.

Domestic tasks kept me occupied until the evening and lighting of lamps. I had something to eat and washed up. It was still raining, so I could not tend Anne's garden as I had promised. For a long time I simply stood at the kitchen window, staring out into the garden and beyond at the gentle slope of hillside. The great trees around the house sagged under the rain, tulips dragged their petals in the mud, puddles were forming in the lawn, the gutters overflowed and a loud, hard splashing of water dominated in the chorus of wet harmonies. The rain lent an unearthly, luminous greenness to the already lush growth. So much for dust unto dust. The human race, Manchester division at any rate, was not returning to the earth, but to the sea. There would surely come a time, and not long, when Manchester and Stockport and our own village would be underwater cities, and one by one the population would slip quietly into the water, struggling a little at first while they became accustomed to their embryonic gills. If not, they would be increasingly confined to their houses until depression carried them off, leaving the countryside to the slugs and those frogs who could still find something to croak about.

When darkness finally came I sat at the kitchen table. There were no books to mark, no urgent letters to write. I did not know what to do. There seemed only two alternatives, read or go to bed. Unwisely, I chose a heavy work on the political history of allegory. It was no competition for Shackleton, whose image forced itself upon my mind at every page, so that I had to read each paragraph three or four times before knowing for sure that I had read it at all. It was a hopeless struggle, which I did not, however, give up, until it had forced tears from my eyes. But at last I began to cry freely, in snuffling, self-pitying sobs. Nothing to do, no one to talk to, no one to write to, nothing to listen to except the rain, nothing to watch except the feverish couplings of myself and Shackleton which flickered endlessly on the mind's screen. I had staked my all on my two so-called friends and they had abandoned me when I most needed them.

There was, of course, a touch of self-indulgence in all this. I could have whiled away a couple of hours polishing the silver or listening to Midweek Theatre, or both. But if there was anything of comfort in the situation it was the grandeur of its hopelessness: I did not feel inclined to insult such solemnity with trivial solutions. That might come later if the mood persisted, but on that first night I could only indulge.

Persist it did. The mornings at least brought human necessities – breakfast, housework, postmen, bills. The afternoons began to clamour with the absence of regular activity. Tea-time, when the very steam on the kettle cried out for company, was the starting-point for the evening's gloom. How much more tea demands to be shared than does any other beverage. To fake tea-time alone is sheer emotional masturbation. Sitting by the gas fire with a large mug of sweet tea, I would have imaginary conversations with Damaris and Anne, talking out the minor happenings that passed for activity during the long, wet days. After a while their figures would merge into that of Shackleton. I would talk to Shackleton for hours, until I was sitting in darkness between the glare of the gas fire and the misted lamplight outside. When it was quite dark I would lay back my head and surrender to my imagination, increasingly lascivious. On the second or third night I began to masturbate.

Thereafter I at least had something to look forward to in the evenings.

Whenever I could think of an excuse to do so I drove into the city, but it was to come back with the conviction that everyone there was busy and happy except me.

On the Saturday morning I was in Lewis's Food Hall, circling aimlessly between the fresh fish, cold pies, condiments, seasonal vegetables and bulk nuts, hoping to see something that would activate my consumer instincts. I stopped and dithered for a minute in front of the coffee beans, wondering if I should come to grips with fresh coffee for once. It would at least use up a bit more time. Turning away, I caught sight of a woman who seemed familiar. She was having frozen cauliflower weighed. Lewis's seemed to have a thing about loose produce. I had always thought it a considerate touch, but at the moment it was a godsend, for the woman was Mrs Shackleton. I blushed, remembering some of the postures her son had recently assumed in my imagination. Of course I would have to speak to her, the only problem was staying calm enough for rational conversation. "Well," I thought, "it's a small world, all right. Well, well. Fancy meeting the mother." I careered through Delicatessen and Prepared Meats. I had a small cousin called Linda who stayed with us for a week once and every time she opened her mouth out came, "IT's a small world after all, IT's a small world after all, IT's a small world after all, IT's a small, small, small, small world." I snatched the thought out of the air as it fluttered by on its way to Bread and Cakes. The wretched parents had given her the record. It was impressive evidence of the value of repetition in learning. Perhaps I might even have got the hang of the laws of thermodynamics if we had had the records at home.

I went for a quick walk round Fresh Dairy Goods, tracking Mrs Shackleton's movements out of the corner of my eye, then went straight up to her and said hello, just as she was getting the change from her cauliflower money.

"Hello, Miss. I've just been buying some cauliflower. Have you ever tried it?"

"Cauliflower? Oh yes, many times."

She laughed, revealing rather old-fashioned false teeth, very narrow and even. I was surprised, because she was not that old, perhaps fifty. "I meant this stuff in here. Of course, it's no good raw, but O grattin it's very tasty. Our Everard likes it with a baked potato. Are you enjoying your holidays, Miss? I expect you need a rest, don't you?"

"I'm certainly getting one. What can one do in this awful weather? It's like living at the bottom of a river."

"How true! Well of course I'm so busy usually I don't generally notice the weather, but I feel sorry for the young people who are going camping. They'll be washed away."

"Or come home. That would be nice for those who only see them during the holidays."

Mrs Shackleton started to move away from the counter, ballasted on either side by two stuffed shopping bags.

"Let me help you with those, Mrs Shackleton."

"What? Oh no, Miss, no." She actually blushed at the idea. "I couldn't have that."

"Whyever not?"

"Well – I'm used to it. They're much too heavy for you."

I felt mildly insulted at the idea that I was too puny to carry a bag of shopping, but more distressed that Mrs Shackleton was treating me so exclusively as teacher, a fragile savant not fully adapted to the rough and tumble of everyday life. Nor did I relish the conversation she might have with her son when she went home. "Guess what, Everard! That sickly-looking English teacher of yours offered to carry these great big bags!"

However, it was not of shopping bags that I wished to talk.

"Just as you like. How are you managing with Shack – your son at home all the time? Are you one of those mums who can't wait to get them back to school?"

"To tell you the truth, Miss, it doesn't make much difference. I do a bit of social work for the church you see, so I'm out a lot and then so is he. He makes his own bed and cooks his breakfast and all that sort of thing. No trouble at all, really."

"So you'll hardly miss him when he goes away?"

"On Tuesday, you mean? No, not really. Though, as you say, they might have to come home if it goes on raining like this. It was exactly like that when we went to the Lake District with Jo and Florence. It got into the suitcases and everything – we had to put all our clothes in the drier when we got home. Rain? I thought somebody had emptied Lake Windermere on top of us, it was fantastic."

"Er ... wait a minute. Do you mean Everard is going camping with the school?"

"Yes, Miss. Isn't that what you meant?"

"No."

"Well, he is. Are you surprised? I must say I was a bit – he's never been much of an outdoor type, but he likes that P.T. master and Brother Eamonn told him it would be a good idea to have a real break before the exams."

"Good Lord. That's – that's really interesting."

"Yes? Well if you'll excuse me, Miss, I must just go and get an Easter egg for Timothy. I do hope you have a happy Easter, Miss. It's been so nice talking to you."

"And you. Happy Easter."

I keeled off into Bread and Rolls and subsequently up the escalator into Ladies' Gloves.

That Shackleton was going camping was hard enough to take in, but that he was going camping with the school party, a party with which Anne had invited me to go and which I had spurned with my heel, that instead of sitting masturbating by myself for another week I could be sleeping under the stars, or at least under the clouds, nearer to Shackleton than I would ever be now for as long as I was to live – these were the unbelievables that slapped at my mind and sent me careering into shoppers in a daze.

Fighting for attention with the fact of my stupidity was a sense that life was conspiring to crush and humiliate me. I had prostrated myself before the image of Shackleton, could I now be surprised if the results of my deviously indulged infatuation were trampling freely over me?

The irony of it made me almost cry out loud – that I had refused to go on the trip on the chance of seeing him in town. It was far too late to change my mind now. When Anne came back to collect her things I would have to smile and be cool, squashing the impulse to mention his name and more or less direct Anne to be alive to his every movement, word, look, and bring back the images as live offerings to slake my thirst.

Of course there was nothing strange about his going. I had always known that he had a kind of friendship with Sammy, presumably because Sammy was incapable of recognizing his quality, and even so had no use for it. Shackleton played cricket for the school. I could imagine them bantering about wides and slips and silly mid-ons among the wind-blown grass on the cricket field, their white flannels flapping, each relishing the manly solitude and self-reliance of the cricketer and indulging to the full the propriety of understatement. At first it had been a shock to think of Shackleton under canvas – as it had to think of him under sail, though that should have been a clue. But it was partly such anomalies in him that were intriguing. I was glad he did not submit to the stereotype his talents suggested. One should be open to all kinds of experience, not reject it on the grounds of ignorance, nothing reveals ignorance more clearly. Shackleton was an artist, and communing with nature and general curiosity were familiar characteristics in the artist. It is only the superficial mind that uses a handbook to characterize human activity.

All this being true, why the hell had I refused to go? Because I had lost my will and my self-respect, and my sense of humour was going down the same road. I sickened myself. More, I was sickened by Manchester, by Lewis's with its infinitely diffuse ordinariness and its nuts in bulk, by teaching, by boys – up to and almost including Shackleton for what he had done to me.

And then, as I barged blindly through the exit, I bumped into someone coming in. A second later, when it was too late, I recognized him as Shackleton, presumably en route to meet his mother in Confectionery. I had been put off by what he was wearing – a thin, yellow pullover with a black and white bee on the front and the legend "Buzz off" underneath. Not surprisingly, I had been distracted by the motif. But the picture before my eyes as I stood back stayed, as though it were burnt into the air. The pullover was collarless and revealed a slightly long neck, the hair loosely curling into the nape, the whole head suddenly that of a dancer, or one of Botticelli's Young Men in mild déshabillé. The eyes were almost tortoiseshell in close-up, and from a slight distance dark gold. He was utterly, devastatingly, achingly desirable, and, realizing it, my whole body was flushed and weakened with sheer lust, so that I almost fainted. I rushed outside and stopped in front of one of the shop windows. My image, superimposed on the stiff plastic dolls with their glistening nylon hair, showed an utterly, devastatingly ordinary young woman in a beige raincoat and two-inch heels, the antidote, as Oscar Wilde put it, to desire.

My car was in Kendal's car park. I ran down Market Street and hurried up to it and drove out of the city as fast as I could. I did not drive home, it could not be borne, but round and round the countryside until I was exhausted and it was dark once more.

On Easter Sunday I got up late and went to bed early, plotting the interval with cigarettes and glasses of British sherry.

On the Monday I picked Anne up at the station. She was her usual serene self, slightly more animated than usual by excitement over the trip. I did not have the heart to burden her with my state of mind, although I was in fact doing myself a favour. To tell a person one's troubles, knowing in advance that they are powerless to help, is merely to erect a mirror in which their awfulness can be more clearly seen. I told Anne that I had had a most interesting experience by myself, and that I had started to write a novel.

We passed a pleasant evening over a dinner of lamb chops, redcurrant jelly, peas, salad and apple crumble, followed by a lengthy investigation into Anne's wardrobe to choose suitable clothes. It was a brief, painful *déjà vu* of the kind of domestic happiness we had not, in fact, often enjoyed.

Sammy came for her punctually at eight o'clock the next morning. It felt as though she were a virgin bride emigrating to Australia in the days of sail. Sammy would make sure of her while they were away, I had no doubt.

When the car had disappeared round the corner I went straight back into the house, up to my bedroom and collapsed in hysterical sobs on the bed. I had never known a moment of such amazing bleakness. It is one thing to be wracked by a hopeless passion for someone who at least qualifies as a prospective mate: it is quite another to be tormented simultaneously by the passion and the loathing of it, where the wish to be free of it was as urgent as the thing itself. And even if I did rid myself of it, what was in prospect that could promise any reward to such virtue? A job I loathed in a place I loathed. Anne would shortly be taken to the altar by Sammy, and Damaris had already withdrawn to tend altars of her own. I was the only one who had not found a future acceptably different to the one we had planned. The knowledge that I was also the only one who was sorry the communal experiment had not worked brought more gulps of self-pity.

When, eventually, the sobs had shaken themselves out, I lay curled up on the bed leafing through possible distractions, lifelines. Not that I was suicidal. The thought never crossed my mind. My future presented itself as graveyard enough to punish my incontinent desires. I tried to compare my own situation unfavourably with that of the poor and the hungry, those languishing in iron lungs or stinking jails, and the anguish of their relatives. But it was no use. I could know, but not feel, such plights, and

I came to the conclusion that it would be a relief to suffer from an external cause, rather than one for which I only had myself to blame. And yet I could not blame myself, I could not see how I had been culpable. This obsession with Shackleton had visited me like the plagues of Egypt, perhaps to try my faith also. My loneliness struck me afresh every now and then, making me reflect that it had always been at the heart of things, that Damaris, Anne and I had never really known each other as we had thought we did and that it was real knowledge that had proved our undoing. Our friendship had been the carefree engagement that precedes the shattering intimacy of marriage.

There had to be someone who could make me laugh, who could reduce my problems to everyday dimensions. Only one image came to mind: Brother William. He was obviously favoured with special insight behind the apparent pointlessness of life. Becoming a monk, probably, would not exactly get me very far, but suddenly an hour or so of Brother William seemed like the prospect of a hot bath after a night on the bare mountain.

The novelty of dragging Brother William out of his private apartments for a gut-level talk about the meaning of life lifted my spirits at once. But by the time I had got the car out I was shaking. I knew I was taking a long step out of the designated channels of my relationship with Brother William. I was gambling on my intuition, and although I was almost sure he would accept my intrusion with his usual calm, the awkwardness of those first few minutes alone with him was horrifying. What would I say? What did I really want to say? Did I intend to tell him about Shackleton? No, never. The only crumb of comfort was that it was still my secret. Then what was I going to say? After ten minutes my nerves failed and I turned the car round, then turned it round again. The disappointment of not going through with it was the greater of two evils.

The countryside was full of pale, watery sunshine. It stirred my nerves the more. One associates sunshine with events of great moment, from G.C.E.s to the return of Agamemnon to Mycenae, as if it is fitting for human tragedies to be played out against a background of nature's indifferent glory. True, there is always more going on in the summer anyway, but when one is being more consciously universal than usual, it seems right to have the symbol of one's universe visibly at hand.

The school was locked and deserted. The brothers' red brick

house, four-square to the wind, was set apart from the school buildings and involved making a long, exposed walk down the path from the side of the gym towards their front door. Some boys were playing football on the sports field over behind the school, but otherwise there was no sign of life.

I stood on the doorstep and rang the bell. No one came at first. I ran my eye in feigned interest over the stumpwork shrubbery around the house.

At last the door was opened, by an elderly woman. I was startled to see a woman. I had not thought of their having a housekeeper. She looked at me suspiciously.

"Hello. I'm Miss Slade, from the school. I was wondering if I could possibly speak to Brother William?"

Her face relaxed. "Oh yes. I've heard of you, Miss. Just wait a minute, will you, while I find out if he's in. A lot of them are on holiday, you know."

"Thank you." She left me on the doorstep. Surely Brother William had not gone away? Didn't he know he had a role to play in my life? Anyway, what did the brothers need with holidays? Going to heaven should cover all that.

The housekeeper had closed the door, and after about ten minutes I began to wonder if she had forgotten me. My body trembled so strongly I must have been out of focus to look at. I listened for sounds of activity inside the house, but all I could hear was the whine of a food-mixer in the distance. Budding lilac trees danced glibly in the breeze.

The door opened again. It was Brother William. I sighed, stirring his cravat.

"Thank God, Brother. You haven't gone away then."

"No, no, this is my true corporeal presence." He beamed, the oriental eyes being temporarily swallowed up. "Did you want to speak to me, Miss Slade?"

"Yes, please. I hope I'm not disturbing you."

"Not at all. I was just sorting out my matchbox collection."

"You collect matchboxes?"

"Yes. You look rather shocked. Don't you think we ought to have private possessions?"

"I'm not sure. It's just ... unexpected."

"Well, I tell you, I made pretty sure I chose an order which wouldn't part me from my matchboxes."

"Actually I have a rather good one here that you might like

– but I'm afraid it says 'Too much sex makes you short-sighted.' It's set out like a test card at the opticians, so you have to read it. Look. I picked it up in the restaurant at Picadilly Station."

"Let me see." He took it over to the window. "I'm short-sighted."

"You'd better keep it then."

"Thank you very much. You shall have a cup of tea for that."

By this time he had led me into a small room at the front of the house, minimally furnished for the reception of visitors. Duck-egg blue walls formed an uneasily sterile background to the faded Turkish carpet, scuffed leather armchairs and red woolly curtains that had obviously come from a much older house. The absence of detail in the room, apart from a coffee-table, a few magazines and a picture of the Pope, ensured that the atmosphere was set by the cold, flawless walls. The kind of room that makes one feel grubby and out of place, as it may well have been intended to do.

My nerves began to sing again as I waited for Brother William to come back. The preliminary banter was over, there would be no evading the issue now.

"There, I've asked Mrs Midhurst to bring it in," he said, as he slid discreetly back into the room and lowered himself into a chair. He crossed his fingers lightly and smiled. "Now then, how can I help you, Miss Slade?"

I swallowed and shook. He was being so nice, my own un-worthiness seemed to grow by the minute. "Well ... it's ... it's difficult ... difficult to ... er ..." I burst into tears.

"Dear me, dear me," he said, leaning forward. "I hope this has nothing to do with me?"

"No! I mean – no. I'm sorry – I don't know ... oh dear."

"Go ahead and cry, Miss Slade. No one can hear you, there's double glazing. Except Mrs Midhurst here –" for she had just come in with the tea "– and she's the soul of discretion, aren't you, Mrs Midhurst?"

"Is the young lady all right, Brother? Would she like an aspirin?"

"No thank you. I'm all right."

"Sure?"

"Yes, thank you."

Mrs Midhurst left reluctantly, perhaps resentful at missing an episode that introduced a welcome touch of *Crossroads* into the brothers' lives.

"I'll pour the tea anyway," said Brother William. "All things pass in time."

When the sobs had shuddered into mere gulps, I flopped back in the chair.

"May I smoke?"

"Please. May I borrow one?"

"Of course. But you shouldn't."

We lit up and drank our tea, Brother William with the discretion of one used to eating in silence, I with noisy, emotional shlurps.

"Well now, what is it?"

"It's absurd, Brother. I'm 'in love' or something. I'm as miserable as sin and I wish I were dead." As the words tumbled out, so did more tears.

"Now let's get one thing clear," said Brother William above the noise, "you're not in love with *me*, are you?"

"No! I mean, unfortunately not, Brother. It's nothing personal."

"I hope you don't mind my asking, but freak behaviour is much more common than one might think. Or perhaps we just hear about it more. But it's interesting that you use that phrase 'miserable as sin'. It's quite often pretty near the mark. Now then, is he married?"

"No."

"Are there other impediments?"

"Actually no."

"I see. Then it's a simple case of unrequited love?"

"In a way. It's not simple. And it's not love, either. I hate being like this. I'm not used to it."

"What are you used to?"

"What?"

"What are you used to? I mean, young people usually form attachments while they're still in their teens. Is this the first time?"

"As bad as this, yes. I suppose I'm a bit peculiar. When I was a teenager I had the odd crush, nothing serious. I'm not a virgin. Not that that makes any difference in affairs of the heart. What I mean is – I used to feel so adult, so much in command of circumstances – but now I feel – just nothing. I realize that I've never really looked at myself before. This – thing – it's so humiliating, it's made me see myself in a completely new light."

"An unflattering one?"

"You bet."

"So, in fact this 'thing', this emotional attachment, isn't the only 'thing', is it? You're going through a crisis of confidence – who am I, where am I going? etc."

"Yes . . . no. Partly both. It's such a mess. I can't tell any more what's me and what's 'the thing'. Yes, 'the thing'. It's a monster, all right. Do you know that passage in *Great Expectations* where Pip tells Estella that he sees her in the wind and the marshes and in the sails of ships and everything? Well, that's the way I feel, only I see him in the chalk and the liver and the faces of 3B and on the pages of their wretched exercise books and they don't exactly meet the requirements of poetic vision – more like double vision, one great big wretchedness superimposed on a plethora of smaller ones."

"Don't you like teaching, Miss Slade?"

"Oh Brother, I don't teach. I just stand there and mouth disconnected rubbish. I really don't know what I'm supposed to be doing, and when I think I do sometimes, it just gets drowned in noise and hostility."

"But Miss Slade, the school is full of teachers, some of them quite good ones. Couldn't you get advice? What about Martin? He's the obvious person to go to."

"I know, I know. But I don't think he ever had the problems I do – he's too imposing. And well, there are just some people one can admit failure to and some one can't, that's all. He's so bracing. He'd brace me up to the hilt superficially and never touch on the mess inside."

"Miss Slade, you're going to roll your eyes in despair when I say this, but I must, nevertheless. What you're experiencing is very common among young teachers, especially graduates who haven't had any formal training for the job. In fact I would say it's the exception rather than the rule if they don't go through something like this. Teaching isn't just a job, it's a completely new life, as – as changing and difficult as having a child yourself suddenly. Don't fight it. Accept the demands it makes on you. Believe me, this time next year you'll feel quite differently. I'd put money on it if we were allowed to have money. And in the meantime you must go and talk with Martin or Brother Eamonn and get some practical help. I'm sure they'll be very sympathetic. And when all's said and done, you have nothing to lose."

"What's the point, Brother? I'm resigning at the end of the year."

"No! Why? Listen, Miss Slade, I would seriously advise against it."

"Why? I'm not happy here and I'm not a good teacher. It would be better for everybody if I left."

"To do what? Is there something you would really rather have done in the first place?"

"No. That's probably half the trouble."

"Then what will you do?"

"Get some kind of job. I can type."

"No, no, no Miss Slade. Leave when you've got on top of it if you like, but not now or you'll carry a sense of failure strung around your neck like an albatross for the rest of your life. It's not worth it."

"Everything in my life at the moment seems to be strung round my neck like an albatross. No wonder I'm depressed."

"It's partly the season, you know. The sap's rising. It always causes upheavals. More tea?"

"Thank you." There was a pause, during which I reflected on how calm I now felt. "Well, perhaps you're right about not decamping from school. I'll give it one more year. But then he –"

I blushed and cast a quick glance at Brother William to see if he had made the connection. He had. He stirred in his sugar in a truly troubled manner.

"Miss Slade, if this passion you have conceived is in any way connected with the school, I must warn you that we cannot support any more scandal at the moment. What with Mr Fallowfield's accident and Miss Cromwell's condition, any more hanky-panky and we'll be due for a public enquiry. I hope you don't mind my being frank?"

"No, that's what I like about you, Brother."

"Thank you. I felt you hadn't come to me to hear platitudes."

"That's right."

"Certainly, if you left the school under a cloud –"

"It would be an albatross etcetera, etcetera."

"Yes. It would be unfortunate. Be patient, Miss Slade. It's only a matter of weeks until the end of the year, and then I have the feeling the problem will take care of itself."

So he knew it was one of the boys.

"And how am I to live until the end of the year?"

"I don't know. But you're an attractive young woman, Miss

137

Slade. You could amuse yourself with quite a choice of young men, I'm sure. Men who would be more – suitable. What about Mr Dacre? He's going through exactly the same thing over you. I couldn't help noticing."

"Better to go out with Mr Dacre than to burn?"

"If you like. You know as well as I do that there are no pat solutions."

"I know. There *are* no solutions, actually. I hope you don't think I've been wasting your time. I could hardly blame you."

"Of course I don't. I feel somewhat helpless, I'm afraid. I know only too well how you feel."

"Really? How come?" My astonishment must have seemed tactless, to say the least, but I had genuinely thought that monks and nuns had some sort of hormone imbalance, like homosexuals.

Brother William laughed. "Because I was once in love, Miss Slade. With a young lady. In a perfectly regular way."

"No kidding? What happened?"

"There was a problem of religion. She was a Methodist. It was more critical in those days."

"How awful! Poor Brother. I do think religion is a pain in the arse. Well, I suppose I can't expect you to agree. Is that why you became a priest?"

"No, no. I got over it long before that. It was mostly infatuation. I was eighteen, she was Althea Rosalie Farquhar of 14 Darford Crescent. But she wasn't very bright, so it all worked out for the best."

"But you see, you've never forgotten her."

"Of course not. I've never forgotten my sister either, but that doesn't mean to say I'd want to marry her. There's no need to romanticize it, Miss Slade. I've never doubted that I made the right decision."

"How did you get over it?"

"I turned my mind to other things. And then time anaesthetizes everything in the end. It's rather sad, really."

"If only one could be guaranteed a few minutes each day when you don't think about them. If only one weren't satisfied with crumbs – worse, actually manipulating circumstances to come by crumbs. That's what's so humiliating. You know, I'd rather go for a walk with this person than go to bed with the entire staff."

"Umm. I wouldn't be so sure of that, Miss Slade. You might

start out by going for a walk, but nature has a habit of taking one by the hand anyway. Do be careful."

"Yes, I will. Thank you, Brother."

"Would you like to see our new kitten? He's called Augustine."

"Oh. Yes, I suppose so."

He took me round to the back of the house and for a few minutes we marvelled over a gangling powder-puff of ginger fur with beady blue eyes, that swiped at our fingers with heart-rending ineffectualness and wobbled after us as we walked away. Brother William was clearly in love for the second time. One would have thought Augustine was the original Model-T cat.

Driving away from the school I could scarcely stop myself from sagging over the wheel with relief and the feeling of amazed exhaustion that must grip survivors of an air crash. I was convinced that Brother William had shown me the way, helped me to throw off my chains, and that all that remained was to rub my wounds. He was absolutely right about everything: there were no solutions, at least not external ones. The cure was within. I must treat the obsession like a disease and be resigned to being an emotional convalescent for some time. Perhaps most people were all their lives. I must learn to direct my energies towards more distant goals, in the real world, not in my imagination. First, then, to thyself be true, and it shall follow as the night the day that albatrosses shall be lifted from the neck. Already I could think more coolly about Shackleton, and tentatively marvel at my infatuation. He was charming, but conceited. He had an excellent brain, but his seeking after erudition had something contrived about it, as if it were a necessary adjunct of his natural gifts that he be seen to the best informed as well as the most talented. Moreover, his cynical enjoyment of the fuss that was made about him was an indication of his immaturity. He had not yet learnt to be humble about his talents, or to accept the admiration they excited with gratitude, as he should accept the talents themselves. There was much, in short, that young Shackleton had to learn.

At home I made myself a cup of instant coffee and took it into the garden. I inspected Anne's carrot and broad-bean seedlings and fortified them with a cheerful word. But the events of the morning had given me a taste for action. It was time to stop this suicidal brooding and rejoin the world of the living. I could have washed the mattress covers, but it seemed to lack drama. There was only one thing for it: Mr Dacre. Brother William had himself suggested it, almost giving the idea the imprimatur. I wondered if that covered going to bed with Mr Dacre if the occasion arose. There was no doubt that he recognized my condition for what it was. Fornication was a sin for Catholics, I knew, but perhaps my being a Protestant lessened the offence. Catholic theology was pretty devious in that way. But then, Mr Dacre was a Catholic, and probably a reactionary one. My virtue would be safe with him, however much my pride would suffer by the liaison. But it was time for a little suffering. Besides, I could not stay alone in the house one more evening.

Mr Dacre stuttered and gasped when I spoke to him on the phone. He wanted to come round straight away and take me out to lunch, but I managed to put him off until the evening.

Afterwards I went upstairs and took the packet of Orthofoam from Damaris' drawer. I closed all the drawers in the chest. As part of my new scheme for a healthy inner life I would in future be perfectly honest with Damaris and tell her that the adolescent hiding of secrets was out of tune with the times and with our age and that I had rifled her drawers because I was hurt by her galloping aloofness.

Mr Dacre – Vernon, as I must perforce think of him now – was clearly in a state of shock when he arrived. He stopped his car violently outside the house and turned the engine off while it was still in gear, so that it juddered and yelped into silence. I watched surreptitiously from behind the living-room curtains. He cursed. Then he looked in the rear-view mirror and smoothed down his hair. It was already as smooth as an oil slick. He was wearing his Prince of Wales check suit. He tripped over the step as he came through the gate and trod on a snail on the path, both calling for more curses. I smiled, feeling calm. Vernon's energies had for so long been channelled into narrow ways, one at least knew where to look for them. He was a potentially dangerous animal and in some respects exercised the same fascination – sex being one of them. It was a pity about the Fred Astaire hair-do; his features were of the chiselled variety beloved of romantic novelists, and he had a firm, well-disciplined body. If one were in the mood to be crushed against an uncompromising chest, his would certainly do. There was almost something erotic about the idea of being swept away by Vernon, as if he were a priest, as if one would be violating rather more mystical codes than those of common sense.

When I opened the door he was frowning and adjusting his tie. He might have been the landlord come to collect outstanding rent.

"I'm early. Sorry."

"Doesn't matter. Do you want to come in for a minute?"

"No, not really. I think it would be better to get on with it."

"Oh. I hope you didn't feel obliged to come out. I thought –"

"I didn't mean that. I just don't like hanging about in people's sitting-rooms."

"Okay. Where are we going?"

"First I thought we'd go down to the Hare and Hounds for a drink and then go for a bit of a drive and have dinner at the Bells of Poever. I've booked a table."

"You've obviously given the matter some thought."

"Would you rather do something else?"

"I can't think of a single thing."

"Right."

He went at a clipped march down the pathway to open the car door for me. I felt as if I were setting off for Westminster Abbey. Courtesies of this kind did not always have that effect, but Vernon's deference made me feel like a fetish object.

Once I was formally in his possession he relaxed a little. He had probably been afraid I would change my mind. We talked of dicky carburetters, his sister's Lagonda, his sister's husband's job with the Atomic Energy Board, touched on quarks and were just getting round to black and white holes when we arrived at the pub. I thought about the conversation while he was ordering the Amontillado, wondering what on earth Jane Austen ever found to talk about.

There was an awkward pause when he came back to the table. Then he said, "Why did you phone me, Carol?"

"Umm? Why not?"

"It's not typical. You've always squirmed when I talked to you and you once told me you didn't like me very much. What's going on? I don't want to be a charity case. I'd rather go without."

"Yes, so would I. Don't get paranoid. I just felt like going out. My friends are away and I don't know many men round here. What's funny about that?"

"I see. So you'll ditch me as soon as you meet someone else."

"Ditch you? Look, we've only been together half an hour, we're not joined at the hip yet."

"Sorry. Sorry. Of course, you're perfectly free. I was just ... very surprised." The sherry quivered under his unhappy gaze. He started to say something, then changed his mind and sat with bowed head.

The good effects of my chat with Brother William started to ebb away before Vernon's nerves. Why did people insist on being three-dimensional all the time? Why couldn't Vernon have left at home the bits of him I could not deal with? My fault, of course, for summoning him to play Dandini when he was cut out for Mr Squeers. Then he said, "I must tell you, Carol, I'm very vulnerable where you're concerned. I haven't often felt like this about a woman – well, never, actually. I suppose I don't know how to behave."

"Yes, I see." Damned if I was going to jump in with re-assurances about his performance so far. My blood ran a little chill, and not just from fatigue. Perhaps I had better be careful before trifling with a man dedicated to the eradication of the sloppy and decadent. "Look, if you're going to lay down conditions already we'd better call the whole thing off. It's ridiculous to expect me to commit myself so soon."

"Is it? Who are you saving yourself for? Some chinless scion of British Industry who'll give you a detached house in Bramhall and holidays in Marrakesh?"

"Well, yes, that would be nice. Honestly, if you think I'm so superficial I don't see why you bother."

"Sorry. Sorry."

"Anyway, why should my choices be limited to you or an upper-class twit?"

"Yes, yes. Sorry." There was a pause. I glanced edgily around at the other drinkers, numbers of whom looked like chinless scions of British Industry. "Look," he said, "I just want you to know that you're the only person I'll ever want to marry, and you always will be. I suppose everyone says that –"

"Yes, they do."

"– but you must admit I'm not a type to muck about."

"True."

"It's corny, but clichés often are."

"I expect that's why they're so popular."

"It's such a new sensation for me. I keep thinking about you – I'm always afraid it will show."

So was I by this time. Unnoticed by Vernon, conversation in

the Hare and Hounds was tailing off as his confessions began to flow. "Do lower your voice, Vernon."

"What?" The horse brasses jiggled. "Oh. Sorry. Anyway, as I was saying, I've got you on my mind all the time. I can't help it – I keep thinking I'm seeing you everywhere. It's an obsession, I suppose. Do you understand at all what I'm talking about?"

"Every word. Believe me, I understand blow for blow. Poor Vernon. Life is a bitch, that's all."

"You mean . . . can I hope? Without committing yourself, could you possibly promise to –"

"No, no, don't get the wrong idea. The bit I understand best is the unrequitedness. That's all I meant. I can't encourage you, Vernon."

"Oh. I wouldn't expect you to love me, you know."

"Wouldn't you? I don't believe it. You'd never stop hoping. I'd hate to have such power over someone. It would ruin my character."

"I doubt it. I'm sure we feel the same way about a lot of things, Carol."

"For instance?"

"Morality. I don't mean sexual morality –"

"That's a relief."

"– but everything else. How best to live. We're conscientious, hard-working. We understand about lesser and greater goods. That's much more important than sexual attraction."

"But Vernon, I am quite sexually attracted to you. It's everything else that's a problem as far as I'm concerned."

"Really? But sex isn't important. A shared outlook is much more important."

"It still seems like a pretty thin reason for getting married."

"You'd be ashamed to marry me, wouldn't you? You'd be ashamed to admit it to the others, even if you really wanted to."

"Hard to say, as I don't really want to."

He was silent for a moment, swilling the sherry round into interlocking crescents of golden sweetness. "Being in love is no guarantee of anything. Look at the divorce rate. They all thought they were in love to start with, I dare say."

"I bet they didn't. I bet the ones who are in love to start with stay together. People still get married for lots of different reasons."

"Well then."

"I wasn't talking about myself."

"Carol, do think seriously about this. I can't bear to imagine you becoming an embittered old maid, waiting for the romance that never came."

"Jesus – I mean, Vernon, I am not an embittered old maid yet. Well, not embittered, anyhow. Ask me again in thirty years and I might have changed my mind, but in the meantime I'm looking round and thinking how many men there are in the world. There must be at least thirty in this pub. I could never promise to be faithful to you. Monogamy is for children."

"What use would they have for it? But still, if that's the way you feel, you could have your freedom. Do exactly as you like."

"What kind of marriage do you call that? You wouldn't get anything out of it at all."

"I don't want to get anything out of it. You don't understand the value of self-sacrifice as a Catholic does. I want you because you're good. I feel that very strongly deep down."

"Vernon, old fruit, that is not what you feel deep down. That is something quite different that you feel deep down."

"There you go again, seeing sex at the bottom of everything. It isn't the case with me."

"Oh no? Then why don't you join the Order? Surround yourself with good men?"

"Because – no you'll laugh at me of course – I had hoped to have some small influence in the outside world. It would be too easy for me to take vows. It would be a pleasure, in fact, like moving into a hotel for the rest of my life. That isn't the best way."

"Well, I think you should try and overcome your scruples. Can we go home now?"

"What? You don't want to go out?"

"Do you mind? I feel a bit battered, what with one thing and another. I thought we were just going to have a chatty evening. But it seems hypocritical to go through all that formal dating rubbish now."

He put his large hand on my wrist and squeezed it, so that I was forced to let go of the glass. "I'm sorry. I'll take you home if you want. It was selfish of me to go on like that. I should have given you more time to get used to the idea."

"I'm glad you didn't."

So instead of dining at the Bells of Poever, Vernon drove me home, and I suggested that we have something to eat there. We were both prosaically hungry after so much intensity. There was not much in the house, but we ended up eating braised sausages and apples, mashed potatoes, tinned peas and banana pudding. Heart-warming, nostalgic family food, its qualities went straight into the bloodstream.

Mr Dacre relaxed and with minimal prompting reminisced by the hour together about his boyhood in Bolton. He and his sister had been brought up by their grandparents. Grandfather had started out in a Jesuit seminary and ended up selling shirts at the local market. Vernon did not know why he had left the seminary. I asked if it was because he had put Grandma in the pudding club, and was accused of being hopelessly romantic. His heart had remained in the seminary. From what Vernon described, his grandfather had tried to run the household on the lines of a religious institution as far as possible, with him as the Father Superior and Grandma and the children as everyone else. He romanticized hardship to the point where he was miserable away from it. I asked if Vernon had thought him cruel. "No. He was impartial, like God. Or so it seemed to us." His mother had married at sixteen. Rumour had spread through the distaff side of the family, and ultimately to Vernon through his sister, Heather, that she only found out about the sexual act on her wedding night. She survived the shock for three years, when she and her husband were killed in a railway disaster. Were they happy? Vernon didn't know. Grandfather had not allowed contact with the father's family because they were Presbyterians. Grandfather had a great respect for learning, which he demonstrated by learning pages of the dictionary by heart.

After dinner we sat on either side of the gas fire in the sitting-room. What with being moved by his reminiscences, touched by his devotion, and woozy on Bull's Blood, the natural chemistry of physical closeness set its mischievous workings in train. I continued to talk in a rational manner, but that sub-strata of the conscious, made so active in use by Shackleton, began to suggest ways in which I might get Vernon into bed. He had taken off his jacket and, at my suggestion, his tie. There is something naked and exposed about a man in a shirt and tie together, like the remains of an artichoke. But I was foxed as to how to cross the gulf that separated our two chairs. Only two yards, but it might as well have been the Ganges in flood. Having got him to take off his tie, I could not even feign interest in its motif. My preoccupation with the problem resulted in long pauses in the conversation.

Mr Dacre was explaining the origins of gazumping, as there had been a rash of it in the neighbourhood. Every deviation in human behaviour had a place in his parabola of cause and effect: he could make a clear cut through all the complexities of life to establish links between, in this case, the gazumper and his lack of discipline in childhood, although he tended to trace all the world's ills to that or television.

"Now I'll bet you any money you like that people who do that had too much pocket," he said. "It always leads to a feeling in later life that easy money is a birthright and a child who has too much pocket money will find it very easy to make friends – he'll not have to stand or fall on his own qualities and that's a bad outlook for adult life, too – he'll be ill-equipped to make friendships on any other basis, and that in turn leads to a lack of empathy with people generally, and a lack of conscience in matters like this."

"So kids with no pocket money are the only ones capable of true friendship? What rubbish. There's more to a person's upbringing than ten pence more or less on the pocket money."

"I only used that as an example of how seemingly harmless indulgences can ruin a child's character. People seem to think that a child will grow up normal, healthy and rational automatically, provided nothing too drastic goes wrong. That's not true. They have to be actively educated, in every respect. You wouldn't suddenly start breeding dairy cows without thoroughly investigating the optimum conditions for their well-being, would you?"

"Not in peacetime, no."

"Well, there you are then."

He sat back, slapping his knees, and we sat in silence for a few moments, thinking about his example.

I suggested coffee. We had to get out of those damn chairs somehow. He followed me into the kitchen and stood about under my feet. It was a small kitchen, with a wobbly Formica-topped table in the middle, ideal for trapping a large, clumsy animal, one would have thought. For my lust for Mr Dacre had now reached a point of no return. I tried to manoeuvre him into a corner – there was always something to be got out of the cupboards, filter papers, biscuits, sugar lumps – all conveniently situated in different parts of the kitchen. But my approach was a signal for Mr Dacre to step dexterously out of my path. He wanted only to hover, like an angel appointed to ensure that I did not trip on a coffee bean. I began to think I would have to let him go without having laid a finger on him.

Under the pretext of being too fascinated by his conversation, I filled both coffee cups with sugar lumps. Then, somewhere between the fridge and the table, I jumped at the sudden screech of a tomcat fight outside the back door. The milk jug crashed to the floor. Mr Dacre leapt for joy. We started to clear the mess up together. Within seconds his arm was around my waist and he was kissing me, though that is hardly the word. It was like being sucked into a turbo-jet: I thought half my face would be missing when I came up for air. We were still squatting in the spilt milk and bits of jug and my legs were getting numb, so I moved away from the mess and lay down on the floor.

"Put the light out," I said. "We don't want to scandalize the midges."

"Are you sure? We shouldn't, you know." He was flushed and dishevelled.

"Put the light out." My tone was peremptory. The fact was I had already begun to have second thoughts. A woman's sensual responses are quite fragile, and their internal balance can be easily and fatally disturbed. While the urge is self-generated it runs along nicely of its own accord, but can go quickly into reverse at the untimely application of pain or brute force. Mr Dacre had been going at me as though I were a thug resisting arrest. My hair had been pulled, my funny-bone banged and my knee squeezed until the patella was almost dislodged from its socket. In the space of five minutes my enthusiasm had plummeted, but Mr Dacre's had reached a peak. I wanted him to get on with it before I lost patience altogether. I knew there was no forgiveness for leaving a man standing in such condition, especially when it was all of my own doing. Speed was essential: with my now more objective eyes Mr Dacre's ridiculous earnestness, accentuated by his inept passion, struck me as of old.

He put the light out and threw himself on top of me in earnest. He had an *idée fixe* that ramming his knee into my groin was a *sine qua non*, and the rest of his technique consisted of biting any part of my face, ears, neck, shoulders and nose that proved receptive to his snapping jaws, all the while pinioning me to the floor by my hair.

147

"Take it easy," I muttered when I could wrench my mouth free for a moment, "we've got all night."

"You're hating it, aren't you?"

"No, I'm not."

"Yes, you are."

"Please, Vernon, don't ask such silly questions. Just get on with it."

"You're angry."

"No, I'm not. But my arm's got pins and needles – could I have it back a minute?"

"Sorry. God, I'm so clumsy. How you must despise me."

"Vernon, please, we can discuss it afterwards."

"You want me to put it in now?"

"For Christ's sake." I sat up and sank my head on my hand. "When you're ready. Which will be quite a while if you don't take your trousers off."

"Must you be so blunt? You're obviously more used to this sort of thing than I am."

"I am not. But I'll get pneumonia if I have to lie on these tiles all night."

"This isn't how I imagined it would be at all."

"Well, perhaps it will make you change your mind about me, which will be a good thing."

"No! Never!" He flung himself back into the fight, kneading and pummelling in what he thought were the right places. Eventually he got his trousers off. I felt assaulted and battered. Surely rape itself could not leave so many bruises. However, another few minutes and it would all be over. I could not avoid the suspicion that Mr Dacre was inexperienced, and a short, sudden climax was therefore to be expected.

It wouldn't go in. I was trying to simulate rapture – with difficulty. Mr Dacre was beginning to panic. His aim got more wildly optimistic. In between heart-felt moans which were meant, nevertheless, to be encouraging, I murmured discreet directions. "More to the left. No, not that far. Up a bit." It was like guiding somebody into a parking space.

After five minutes or so of this, I sensed that all directions would be in vain. He had collapsed.

Without further ado I rolled Mr Dacre off me, got up and put my clothes on.

Mr Dacre remained lying face-down on the floor. I stood looking at him, trying to be angry in the hope of diverting imminent tears.

"Now listen," I said, "don't apologize. It was my fault, the whole thing."

He slowly raised his torso from the floor, his head hanging. "Well," he said, "you had to know some time."

"Know what?"

"I've never done it before."

"Oh. Oh. Really? I'd never have guessed."

"That's right. Make fun of me. I asked for it."

"No, really, it wasn't obvious – not that – I mean – well, it doesn't matter. People have off days, anyway. You mustn't get a thing about it."

He sat up and hugged his knees, his head bowed. I thought he too wanted to cry. I tried to think of some positive aspect that could be isolated from the total experience, given a bit of a polish and used as a pointer to better things. In vain. Hope was the only answer. I should have considered that he might be a virgin, except that it was inconceivable that a layman of thirty-four or –five would be these days. It obviously had everything to do with his moral scruples and nothing to do with his virility. I could have respected another man for that – Brother William, for example – but Mr Dacre's morality seemed to be a thing of duress, not free will. I still felt sorry for him in his present woebegone condition, but could not offer any consolation without sounding priggish or patronizing. The kindest thing would be to pass the thing off as lightly as possible and forget it.

As Mr Dacre put his clothes back on I reflected that only a frustrated virgin could conceive such a pure white passion as he had done for me. Sex can be a grubby business, very little idealism about the love object survives. "Once a man's got what he wants ..." as Muriel used to put it in her folksy way, stirring Bird's custard with feeling and gesturing with her bejewelled hand. That was one good reason for sleeping with Shackleton: it would lance, as it were, the boil of my obsession.

Mr Dacre had taken a terrible tumble. He sat at the kitchen table with his head in his hands.

"It's a judgment," he said finally. "Unlawful copulation. It was bound to fail."

"Thank you. That certainly puts me in an attractive light. Don't be juvenile, Vernon. Do you think God was sitting up there just waiting to pull the switch on you – like a kid with Meccano? Come on, you're making God out to be less than human, not more."

"Please don't talk that way, Carol. It's blasphemous."

"Rubbish. I'm not a Catholic. Thank goodness. Do you intend to abstain for the rest of your life? Have no *vie des sens* at all? God made you for that too, you know."

"Yes, but only in lawful marriage."

"Then for heaven's sake fall in love with someone more suitable."

He shook his head. "What does it matter? The body isn't important. Everything about us that is essentially human is non-physical."

"So? What's so great about being human, anyway?"

"Humanitarianism. Intellect. No animal says, 'I am an animal.'"

"How do you know they don't? How do you know that every animal doesn't put itself at the head of the natural order?"

Vernon just shook his head again, as at the burbling of a child. "I must live in my own way, Carol. It's too late now for me to become a free-thinking, free-loving, free spirit, or whatever it is you're hinting at. I just can't do it – as you have seen."

"You give up too easily. Your own way is an easy way for you. You'd rather go your whole life without sex than put an ounce of faith in God's forgiveness."

"You may be right but, as I said, it's too late to change. Can you really see me growing my hair and shaking my fist at the heavens?"

"There's no need to do anything so drastic, though you could go easy on the Vitalis. Just loosen up a bit. I'm not suggesting you chuck in your job and go to Tahiti. And ... and about the sex thing –"

"Please –"

"All I want to say is, don't take any notice of tonight. It was me, I was in a funny mood. Once you get the hang of it it will be plain sailing, honestly – like swimming, or riding a bike."

Mr Dacre laughed, at my earnestness I think. But I did not want him to leave with the idea that there was anything wrong with him that a little more practice and a little less banana pudding could not put right. There was, in my opinion, but there was nothing to be gained by saying so. It was too late for him to change; he would continue working off his energy in pursuit of his scorched-classroom policy.

He stayed for another half hour or so. We said goodbye without risking any more physical contact. I watched him down the path, crunching snails as he went. My spirits sagged. I closed the door and leant my head against it, oppressed by the old familiar *lacrimae rerums*. But at least I had not thought of Shackleton for four hours on the trot. My attention had remained diverted at least for that time.

But the very thought opened the mind's door to Shackleton. His image slithered in, engulfing remnants of neutral thought, like an amoeba absorbing its food. How different it would be with him. Even if he were not a practised roué, it was inconceivable that he would be anything but sensuously co-ordinated, unhurried, confident, detached. Any little awkwardness would be surmounted with grace and humour. Oh, oh, oh, how I burned! It was so bad I had to laugh. Of course it had been ridiculous to try and substitute Mr Dacre. I was possessed of a devil, it was useless to run away from it. So, what to do? To Mr Dacre I had espoused the cause of sensual indulgence as one of the main pleasures, if not purposes, of life. Did I have the courage of my convictions? I decided to find out. Whether I indulged or fought the obsession, the likelihood of my nobbling Shackleton was about the same. So why not stop fighting it? Psychologically it would be much healthier. I did not want to get drummed off the staff for corrupting the innocent, but if there were a legal way to nobble him I would try and arrange it. There was nothing so unnatural in the idea – what was five years here or there? It was the school uniform that was the real barrier.

In bed that night, I lay awake for some hours ruminating on ways to get it off.

Sammy brought Anne home on the Saturday morning, before term was due to start on the Monday. She had caught a terrible cold and Sammy all but carried her into the sitting-room. His expression was grim.

"She's not to come to work on Monday," he said, pointing a finger at me, his granite jaws clenched, eyes glittering. I could not help thinking it a shame that Sammy had such a *vox populi*; a B.B.C. accent would have transformed him into a thing of real beauty. "I'm putting the responsibility on you."

"Well, thanks. You drag her out to the wettest place in Europe for a camping holiday and then expect me to deal with the consequences. Am I supposed to chain her to the bed or what?"

"Do what you like, but if I see her at school on Monday, you'll answer for it."

"I've only godda code, Sammy," snuffled Anne, looking at him from over her handkerchief, which hadn't left her nose since she came in.

"I know, but there's Siberian flu about and I don't want you catching it. You're not strong."

"Don't you think you're rather overdoing the male protector bit, Sammy?" I asked. "How do you think Anne coped with the common cold before you came along?"

"I'm not interested."

"You're just feeling guilty because if she hadn't gone she wouldn't have got ill."

"Maybe. So what?"

"So bugger off and let her get to bed."

Sammy looked at me as if only deciding which of my eyes to slug.

"I'll go, now," he said at last. "I'll just bring her things in." He briefly took Anne's hand and squeezed it.

After seeing him off the premises I went back to Anne, who had leant back in the chair but otherwise not moved. She still wore her becoming bright yellow rubber coat and matching boots. One had to admire Anne's capacity for producing outfits to suit the occasion.

"Want to go to bed?" She shook her head and stared at the mantelpiece. "How did it happen? Did Sammy take you skinny-dipping in Grasmere?"

"Doe."

A faint blush suffused the pale skin above the handkerchief. Her little nails were incongruously dirty, the varnish chipped and a long scratch crossed the back of her hand and disappeared up the yellow rubber sleeve. Probably he had taken her for an amorous ramble through the undergrowth and stifled her protests under a blackberry bush. It was hard to say where my sympathy lay. Anne was so pretty and passive, a real pushover, I could see how for a man like Sammy it would be like picking an apple off a tree. But she was our apple. To understand is not always to forgive. "Well, did you enjoy yourself before you got ill?"

"Yes, dank you. Could I possibly have some tea, Cardo?"

"Of course. How thoughtless of me. Something to eat too?"

"Oh doe." She spoke with feeling, but hardly daring to move her head, which looked painful even from the outside. "I'm sorry to be a bovver, Cardo."

"Nonsense. To each according to his need, and whatnot."

It was, in fact, a pleasure to nurse Anne. She was so fragile and grateful. A little frustrating that her condition, which seemed to have affected the brain as well as the nasal passages, precluded my pumping her for snippets about Shackleton. It was obviously painful for her to think, never mind talk, and for the whole of Saturday and Sunday she lay dozing and snuffling on the sofa, covered with blankets and copies of *Family Circle*, looking romantically consumptive.

Damaris came back on Sunday afternoon. She arrived by taxi. She flung her briefcase to the ground and pulled me into her arms in a single movement. I got a close-up of her new cape, embroidered overall in red wool and her newly-washed, un-combed hair.

"You're cheerful," I said. "Did you finish the *chef d'oeuvre*?"

"Fuck the *chef d'oeuvre*," said Damaris. "It's rubbish. I've decided there isn't enough Celtic gloom in my blood for that sort of thing. I'm going to start another one – much more realistic, about the cotton mills."

"A-ha. More spinning choruses?"

"Maybe. One could use the actual sounds of the machines, don't you see?"

"Yes. Chorus of spinning jennies and French horn. I can see that. And the wailing weavers. Yes, it has possibilities, really."

"I thought I'd take one of the Luddites as the hero. It's got to be dramatic and direct and yet – universal. Man against Progress – know what I mean?"

"I think so. It also sounds a teeny bit familiar. Are you sure nobody's done it already?"

"Who cares? Mine will be better."

"Good, good. You've obviously given it some thought."

"Yes. It's going to be like a fable – Everyman, or Noah – with lots of action. Something that a child could understand, but only an informed adult appreciate."

"Isn't it going to be rather expensive to stage if they have to smash up a couple of carding engines every night?"

"That can be done with back projection. I've no objection to using modern techniques."

"Perhaps you could dispense with the orchestra altogether. Just score the whole thing for oiled cogs. That would be cheap."

"Someone would still have to play them."

"True. Anne's got a stinking cold."

"Oh really? Where is she?"

This conversation had been conducted in the hall. It cheered me. Damaris was herself again, quirky, direct as a bacon slicer, hopelessly out of touch with reality. Perhaps I was being unfair; perhaps her opera would get written and would be a success. But that was really unimportant. She knew herself in the commitment to writing it. After all, Damaris would never make it as a wife and mother with a part-time job, why should she not live in the make-believe world of creative activity?

Anne, too, cheered up as soon as Damaris entered the room. For the rest of the day she entertained us with a lively, self-mocking account of her abortive trip to Finland. She had actually spent most of the time with an old college friend in Edinburgh who had agreed to write the lyrics. This "friend" had actually got one foot into show business – he was musical director with a small theatrical company. This news cheered me further. He could presumably give Damaris practical advice and temper her fantasies a bit. I was impressed by her flush of self-confidence. It was infectious. I felt that in the coming term all things would go according to plan.

The summer term is always strung out on a nerve. The tantalizing promise of summery sensual indulgence, apricating, swimming in clear waters, lying in sweet grass; a new, Sunday-supplement you just around the corner. But while the term lasts one must live with the pressures of study and examinations, suppressing the instinct to go native, perhaps indulging guiltily at the weekend and the guilt increasing the panic and tension.

The school was zinging with tension from the first day. So many Waterloos to be faced before it was over, phases to be brought to a close, syllabuses to be finished. And then the form outings and the sports events and the visits from educational and ecclesiastical potentates. The specialness of the summer term filtered right down through the school. All forms had exams and some arrangements for fêting the season.

Now that I too had my own plans to bring to fruition I shared positively in the atmosphere of nervous anticipation.

But before I could get to work on Shackleton there were two other problems to be surmounted, Mr Dacre and Grass. I dreaded encountering either of them, and yet it was inevitable that I would do so on the first day. I had decided not to tell Damaris or Anne about the fiasco with Mr Dacre; it reflected badly on both of us, but I must admit I was more concerned about myself. There are times when confession is good for the soul, and others where the offence can only be mitigated by silence.

Mr Dacre was in the staffroom when I arrived. He glanced at me nervously, but did not interrupt his loud defence of Conservative agricultural policy to the Head of Biology, which I suspected that he had staged to cover my arrival. Seeing him in the flesh, upright, fully clothed and in possession of all his faculties, reassured me that his desire to treat the incident as though it had never been was as great as mine. I felt grateful, my jaws stopped jabbering together, and I hovered near Mr Dacre until a suitable opportunity arose to say a pleasant word to him. When it did, we chatted stiffly about nothing, I rather overdoing the gracious enquirer, he sticking to his yo-ho-ho-and-the-Devil-take-the-hindmost nonchalance. But I was, nonetheless, reassured.

3B and Grass would be next. This time I was really determined to take no nonsense from them. However, I looked forward to facing them as I would to a chat with a Mafioso whose grannie had fallen under the wheels of my car. I tried to divert my nerves into sparkling chatter with other members of staff. Standing by the window with Terry Yeats – tanned from his sojourn in Corsica – my attention was caught by the sight of Shackleton getting out from behind the wheel of a Morris Traveller.

"Good God," I cried, "that's the limit. They'll be demanding drive-in lessons next."

"What?" Terry followed my eye. "Oh no!" He giggled, delighted. "He's on wheels. Well, it'll be frying every night from now on I daresay."

"Really, Terry! Shackleton's not a practised roué already, is he? Can precocity be so all-embracing?"

"No, worse luck. Or if he is, he's discreet. I wouldn't put that past him. No, if he had fleshly lusts of any sort there'd be more hope for me."

"You think he's pretty bloodless, then? That would be tragic. All the unrequited love due to be heaped on his shoulders."

"I wouldn't say bloodless, but he is a cold fish. He knows

155

people get into a stew over him, and he pretends not to notice, but he doesn't pretend hard enough not to take advantage of it. He's rather calculating in that way. One tends to placate him, like a god."

Terry's expression was rueful as he looked at the now abandoned Morris Traveller that had conveyed Shackleton to school. I would have liked to know in what way Terry had come by his information, but he would never have told me so I did not ask.

"I suppose one shouldn't expect his emotions to be as well developed as his brain."

"No, one shouldn't," said Terry.

Seeing Shackleton, lovely as ever in his freshly dry-cleaned blazer with the striped braid trim, lifted my spirits. The less developed his emotions, the better for both of us. Let it be a purely aesthetic exercise.

I went to 3B after morning break in still buoyant mood. Grass was sitting at his desk, gouging it with a compass.

"We're going to do *Julius Caesar* this term," I said, "and nothing but *Julius Caesar*, and if we don't finish it you can come in during the holidays until we do, is that clear?" A new approach to structuring the lessons was long overdue. I was tired of messing about with vapid texts on taxidermy and the common cold, snippets from newspapers illustrating "style", trying to stimulate the flow of eloquence and imagination with tales from the B.B.C. or photos from Sunday supplements, finishing off the lesson with a poem "if time allows". Perhaps Mr Dacre had influenced me, but I felt it was time to eradicate the woolly and the optimistic, abandon modern thinking on the subject and follow my instincts, which were to do one thing at a time and do it thoroughly. Order was lacking in the lives and minds of 3B. It would not in future be lacking in the English lessons as well.

3B moaned and wriggled. "Is that Shakespeare, Miss?" asked Riccio suspiciously. "Shakespeare's dead boring. Me bruvva said."

"It's much more likely that your brother is dead boring, Riccio. Shakespeare was a man, a very human one, and if you can rid your minds of infantile prejudices you will come to appreciate that he is a marvellous entertainer."

"Yeah, and that's not all," said Grass at large, "Shakespeare was a horny little runt, wasn't he, Miss? They cut out all the best bits in school editions, though, don't they, Miss? Like in the bibles we was given by the Edification Committee."

3B laughed dirtily.

"Sod'em," shouted an unidentified wit at the back of the class. My gorge was rising, but I was now practised at remaining outwardly calm.

"I should have thought you had enough dross in your daily lives without having to bring it into the classroom as well. Of course Shakespeare was no angel. That's one of the reasons why he could write so well about human frailty. But there must come a time when you stop thinking that the only interesting things in life are in the pigswill. It's childish."

"Not for the pigs, Miss," said Grass.

"Of course you can make your choice, Grass. But if you intend to take your place in human society I suggest you revise some of your attitudes."

"How will reading *Julius Caesar* help me do that, Miss?"

"Well, not reading *Julius Caesar* certainly won't. To adapt a well-known cliché, reading improves the mind if you have a mind to improve. The choice is yours."

"But that's only your opinion, Miss," piped up the Chihuahua.

"I beg your pardon?"

"He's right, Miss," said Dapper. "Why do we always have to take the teacher's word for it? Everyone knows Shakespeare is boring. Why can't we read Mary Stewart, Miss? She writes real good stuff. Nothing smutty, either, Miss."

"You can read Mary Stewart whenever you please. The chances of your reading Shakespeare in your spare time are virtually nil." I was surprised and a little shaken to have Dapper and the Chihuahua taking sides with Grass against me. I could usually depend on their neutrality at least. The allotted thirty-five minutes and my mood of iron resolution began to ebb away.

"But that just goes to show that Shakespeare's boring, Miss, if we'd never read it voluntarily," opined Baxter.

"Yeah," said Cod, "why can't we read *Red Shift*, Miss? I've got a friend at Eccles Grammar reading *Red Shift*."

"Then I suggest you transfer to Eccles Grammar. Any other questions? You can always complain about the syllabus through the usual channels, but at least until the end of this term you will have to put up with my choice of text."

There was a further swell of groans.

"It's all right, lads," said Grass, "it won't be so bad. Like I said, Shakespeare was a horny little runt. All his poems are about lust, aren't they, Miss?"

"That's enough, Grass."

"I know all about it, 'cos me Dad said. And not only that, but he was kinky with it, me Dad said. Into whips and things, wasn't he, Miss?"

"I will be if you don't keep your mouth shut, Grass."

"Ooooooooooh, Miss!" I saw my mistake at once. The joyful reaction of the class erupted in dirty laughter and catcalls, anticipating the scene should I go through with my threat.

"Will you do me after?" shrieked Gottfried.

"And me! And me!" came from various parts of the room.

I was speechless with rage, at Grass, certainly, but also at the speed and totality with which 3B had dismantled my intention to be decisive and inflexible. I stood glowering at them ineffectually, one hand clasped on the desk in an attitude that I hoped would be vaguely reminiscent of Mr Dacre in similar circumstances.

Grass was rising to the occasion. His voice had become shriller and his colour higher as the intoxicating malleability of his audience went to his head.

"*And*," he shouted over the noise, "he was a fag like Mr Fallowfield. Me Dad said. Him and the Duke of Southampton screwed each other's balls off."

The reaction to this took the roof off. Grass was contorted with soundless laughter; most of the others were in an equivalent condition. They presented the most loathsome, Hogarthian scene I had ever witnessed, cackling and shrieking and shouting, snots and tears, spittle and chewing-gum flying freely about the place. It was a madhouse. They were not human and, what was worse, lacked even the dignity of animals. It was impossible to categorize them, they were no more than personified excretions.

After standing for some moments in hysterical silence, I said only, "The *Earl* of Southampton", and left the room.

The corridors were empty. I ran rather than walked down them, and up to the staffroom. Brother William was the only person there, lovingly making amendments to the timetable.

"Where is Mr Dacre?" I said, with some difficulty. To my horror I realized that I was no longer in complete control of my speaking apparatus: my breath seemed to be missing when I wanted it and it was difficult to control my mouth. I tried to breathe deeply, to get some semblance of order into my thorax.

"Mr Dacre? Oh – umm, let me see. Ah yes. Upper Sixth B, in their room. Anything wrong, Miss Slade?"

"N – o, thank you, Brother." I ran out of the other side of the staffroom towards the sixth form ghetto. I did not even knock before entering. Mr Dacre was drawing a diagram on the board. A few desultory sixth formers were taking notes.

Mr Dacre looked up and blushed. "Miss Slade! You wanted to see me?"

"Yes, please." I went outside and waited for him.

When he came he said, "What's wrong? 3B?" I nodded. "Grass?" I nodded again.

"That boy – he's ... unspeakable ... he's – just – well ... as you see – un – speakable."

We walked quickly back towards the staffroom, I skipping a step here and there to keep up with him. Just outside the book store Mr Dacre stopped me.

"It's better if you stay here," he said. "Have a cigarette and try to calm down."

"Okay. Vernon, I don't want to go back to that class anymore today. I can't. I'd break down."

"Don't worry. It's over half-way through the period. They can sit in silence until the bell goes."

"Thanks. Thanks a lot." I put my hand tentatively on his tweedy sleeve. He looked at it without curiosity. I was still just sufficiently in command of myself to notice that he was quite calm. It was I who was choked with murderous intent.

For a moment I stayed, motionless, in the store room, preparing myself to meet Brother William. When I went in he turned round and smiled.

"Trouble in the ranks? 3B, I suppose?"

"Yes."

"They're killers, that form, I'm afraid. That's why we gave them to Mr Dacre, quite frankly. He's the only teacher who can control them. Shocking admission, isn't it?"

"They didn't kill Mr Fallowfield, did they?"

"Good Lord, no. I don't think so. That was an accident. I meant it figuratively."

"Nonetheless, I think you may have hit upon something there, Brother."

I sat down in a dark corner and closed my eyes, trying to control the thumping of my heart, which seemed to be flinging itself, kamikaze-like from one side of my rib cage to the other. The thought that Grass would at that moment be screaming his head off under the impact of Mr Dacre's squash shoe gave me a thrill of achievement. I was only sorry he would not use his track shoes with the little spikes. At last I had carried out my threat. Revenge was sweet. I hoped Grass would be hospitalized for a week. After all, it was only his vile flesh that suffered: flesh recovers. I, on the other hand, would be haunted by the humiliation of teaching 3B for the rest of my life. Would they ever know what they had done, when they were grown up, full-time housebreakers, loan sharks, purveyors of wholesale tat, respectable launderers of stolen cars? Would they ever give me a remorseful thought and caution their offspring to lay off the greenhorns? Like shit. I ground my teeth. Pity can only succeed to comprehension, and they were incapable of it. No understanding, no conscience. Albeit the parents were more at fault than they to begin with, there was no doubt that they had long since embraced their elders' moral vacuity of their own free will. And as for Grass, he could have been brought up by a consortium of fun saints and still have found his own loathsome way to self-expression. About him my conscience was clear. The only thought that nagged was that if the undoing of Grass did not work a permanent improvement in the behaviour of the class, my position would be worse than ever. Not only would I have failed to raise my standing with 3B, but I should have thrown off my habitual pacifity to no avail. This blood-lusting creature that I had become was a stranger to me. Perhaps it was the real thing, repressed for years under the yoke of lack of opportunity. But unfamiliar it certainly was. It was alarming, looked at objectively. I had not so much as trod on a slug on purpose before. Would I end up by mugging old ladies, or going for Muriel with a frozen Aylesbury duckling and calmly pickling the pieces for the church fête? If only I knew whether psychotic killers were born or made. I had to get away before I found out. Next year would see me away from this place and its provocations to violence, even if it meant joining the Wrens.

Mr Dacre came back just before the bell went for the end of the lesson. He looked as if he had been running, though of course he had not. A lick of oiled hair had been worked loose by his exertions and he smoothed it back into place.

"No need to worry about him any more," he said, without looking at me.

"Thank you. I'm sorry to have asked – it's so feeble –"

"No!" Then he did look at me. "It would have been feeble not to. If you start feeling guilty about it you'll lose your grip on them again. They don't want that. They've been asking for it. You have to understand the mentality. They're inarticulate as a group, and by themselves, of course. The trouble they were giving you wasn't gratuitous, it was a message, a message that they wanted you to take control, to show you mean business. Now you have. They'll be satisfied."

"Have I?" My participation had been vicarious, but Mr Dacre's words smoothed the remaining wrinkles in my conscience.

To my fancy the entire school must have heard about the incident. I imagined that they all looked at me differently, with circumspection. Walking to the library I encountered a group of 3B. Their faces fell, conversation ceased, they shuffled past with lowered eyes and muttered "Good afternoon, Miss"-es. I was gracious, trying to keep my satisfaction within bounds. Certainly there was not a squeak of unsolicited comment from the other classes that day.

At four o'clock I was anxious to see Damaris and tell her what had happened. It was fortunate that Anne had been sick at home: it would give me an opportunity to relate the incident in my own way, so that she would understand – which she otherwise might not. But Damaris would. Her support would be instant and wholehearted, especially in her present obstacle-squashing mood.

When she did not appear in the staffroom I went to look for her in the hall where she had had her last lesson, but it was empty, so I went on to the music rooms which were isolated in an extension block beyond the hall, with the new library above. Someone was playing the piano, a soupy piece of Ravel that I knew to be one of Damaris' favourites, but the playing was too good to be her. I put my head round the door.

Visible through a ramshackle forest of tin music stands was the rear view of Shackleton, playing from memory, with the occasional bar repeated, as if to give the impression he took practice seriously. I shut the door noisily and he stopped playing and turned round. His expression at once changed from neutral pleasantness to open hostility. He gave me a long, cold stare and resumed playing. I was panicked. It was unnerving enough to have by chance found him alone in the remoteness of the music room, but more so to realize that he had a momentous bone to pick with me. I tried to organize a few thoughts as to what I could have done to upset him, but I was too anxious for the scene to begin.

"Have you seen Miss Fotheringay, Shackleton? She was in the hall last lesson."

"No, I haven't seen Miss Fotheringay, Miss Slade. But I understand from Mr Yeats that the music staff is meeting in Brother Basil's office with a view to discussing the acquisition of challenging brass for the school orchestra."

At first I stood in the middle of the room, trying to decide how to react to this piece of childish petulance. I was angry. But Shackleton's voice was not as steady as his supposedly crushing words were meant to suggest. I stared at his bent head. The hair was getting a little too long now, a shiny frond dangled over his blazer collar like the paw of an idle cat. His peevish tone bolstered my sense of greater maturity, even though I would have given an arm and a leg to put my hands on his shoulders and press that elegant, youthful head against my stomach.

"What's the matter with you, Shackleton? What's all this outraged diva act?"

The music stopped. He sat with his hands in his lap, silent. This was absurd. Was I supposed to coax and admonish by turns until he talked, like trying to get a highly-strung filly into a horsebox? It was tempting to leave the room with matching hauteur, but I had to get to the reason for his hostility. In a way it was thrilling. Anger is a very personal thing.

"Have you nothing to say?" No, he had not. "Your silence is verging on insolence, Shackleton. I suppose you think you're too eminent to observe the usual formalities. Or are you just brushing up your artistic temperament?"

Shackleton began to tidy his music in a nervous manner. "Why don't you send me along to Mr Dacre to get beaten? Or do you only specialize in boys smaller than you are?"

So that was it. He, at least, had heard about the taming of Grass. "I don't see what difference it should make to you what measures I take to deal with that form."

"I'm sorry. I can't help having an opinion, can I? Excuse my 'insolence' in expressing it."

"And what do you suggest that I could have done instead? You have no idea how impossible they are to control."

"If you can't control them you've got no business being a teacher. I never have any trouble with them."

"You insufferable prig! There's no comparison on that subject. For one thing you've only had them for twenty minutes, and for another they idolize you because you led your team to victory in the All-England Inter-Schoolboy Paraplegic play-offs, or whatever it was. You try teaching them something they don't want to know – you'd soon have that smirk off your face. And anyway, how dare you say I've no business being a teacher. How dare you! Not Solomon in all his glory would judge me for reacting to such provocation, but you – the great white hope of The Blessed Ambrose Carstairs – you have special insights, I suppose?" Although my words sprang from genuine resentment, I could not help being proud of their coherence. It was pure luck that they came to me then, and not the day after, as was usually the case.

Shackleton got up. He picked up his music and replaced the stool neatly under the keyboard. "I'm sorry. I must have misunderstood your character. I had the impression you were against the use of violence."

"I am! I still am. Don't you see? Can't you attempt to imagine what I must have suffered to get to that point?"

"I can assure you you aren't suffering as much as Grass is. I saw him a few minutes ago. In the sickroom."

"What? What's he doing in there? Is he all right?"

"He'll live. He's just been sick, that's all."

"Oh no! No, I don't believe it!" My stomach heaved. What had I done? No boy that I knew of had not been able to carry straight on with the lesson after chastisement. "Are you sure? I mean, are you sure that's the reason?"

"Why don't you go and see for yourself? If you'll excuse me I have to go now."

"No you don't." I caught his arm as he walked past. "You bloody well stay where you are and listen to me. You're not going to sling all those pious accusations at me and then just swan off." We glared at each other, our faces not six inches apart. His was flushed, and I felt mine was too.

After a moment I let go his arm and began to pace up and down the room. "Look, I should be truly sorry if Mr Dacre has carried his zeal to excess, but if you had seen the state I was in by the time Grass had finished with me you wouldn't be so damned sanctimonious about it. I have never in my life heard such foul language, been subjected to such insults – teaching 3B is like being alive while your entrails are removed. I've never known anything like it. I come from a normal home where the worst thing I ever heard was the occasional 'bugger' and sex was never mentioned at all. Can't you imagine what it's like to be forced to listen to the combined excreta of 3B's minds day in day out, to continually have one's authority spat on – literally in some cases. One can't teach in an atmosphere like that. There comes a time when gut reactions take over, when that's all that's left to trust. Okay, I'd much rather have found some non-violent solution – but what? There's no central authority in this school, we're supposed to make our own discipline. So I sent one of them to Brother Basil once. Do you know what he made him do? Polish the chapel floor. In one of my lessons! The kid came back all smiles, boasting about what a cushy job it was. Of course, Brother Basil gave him the machine to do it with and everything." Shackleton had remained unmoved while I spoke, standing with his arms folded, gazing out of the window. "Oh come on, Shackleton, Grass was asking for it."

"I'm glad for your sake that you can justify your actions. It's a pity you weren't a Nazi at the beginning of the war."

I went up to him and slapped his face, very hard. He stepped back and put his hand to his cheek, where the outline of my fingers slowly filled with blood. I was shaking and speechless. Then, contrary to my intention in slapping him, I was the one who burst into tears. The world had come to an end. I was lost and without resources. Not content with advertising my impotence with 3B by getting Grass creamed, I had followed it up by swiping the face I most wanted to caress. I leant against the window and sobbed silently, covering my face with my hands.

I do not know how long I stood there, but when I calmed down and turned round Shackleton was sitting on the piano stool, his hands clasped between his knees, head thoughtfully bowed. I was surprised that he had not left, and said so.

He looked up, his expression of equal caution and regret. Distressed as I was, I could not help being struck by his beauty, that was the only word for it.

"Well, *I* asked for that, I suppose," he said. "I'm sorry, I shouldn't have said that, it was unfair. And anyway, it was wrong of me to get so indignant without explaining why. There are things about Grass's home life that perhaps you don't know. I do, because my mother is a sort of unofficial family counsellor for our local church and she knows the father. Grass is a special case, you see. It's just unfortunate that he should have set himself up like that. If you knew his background you probably wouldn't have acted as you did."

The blood drained from my head in a single gulp, like a sea anemone cringing at an alien touch. Shackleton's quiet confidence in my ability to make judgments in such matters only rubbed salt in the wound. "Wait a minute. What are you saying? Grass once told me some story about his father assaulting him, but Mr Dacre said it was a pack of lies."

"Mr Dacre? What does he know about it?"

"He had the father in for a talk. He said the man was a harmless bus driver and shed tears over it and whatnot."

Shackleton blinked. "And you believed him?"

"Well – yes. God help me, what a choice! Grass or Mr Dacre. Of course I believed Mr Dacre. He's basically very moral. If he'd suspected the man was a pervert he wouldn't have let him get away with it for a minute, even if it meant siding with Grass."

"No, you're right. He probably did believe it. My mother said the man's virtually schizophrenic. But the fact is he is a pervert, and he does assault Grass. They've got bus-loads of social workers on the case and there have been several attempts to get Grass into care, but he himself has resisted it. The nearest suitable place would mean he'd have to go to another school and he doesn't want to. He made out quite a moving case against having his education interrupted, apparently."

"I can't believe this. I feel sick."

"Here, sit down." Shackleton fetched a chair and placed it behind me. This had to be the final version of the truth about Grass. Shackleton would have no reason to lie. My action now struck me as crass and blundering, insensitive, immature and bestial. 3B had done their work well. They had reduced me to their own level of primitive response, only I was more to blame because I was acquainted with reason and temperance. I had re-acted to provocation with simplistic hostility, as though it had been pre-meditated by adult minds. I felt crushing shame, and buried my face in my hands and groaned.

"Listen," said Shackleton, clearly embarrassed, "don't blame yourself entirely. You're right about me being sanctimonious. I'd probably have done the same as you in the circumstances. It's always hard for new teachers."

His expression was so kindly condescending that I had to smile.

"Shackleton, people like you wouldn't have the problem in the first place. There's something about you that even troglodytes like 3B recognize as natural superiority. The rest of us have to work at it." I was in a mood for self-abasement, and besides, there was a nice ripple of masochism in abasing myself before Shackleton. He blushed and doodled, Sooty-like, on the piano stool.

"I don't think that's true at all. I don't know why you should say that."

"Don't you really? Observation. You just strike me as the sort of person into whose lap things fall. Or hadn't you noticed?"

He shrugged. "Perhaps. I suppose I am lucky to be good at most things. I wonder sometimes, how much gratitude is appropriate, if other people get something out of it too. I mean, how much one should accept from people."

"Depends what it is. Or rather, what your acceptance will cost them. All our actions have consequences, even the passive ones."

"Do you say that for any particular reason? Are you thinking of any particular consequences?"

"No. I don't think so, I'm just a bit shaken by the realities of cause and effect just now. Like believing Mr Dacre instead of using my head."

"Umm. I was surprised by that. I thought you didn't like him."

"I don't. Probably all the more reason why I thought believing him was an act of pure objectivity."

"But does he strike you as more normal a man than Grass is a boy?"

"All right, all right, don't rub it in. I've seen the error of my ways. Now, what can I do about it?'

"Sorry, I don't know."

"Apologize to Grass, I suppose. That will be humiliation enough to start with."

"He's probably still in the sickroom."

I laughed. Shackleton was eager to see my purification set in train. We both stood up.

As we had been talking, the music room had gone dark with the unnatural gloom of a threatening summer storm. Outside a strong wind tore at the trees and their leaves fluttered, the pale undersides exposed and flickering in the green light. We stood facing each other. He was clearly visible, but strangely transformed by shadow into something more substantial than normal.

"Shackleton, why have I been talking to you like this?"

"Like what?"

"As if you were almost human."

"Well – that can't be it."

We laughed. Perhaps I inadvertently put out my hand. Perhaps he did. Then we kissed. Our bodies suddenly seemed to have nothing else to do. It was liberating, kissing him, like finding out one can swim, or a baby rolling over by itself. Our mouths and tongues slid together effortlessly; it was pure sensation, no clumsy technique; it would have brought a corpse to life.

Suddenly he pushed me away.

"What was that?"

"What?"

"I think there was somebody at the door."

"Really? Did you see who it was?"

"No. Wait a minute." He went to the door, opened it and looked cautiously into the corridor.

"Well?"

"A brother. I don't know which one. Just saw the skirt whisking round the corner."

"Could he have seen us? We're not exactly in a direct angle from the door."

"No, but why would he look in if he didn't want to see if there was someone in here? Well, we'll find out tomorrow. Never mind, you said you didn't like teaching anyway."

"Don't joke. I could probably be prosecuted under the Children and Young Persons Act."

"I'm over eighteen, as of last week."

"Congratulations. Even so it would be embarrassing. It would 'jeopardize my position' or something."

"Don't worry. He probably didn't see us. If he had, he'd probably have raised the alarm."

"Perhaps it's just as well. This is no place for a liaison dangereuse."

"Have you any suggestions on that subject?"

He looked at me uncertainly. I sustained a series of hot and cold flushes. Now was the time for sensible caution. What would Muriel advise?

"Not at the moment. Have you? Where do you normally take your girlfriends?"

"Home, usually. The parents are out a lot, and they're very trusting."

"Hardly suitable in this case. But I'd better be going now, or you'll get yourself raped. I'll go and see Grass first. Then I must get home. Anne is ill."

"Yes, I know. Give her my regards, will you? And Miss Fotheringay, of course. Is she all right, by the way?"

"As far as I know. Why?"

"I haven't seen her around much lately."

"She's writing an opera."

"Ah! I thought she looked more artily rumpled than usual. Do you want me to come with you to see Grass?"

"No, thank you."

He opened the door for me.

"Well, goodnight, Shackleton. Sleep well."

"Goodnight." He made as if to kiss me again, but I stepped back.

"No, not here anymore. L'Eminence Brune made me nervous."

"All right. By the way, hadn't you better stop calling me Shackleton? At least in private."

"No. It's more erotic. What's the point of seducing a schoolboy if he's going to pretend to be grown-up?"

I blew him a kiss and more or less levitated down the corridor in the direction of the sickroom. My parting words, though not strictly true conveyed my general mood. The attraction had been mutual, neither of us had initiated anything, but nonetheless the feeling was strong that I had triumphed over something. Perhaps merely the conviction I had been labouring under in recent months that life was a tortuously fragmented disappointment, that wanting something was no more than a preliminary to being denied it. I was at last getting something I wanted. It was, of course, necessary to isolate this triumph: it was not a thing that could go on the curriculum vitae. But it was already so apart from the normal that it was no effort at all to keep it so. I did wonder fleetingly if it would all end in madness, but if I had had to choose between madness with Shackleton and sanity without him, he would have won. But my mood was so light that I could consider no such prospect seriously. One day, quite shortly perhaps, I would make love to Shackleton. It was enough to transform the world into a promise of pleasure and fulfilment. This sensation of breaking codes, defying conventions, made me feel curiously more secure about The Future, as if I had turned aside from the ankle-wrecking path through a wood into the dark trees and suddenly found that they were their own protection from the fears they held.

Grass was not in the sickroom. The army blanket on the hard couch had been thrown aside, so I assumed that, barring life after death, Grass was ambulatory and had gone home. The frustration of not being able to follow the scene with Shackleton by one in which Grass forgave me with an off-hand "That's all right, Miss" was great. It became necessary to find Grass and make my excuses. I did not like to think of him walking around thinking evil of me: it gave him too much power. It was imperative that I speak to him. I went to Brother Basil's office.

Anne's desk was bare except for two empty letter trays and a shrouded typewriter. There was no answer when I knocked on Brother Basil's door so, flushed with anti-establishmentism, I took the keys from Anne's desk, blessing the Utopian security arrangements. It took a while to find Grass's file in the cabinet. I took it out and memorized the address. The file was surprisingly thick. Panting a little, I flipped though it. There were many letters, typed ones with the crest of the local authority, scrappy ones hand-written in biro on lined paper with no punctuation, copies of school reports, I.Q. tests, medical data, an X-ray of his ankle and what appeared to be a psychiatrist's report. I began to read it, but was disturbed by the sound of footsteps in the corridor and quickly re-locked the cabinet and put the keys back in Anne's drawer.

Brother William put his head round the door. He frowned and came into the room, closing the door with pregnant precision.

"Oh, hello, Brother. I was just looking for something that Anne asked me to –"

"Never mind that, Miss Slade. I must talk to you seriously for a moment. Please sit down."

Brother William was in unusually grave mood. I knew at once that it was he who had come in to the music room and observed Shackleton and me in the act. I was sorry it was he: he had been so sympathetic.

He propped himself up against Anne's desk, feet crossed before him, hands supporting him on either side. I sat in Mrs Prudhoe's swivel chair, trying to suggest nonchalance.

Brother William began. "The role of Peeping Tom is not a dignified one, Miss Slade, I know that, but what I saw going on between you and young Shackleton just now forces me to reveal myself as such."

"I'm sorry about that, Brother. It was the first time anything had happened and I can promise you that nothing will happen again on school premises."

"Is that all you have to say? Is that supposed to make it all right? I'm astonished, Miss Slade. I have always liked you, taken you for a sensible, level-headed young woman. You're behaving now like a mindless harpie. I don't recognize you."

Brother William's vocabulary, if not his voice, conveyed emotion.

"Steady on, Brother. I know 'harpie' isn't strong language these days but I presume it was when you last used it. Quite frankly I think this is a private matter. You'd be entitled to get me drummed off the staff but not to call me names which you, at least, think offensive."

"You were anxious enough for my opinion when you were looking for consolation."

"That's true. I'm sorry. But there doesn't seem much to be said now."

"I disagree. Let me get one thing clear. The person you spoke of when you came to see me; that was young Shackleton?"

"You're rubbing in the 'young' rather, aren't you, Brother? I'm only twenty-three myself."

"Miss Slade, the factors governing your relationship with the boy are not your respective ages, but the fact that you are a teacher in this school and he is a pupil, that you know him exclusively in that capacity. That is where the offence lies. But I'm not principally concerned with your position. Your moral life is your own affair and what you do away from the school is none of my business. I'm only concerned with your behaviour as it affects Shackleton. While he is a pupil at this school it is our duty to protect him from the designs of unprincipled teachers."

I blushed and glared at Brother William. He was no more than utterly grave, there was no anger in his voice or expression, only regret and distaste. The friendliness verging on affection which I had sensed in him had gone, he had become a mouthpiece of officialdom. The implication that he viewed me now as no more than a randy non-Catholic was deeply hurtful. I had valued his good opinion: his failure to take a more broadly cosmic view of the incident seemed like a betrayal. To myself my conscience was clear, but Brother William's opprobrium still made me feel dirty and I resented it.

"Why do you imagine that it was all my doing, Brother? Shackleton is no innocent. He knows what he's doing."

"Does he? Come, come, Miss Slade, be honest. Perhaps a young boy like that might well think there was something glamorous and exciting about a little 'romance' with an attractive young teacher – an innocent kiss in a dark corner. I can understand that. But you obviously expect it to go further. And you are more experienced. I have no means of knowing if you subscribe to a moral code at all, but the fact that you have already let things go so far suggests to me that even if you do, it is one that could only be a threat to the moral life of an innocent boy."

"Innocent? You can't use that word, Brother. I'm afraid I can't accept it. No boy who had been educated in a school like this, in an age like ours, in an area like North Manchester could possibly keep his innocence intact unless he were deaf, dumb and blind. I suppose we are talking about the same thing? You suppose that Shackleton is still a virgin?"

"I have no doubt of it. He's a high-minded, responsible young man from a good, Catholic home."

"Brother, please don't joke. Do you think the image that Shackleton presents to you tells the whole story? Of course he behaves like a five-star Catholic youth as far as you're concerned – he has his university entrance report to think about. But these days, 'good Catholic homes', whatever they are, are no match for the outside world. Why I've learnt things about the sex life of Catholic boys that would make your hair curl. Half 3B have slept with their girlfriends, you know. They brag about it."

"Probably they do, because that's all it is – just boasting. Of course they think that's grand. They have to give their peers the impression that they're sexually experienced. But it isn't so. Most of them are extremely shy with young girls."

I could only stare at him. We were talking about two different sets of boys. "Be that as it may, Brother, we're talking about Shackleton. He is not shy with young girls, or with anyone else. He must have had a dozen offers at least and he admits to accepting what he's offered. You can't think that a boy as attractive as that would still be a virgin at eighteen?"

Brother William gave an exasperated little gasp and shook his head. "Dear, dear, Miss Slade, this is the only trouble about introducing a non-Catholic element into the school. You assume that young people will have sexual relations before marriage: Catholics do not. It happens, of course: we're not naïve. We know what goes on. But one cannot start acknowledging it or it would act as an inducement, don't you see? When a couple are deeply in love they sometimes get carried away – it's all to easy. But to assume that our young men jump in and out of bed with anyone who is willing – well, I think it is you who are being naïve. The permissive society may have got its grip on the area of London that you come from, Miss Slade, but up here we subscribe to more traditional modes of conduct."

"I'm sorry, Brother. We must beg to differ. I don't think you know the animal you're dealing with."

"Animal. That's the difference between our points of view, Miss Slade. Shackleton is not an animal to me. He is one of God's children. It's his immortal soul I am trying to protect. If he once commits such a grave sin others will follow. It will become a lifetime's habit. That is why I must insist that you promise me to have nothing more to do with him, or I'm afraid I will have to bring the matter to the attention of higher authorities."

"The Pope?"

Brother William said nothing. I felt the cheapness of the joke, deepening my sense of being hard–done–by.

"Well, anyway, what happened today was spontaneous, Brother. At least I can promise that I will not do anything to continue the relationship."

"That's not quite good enough, Miss Slade. Shackleton may be so infatuated with you that he acts unwisely. You must be prepared to be firm with him."

"Brother, I can only be responsible for myself. After all, Shackleton is the one who is fortified by a good Catholic home, not me. If you're still nervous about his ability to resist my wiles you had better talk to him."

"Have you no compassion, Miss Slade?"

"Compassion? What are you talking about, Brother?"

"The seduction of innocence is a terribly cruel thing."

"But he – Oh, what's the use. You're determined to think of me as a trainee Marquis de Sade. I've given my promise that I won't waylay him down a dark corridor, or anything. I don't see that you can expect more."

"Very well, I will have to settle for that. But I will be watching you, Miss Slade."

"Thank you, Brother. That should certainly keep me safe."

"Have you got what you came in here for?"

"Yes, thank you."

"Then I'll see you out."

Brother William's extraordinary image of me as a child molester drove all other thoughts momentarily out of my head. Could it really be true that the brothers thought they presided over a unique collection of six hundred and fifty virgin boys? He had accused me of cruelty: how much more cruel to bring up adolescents in a moral cocoon, beyond which the realities of modern life waited to ensnare and disillusion them. Surely, if his version were true, they must eventually come to reject their moral education whole-sale, as having no relevance to the way things were. But I was sure that his version was not true. The detailed sexual knowledge as revealed by 3B and others, could not be the result of hearsay only, although it might be liberally spiked with mere boasting. A considerable number of them had at least experimented. Besides, they *were* animals. Their sexuality was at its most dangerously imperative and unmodified by a social context. Probably even Shackleton, in his more private and refined way, had passed through this stage. But Brother William had successfully planted a seed of doubt in my mind. It was just possible that he was right about Shackleton. If it were true, then I would be culpable in leading him into a situation which he had not anticipated. I longed to discuss the matter with Damaris. Here was a test of my sincerity. If I were to live up to the standards I had set for her, I must confess and confide. In the past I had always loved such fulsome scenes, but then they had been part of the warp and woof of adolescence: now they demanded more energy and more faith.

Damaris was actually pacing up and down the lane outside the cottage when I arrived.

"There you are. Where have you been? I didn't see the car. I thought you must have gone home without me, but you hadn't."

"I know I hadn't. The car was round the back. Sorry. Were you worried?"

"Yes. I was just thinking, if you had an accident, how would they know where to find us? I bet you haven't changed your address or anything."

"People always find people. You'd get in touch with the police after twenty-four hours, I suppose."

"Oh, before."

Damaris was leaning in at the window of the car, examining me at close quarters. Her anxiety had evidently been so great that it took more than my mere arrival to assuage it. She was looking good these days: creative dishevelment, at least when accompanied by weight loss and trimming of nails, suited her. She was looking less gigantic, more supple: less Amazon, more Bloomsbury. In other ways too, she seemed to have acquired more ease, as if the creative effort of writing *Peterloo*, as the opera was tentatively called, absorbed the bizarre and theatrical elements, leaving the Damaris who faced the world more at one with it.

"I'm sorry you worried. I'll explain what happened over a cup of tea."

"There's no time for that. We've got to get supper on."

"Give us a kiss, then."

"What?" For a moment Damaris looked startled, then she laughed and lunged at me with one of her big, sloppy kisses, accompanied by chewing noises.

Anne was in bed, asleep and had been when Damaris got home. I was relieved. It would be easier to get down to soul-baring with Damaris. Instinctively I felt it right to protect Anne from knowledge of my depraved nature, at least I did after talking to Brother William.

Damaris had heard about the harrowing of Grass, and I was confident that in the course of discussing this and explaining my change of heart, I would be able to mention meeting Shackleton quite naturally.

Over supper we discussed the problem of discipline under an idealistic, non-teaching headmaster at some length.

"It's all a question of confidence," said Damaris. "Boys are like wild animals – if they smell fear they'll pounce. We've both had it with this year's classes but next year it will be better. I have no feelings left where boys are concerned. I think they'll sense that at the beginning and show some discretion."

"That's all very well, but how do you get them to notice that you've entered the room in the first place?" I sighed. "You intend to stay on, then?"

"Why not? The holidays are useful for writing and the money's useful for living. I can't think of anything else that would give me as much freedom, really. Anyway, I'll go on with it until I'm receiving commissions in every post. Besides, I like living here, don't you?"

"Yes. But suppose Mrs Lawford gets better?"

"No chance. They never do. It's only a matter of time. Then the place will probably be sold and we could buy it. Even without Anne I think we could afford it."

"Wouldn't we have to get married first?"

"If there's any trouble on that score I would rejoice to make a sex discrimination case out of it."

"We'll end up like Jarvis & Jarvis in *Bleak House*."

Time was getting on. Damaris was on her fourth post-prandial cigarette and would shortly be making moves to wash up, after which she always went to her room. I dreaded the artificially inseminated conversation.

"By the way, I saw Shackleton today. He was asking after you."

She raised one eyebrow and re-crossed her legs with vigour. "Really? Touching. Why?"

"He said he hadn't seen you around as much. I told him you were writing an opera. That seemed to satisfy him."

"I wish you hadn't."

"Why?"

"I just wish you hadn't. I don't want everyone to know."

"Sorry. I didn't think that Shackleton was everyone. I thought you'd think he was a special case."

"He is. Very. But if you don't mind I'd rather not communicate with him through third persons."

"Sorry." There was a pause. I felt admonished.

"Did he say anything else?"

I drew a deep breath and the door bell rang. Cursing, I went to answer it. It was Sammy, come to inspect Anne's condition. I put him in the kitchen with Damaris and went upstairs to wake her.

It was dark in her room but in the shaft of light from the open door I saw her roll over and squint at me.

"It's Sammy, Anne. Shall I send him up?"

"What? Oh no." She put her arms across her eyes. "I don't want to see him just now. Can you tell him I'm asleep?"

"It will be a bit hard. He can hear our voices."

"But I really don't want to see him, Carlo. Please put him off."

I was surprised and a little annoyed. It seemed perverse of her

175

to start developing powers of resistance which would mean my having to get rid of a rampant Sammy. "Is there anything wrong?"

"Doe."

But there was the unmistakable false register of tears in her voice. I groped my way over to the bed. "Are you all right?"

There was no reply, except for the sporadic release of sobs between rib-cracking heaves of breath. "Hey, what is it? What's the matter? Don't cry, Anne." I had never seen Anne cry, had rarely seen her betray any emotion stronger than contentment. It was mildly shattering. I put my arms round her and she hugged me.

"It's – just ... flu, I expect. You get – depressed – hic – with the flu."

"Yes, yes of course. Don't worry. I'll keep him out even if it means pouring boiling pitch down the stairs."

"Hic – thanks."

Sammy was all for running me through with the packet of After Eight he had brought for Anne when I told him she was too tired to receive him. He made a step towards the stairs, but I flung myself across his path and looked and threatened in deadly earnest. Sammy was a simple fellow: he retreated, sensing some dark female mystery into which it would be dangerous to probe. He declined tea and, accompanied by both Damaris and I, left quietly, with many a troubled glance at Anne's closed bedroom door. I watched him leave from the darkened sitting-room, to make sure he did not go round the back and up a drainpipe. When the tail lights had safely rounded the bend in the lane I returned to the kitchen. Damaris had already gone upstairs. Feeling like a coward, and a relieved one at that, I gave up the idea of telling her about Shackleton and me. In her current mood of self-awareness she would only caution me, but in more kindly words than Brother William had chosen, not to be a fool. But Damaris had never suffered a pure physical passion: her one night of love with Terry Yeats seemed to have cured her of whatever it was that was motivating her at that time – curiosity or hysteria. If I had thought it would cure me I would have done it myself, but in my case there was no cure, only expurgation.

The next day was 3B-free. I kept an eye open for Grass but did not see him. The distant possibility that Mr Dacre, and by implication I, could be prosecuted for Grievous Bodily Harm troubled me. Why had Grass so behaved as to turn my sympathy back into vicious rage? It was as if anger and disruption were the only level on which he felt comfortable with adults. He obviously took pleasure in manipulating their behaviour when he could: there must have been a strong element of revenge in his wanting to see adults whom he basically liked roused to punitive anger. I had not realized how desperate a child can be for attention. It was to my shame that I had fallen in to his cock-eyed scheme of human relationships.

Our lunch table was observing monastic silence. Mr Marple was due for his classroom assessment visit and twitched in lonely angst. Mr Dacre was quietly proud and protective, Brother William solemn. I wanted to show him that I was unmoved by his aspersions, but all my bright remarks futtered and died. Shackleton I had only seen at assembly, and I had to arrest my head physically from swivelling round in his direction. It was a question of watch and wait. One stolen glance and Brother William would haul me off to the Education Committee. Insofar as I could I would keep my promise about not pursuing Shackleton: I had not needed to so far anyway. I was sure he would make the next move himself.

A week went by with no more than a brief greeting in a corridor, a meaningful look and a hasty glance over the shoulder for Brother William. And then another. And another. It confounded me that the affairs of the school should leave so little room for manoeuvre to affairs of the heart, or wherever my craving for Shackleton was seated.

My time, and to some extent my attention, was claimed by composing examination papers, seeing they were typed and preparing classes for them. The anxiety that the younger boys in particular exhibited at the prospect of examinations was heart-rending, or would have been if the experience of teaching them during the year had not turned my heart to stone. The staff gloried in the dispensing and disposal of so many fates. In the case of the G.C.E. candidates, and perhaps the preceding year also, it was understandable: lives could be ruined by the result. But the solemnity with which even the first years' papers were drawn up (Draw a sketch-map of Yorkshire, showing the coalfields. Conjugate in the perfect tense, *manger*, *boire*, *s'assayer*, *être*. How does a light-switch work? Give the formula for: sodium nitrate, gold, oxygen, magnesium. Write an essay on EITHER A Football Match OR My Grandmother) was fascinating. There was no doubt, though, that there was a certain sweetness of revenge in the task. It was such a beautifully legitimate excuse for the exercise of indisputable authority. For all the pain suffered during the year, here was a chance to inflict some in return, to make the little buggers squirm and sweat while posing god-like detachment and even a little gracious sympathy. It was with difficulty that I refrained from giving 3B a bit of *Beowulf* to translate, or an essay on the Swedish economy.

But their reactions were not necessarily predictable. Since the Grass-cutting, as Damaris rather unfeelingly put it, 3B had changed drastically. It was evident from the first lesson after the incident.

When I arrived at the classroom they were sitting silently at their desks with their books in front of them. It was a shock, but not an unpleasant one, that needed some adjusting to. Grass himself was at his place, wearing no bandages or showing any other signs of severe damage. This was a relief. I determined to speak to him after the lesson. He sat bolt upright, his big, pale eyes wide and fixed on my face with his old expression of mock deference. It was tempting to respond to the exemplary behaviour of the class with exemplary joviality and general niceness, but I remembered Mr Dacre's dictum that any sign of repentance would be pounced on as weakness and would bring 3B about my ears again. It was, after all, only Grass who had suffered by my combined bad judgment and inexperience. Besides, at first I attributed the change to fear of Mr Dacre. It was only after the third or fourth lesson that I realized a more powerful group instinct was at work.

3B had sent me to Coventry. They were working to rule, with a hard-line union solidarity that proved impossible to penetrate. They answered questions in monosyllables, read when assigned to do so, all in a solemn, cold, implacable correctness that was so thoroughly carried to extremes that it would have been amusing if I had been capable of detachment. Now the door was always opened for my entry or exit, my dropped chalk rescued with meteoric speed, my books carried to the staffroom, homework given in on time with all the attendant rubric strictly followed, all in silence, without expression. Their ability to keep it up surprised me. I thought their natural restlessness would get the better of them in time, but it did not. Had I not had Shackleton to think about it would have obsessed and possibly destroyed me. As it was, I was able to match their *froideur*, and retain my composure.

It was at all events better than the state of affairs that pertained before. Slightly.

Grass was one of the best exponents of the new mode. After the first lesson I called him out into the corridor. He came promptly and stood with his hands respectfully clasped behind his back. We were surrounded by itinerant classes and the atmosphere was not conducive to intimacy, but my intentions were still powerfully good.

"You wished to speak to me, Miss?"

"Yes, Grass. I'm sorry about what happened. Your behaviour was appalling, it's true, but I would not have sent you to Mr Dacre if I had known what I know now. You see, when your father came to see Mr Dacre, he convinced him that you had been lying, and I'm afraid Mr Dacre subsequently convinced me. I'm afraid your behaviour made me want to believe it. But now I have been further informed, and I realize that I haven't helped – that it would have been better to take some other course of action. Well. That's all. I'm sorry."

I felt rather proud of the frank humility of this speech. It had not been easy; my heart was pounding. But surely Grass could not fail to appreciate the rarity of my approach, my obvious sincerity and desire to put his needs as a human being before my dignity as a teacher. He did, however. He said nothing. We looked at each other for a minute, while my tentative smile froze. Grass's expression did not change.

"May I go back to class now, Miss?"

"Yes."

Thereafter I made no more attempts to mollify Grass. He was extracting his slow revenge anyway.

As the term moved into the end of May and Shackleton and I had still inexplicably managed to avoid chance encounters, doubts set in. I was tortured by the idea that there had been no developments because he did not anticipate any, that the incident had been of no significance to him, that brief crescendo in the music room. Surely, even for him, it had been bizarre enough to linger in the memory for a month or so? Or perhaps he thought of it as just something to be laughed about among his friends, or used to furnish a post-coital chat with his molls. The existence of at least two of these I was sure of. It was this last possibility that particularly haunted me. A woman in possession of a coveted lover is a merciless creature, glorying in the heartache of her rivals. I had no wish to be an object of derision to an unformed mind. It put years on me to think of myself from their point of view.

And as time went by, the G.C.E.s drew nearer. Shackleton would have his first exam shortly, and it would then be out of the question to expect him to spare a thought for anything else.

In this respect I underestimated Shackleton.

The wretched youth was breaking all school records by taking English, French, Latin, German, Music and Art. The teachers involved were all of a twitter lest their own subject should suffer under the pressure, and snide remarks to this effect were bandied freely about the staffroom. They all anticipated taking the credit of his almost certain "A"s to themselves. It was torture to hear him discussed by others and have no excuse to join in.

On the day before his exams began I did run into him in the library. Under the pretext of discussing a particularly knotty passage in *Much Ado*, I motioned him into the glass-sided office in the corner of the library. We stood side by side, directing our words and looks to the open book on the desk.

"Well, Shackleton, your hour has come. I suppose you know that if you don't get straight 'A's there'll be mass suicide in the staffroom?"

"Don't tempt me. Do they think I'm a robot?"

"Are you really worried? You don't look it."

"I'm not. Well, a little. As much as is conversant with common sense."

"You're odious. I hope you fail the lot."

"Thank you. Anyway, why have you been avoiding me?"

"I have not been avoiding you. I thought it was the other way round."

"Oh dear. That's the way tempus fugits, isn't it? I didn't know. You could easily have been toying with my affections. I'm only eighteen, you know."

"I had to swear to Brother William that I would leave you alone. He thinks I'm a threat to your virtue."

"Dear Brother William. He didn't say anything to me. So I suppose I can bother you if I want."

"Yes, I suppose so."

"Well, then, how about a drink tonight?"

"What? Are you crazy? You've got an exam in the morning."

"But the best thing to do would be to take my mind off it."

"I daren't, Shackleton. If we were seen boozing the night before your first paper – well, it smacks of unprofessional behaviour even to me."

"When then? I can't not see you until after the exams. That's in three weeks."

"Can't you?" I said the words on a convulsive gasp and leaned on the desk for support. His nearness was producing coloured spots before the eyes and a sinking dizziness throughout the body.

"No. What about next Saturday? I don't have a paper until Tuesday."

"No, no. Not until you've finished."

"Please."

"No."

How I produced such heroic resistance I do not know, unless it be our old friend sado-masochism. Probably the forces of convention where he was concerned had lain so idle for so long that they were able to spring to life with renewed vigour when his best interest called upon them. "Anyway it would be best to wait until the end of term, to avoid complications." This was turning the knife in the wound. The longer we waited, the more likely that his interest would cool.

"The day after the end of term, then. That's a Wednesday."

"All right. Where?"

"I don't know. Not my place, I'm afraid."

"Tell you what, we could go to Haworth. I've always wanted to. Besides I'd be happier if there were a semblance of educational purpose about the liaison. Will you have the car?"

"Probably."

"Then get on the road to Todmorden. I'll meet you somewhere between there and Hebden Bridge. Just find somewhere to park and I'll pick you up. Or vice versa. Whoever gets there first. The twentieth July, about ten-thirty."

"Okay."

"But if one thinks of Leonardo's speech about the fallen Hero – it's such a beautiful piece of centre stage rhetoric – 'But mine, and mine I loved and mine I praised,/And mine that I was proud on; etc. They had to sound convinced after all, or the plot wouldn't hold water. And of course, he's also getting over their subconscious fascination with corruption. A lot of his characters suffer from sexual double-think. Well, who doesn't?"

"What are you talking about?"

"Mr Lewis."

"Oh."

Martin had come into the library and was heaving to in our direction. When he joined us I explained the problem that we had ostensibly been discussing and for a pleasant half hour we chatted about undercurrents in the Bard.

For the weeks that remained of the summer term I went about in a semi-comatose condition. The weather was hot. In the early morning the sun soaked warmly into my body, stirring the blood. The day was given over to the supervising and marking of exams, the evenings to beer in pub gardens, sometimes Damaris and I alone, sometimes with Terry, Sammy and Anne or some of the other teachers. There was a pleasant camaraderie among the staff at this time. Without realizing it, I had been subtly knitted into the scholastic mesh. I began to appreciate the sense of belonging. It was a new sensation. Previously I had only belonged to things to which I did not want to belong, like Worcester Park. If only one could have continued as a member of the commune without having to teach.

Not having to teach was like having a plaster removed: I bloomed in the sensation of regained freedom. I had not realized how completely the year had sapped my energy until the pressure was lifted and the dregs revealed. I was content to sit for hours at the desk, staring out of the window while the boys scribbled and sighed. The prospect of the rendezvous with Shackleton used up every flicker of mental activity. As to consummations and the like, I had no idea when or where or even if: the fact that he wanted to be with me was a consummation in itself. And he would officially have left school and the loving protection of Brother William.

My faculties were not so defunct, however, that I could not notice there was something wrong with Anne. Always quiet, she was now almost a ghost. Since the flu she had never recovered her small appetite; when spoken to she tended not to hear. She had lost weight and there were curious blotches under her eyes. Altogether she was beginning to look like Keats aged twenty-five. She spent a lot of time with Sammy but the affair did not seem to be bringing her much joy. Once or twice I asked her how things were going between them, but all she ever said was "All right", and lowered her eyes.

Then one day in the ladies loo I got a nasty shock. Anne was in there washing her hands. She jumped when I came in. Her eyes were red and her face mottled and damp, but that was not what alarmed me. It was the smell of sick. There at the very sink where Miss Cromwell had thrown up before. Was I still supposed to believe in Brother Basil's innocence? But of course, it was much more likely to be Sammy, and it came to me in a flash that he was the obvious candidate in Miss Cromwell's case too. All that lean muscle, chiselled profile and Paul Newman eyes, Miss Cromwell would probably as soon have thought of resisting the laws of gravity as his natural imperative. But the idea of Anne, delicate, perfectly made, benign, blameless child-woman that she was, the thought of her having to go through with an unwanted pregnancy or an abortion made my own stomach heave.

"What's the matter, Anne? You've been sick, haven't you?"

"Yes. It's nothing." She dried her hands on the roller towel and delicately wiped her mouth.

"What do you mean 'nothing'? Of course it isn't. Why won't you admit it?"

"Please don't make a fuss, Carlo. I have to go back to work, now."

"Darling Anne, I'm not trying to be nasty, but it's so obvious, suddenly, what's wrong with you. You know I only want to help. Good God, I'd be the last person in a position to criticize. You must trust me."

"Please stop it, Carlo. I must go."

"No you mustn't. We must talk. How can you shut us out at a time like this, Anne? It's very hurtful."

"Carlo, I must get back to the office. Please let me past."

Anne was getting hysterical. I could not very well detain her against her will, so reluctantly stood back and let her leave.

That evening I told Damaris my suspicions. They were not news to her.

"What a ghastly cock-up," she sighed, in low tones so that Anne, who was in the bath, would not hear. "What are we going to do?"

"What can we do if she won't admit it? We can't tie her down and get a urine sample."

"I suppose she'll have to marry Sammy."

"Oh no. He's such a troll."

"But what's the alternative? Perhaps the parents might adopt it. They're fairly phlegmatic. At least I think that's what they are. They could be permanently unconscious."

"The trouble is, I don't think she could stand an abortion psychologically. You know the trauma she had that time she put the garden fork through a worm. But I don't think she could stand to have it either. We'll have to get her to talk."

"No." Damaris held up a warning finger. "Don't force her to. Anne is a creature of instinct. The kindest thing we can do at the moment is just be around if she wants us — not start making demands."

"You're right. But it's so agonizing."

"Well it's worse for her, so there's no need to feel sorry for yourself."

We did out best, in the weeks that followed, to lard Anne with subtle assurances of our support and affection, in the hope of easing the path to confidence, but she said, literally, nothing. Mesmerized as I was by the 20th of July it was hard to give the matter the attention it deserved. I postponed worrying about it until the 21st. Exactly what the difference would then be I did not know. I presumed that the tension at least would be relieved, a bridge crossed, a corner turned, a hurdle jumped, or that I would in some wise have landed in calmer waters. Until then I was as incapable of relaxed thought as if I had been preparing for my début at La Scala.

The last week of term was celebrated with class outings, visits to the cinema, nature walks with picnic and a total breakdown of discipline, at least in my classes. I was past caring. Nominally we went over the examination papers, but there was no attempt on either side to disguise the fact that we were just filling in time.

3B's silence was finally going under. The prospect of getting rid of each other was too pleasant to be left unexpressed.

But when I walked into their classroom for the last time, I thought they had changed their minds again. To a boy they were standing to attention behind their desks. They said the prayer with fervour and sat down in silence. I had told them to choose a poem to recite to the class. Several of them seemed to have done so. Hands were eagerly raised, poems recited, laughter and applause followed.

"Now then," I said, "time's nearly up. Who's going to do the last one?" For once I had really enjoyed the lesson and experienced a flicker of reluctance to part with 3B. Heads were turned in the direction of Riccio, who stood up sheepishly.

"Me, Miss."

"All right. Come out to the front then."

There was some giggling as he shuffled up to the front of the class. I suddenly had a cold flush. There was something afoot. Had they planned a final *coup de grâce* for me? Grass's bold grin seemed to confirm it. They would know that on the last day of term they could act with impunity. I gripped my hands together under the desk and tried to adopt an expression that would adapt to any emergency.

Riccio was blushing. "This is called 'Miss', Miss."

"I see. Well go on."

He cleared his throat. The tension in the class was at a peak. Most of the boys were about to rupture with suppressed laughter. Riccio broke down and giggled a couple of times, but there were loud shouts of "Get on with it, you turd" and similar, and he eventually began thus: "'Our Miss is a tartar/She makes us work hard/With poems and pronouns/And plays by the Bard./She puts us in den./And gets our backsides thumped/And gives us extra homework/When she thinks that someone's pumped.'"

At this the tension broke and the entire class, Riccio included, became apoplectic with laughter, to the point where death by choking was only minutes away. I smiled, tensely. If it got no worse I could endure it.

"Is that it, Riccio?"

"Oh no, Miss." He gasped and wiped away the tears.

"Let's hear the rest, then."

After a few minutes and further false starts, he pulled himself together and continued. "'But our Miss is pretty/Her hair a silky mane,/And eyes like speckled pebbles/When they're wet, like after rain./We like it when she's angry/And her cheeks get red as fire,/And we like it when she's smiling/And the sun comes out once more./We couldn't have a nicer one/And we've learnt some grammar too/So we've bought these flowers/And something else/To say that we love you.' That's it, Miss. You can keep this."

He handed me the paper on which the poem was written. It had been copied out in a fair hand and decorated with emblems dear to their hearts – stock cars, little football players in the colours of Manchester United, and a small sketch of what I took to be me, wagging my finger. As he handed it to me, Cod and Baxter bashfully approached from the back of the class, Cod holding a sheaf of flowers in cellophane, of the kind one normally puts on a coffin if one cannot afford a wreath, and Baxter a large box in wrapping paper.

I was speechless with emotion, my cheeks so hot with blushes I thought my hair would ignite. The shock had dismantled my composure. Deafening applause greeted the end of Riccio's recitation and the presentation of gifts. I struggled for words.

"Really, boys, I never expected – I don't know what – oh dear –"

"Go on, open it, Miss," urged Baxter, as I stood with flowers in one hand and giftbox in the other, dazedly looking from one to the other.

"Oh ... all right." I handed the flowers back to Cod while I opened the box. Inside was a black and white powder puff with bright green pinhead eyes and ears laid back in terror as the lid was removed. My heart melted like a plastic bag. I picked the kitten up in one hand and held him up to show the class, who oohed and aahed with one voice. The kitten clung to my hand and squealed.

"We didn't actually buy it, Miss," said Cod, twitching with honesty. "Baxter's cat had four, see, and if you can't keep it he'll take it back."

"Of course I'll keep it. It's the nicest present I've ever had. Oh dear." I sniffed to draw back the tears.

The bell rang for the end of the period. "What are you going to call it, Miss?" someone shouted.

"3B, of course. What else?" They all laughed and applauded again. As they filed out of the classroom they looked in at the kitten and tickled him and cooed, and said "Ah, 'n'e cute, Miss?" I was stunned and could only smile and gasp a little. I had imagined the only use they would have for small animals was as dartboards. Gushes of suppressed affection welled up in me. I looked at each kindly face in wonder. Was this really 3B I saw before me? My only disappointment was that Grass alone went straight out without looking at the kitten or saying goodbye. But I could not begrudge him his pride. I would have done the same in his place.

When the classroom was empty I sat at the desk contemplating my gifts. The sudden reversal in 3B's attitude had caught me in a weakened condition. Kindness was more than I could endure, and I duly sobbed for a few bewildered moments. There was so much about 3B that I did not know, the fact that they could respond to simple pleasures, and conspire, not only in hostility, but in good will also. And probably much more that I would now never find out. My attitude to them had been doomed from the start. Why had it never occurred to me to try being nice to them? I addressed the question to the kitten, who miaowed in a miniature voice, like a fairy, and sent out a thread-like jet of piddle in response.

The next day was the last of the term. In the evening a large group of staff went out to a pub in Cheshire, and afterwards to Martin's house. We drank and were jolly and got home at half past three. But when I got into bed I could not sleep. Tomorrow was the day I was meeting Shackleton.

It was not excitement that kept me awake. I tossed and turned, trying to pin down exactly what it was. Why wasn't I feeling like a child on Christmas Eve, but rather, like myself before a job interview? Perhaps it was simple nerves, the fear that he would not turn up or that we would have nothing to say to each other. But no. They weren't the reasons. At whatever hour of dawn it was, I finally faced it. Cold feet. I didn't want to go through with it.

A humiliating admission. I sought the reasons for it. Perhaps it was to do with the more positive aspects of my rôle as teacher that I had been experiencing over the last few weeks – the accolade from 3B, the socializing with colleagues. I had begun to think of myself as a teacher, as opposed to someone who had wandered off the street by mistake and had a timetable thrust into their hand. It was not that I thought of Shackleton as any less desirable, or that I desired him less. It was just that I was viewing with a fresh eye the indignities attendant on the affair – meeting surreptitiously down a country road, slipping a contraceptive into the make-up purse. The details were so degrading: I couldn't do it. Worcester Park would cry out for vengeance. The thought that I might, at some advanced age, eke out my pension by telling the *News of the World* how I slept with the Master of the Queen's Musick no longer raised the quality of the experience to acceptable levels. At the same time I despised myself for falling victim to the ogre Convention. Had I met Shackleton in any other circumstances I would not have had any qualms. But now the school blazer seemed to cloak him in inviolability. I found that I feared the contempt of my peers more than I had thought. There was no justification for this fear in cosmic terms, in fact I regarded it as a craven instinct. But, craven or not, it **was** powerful, and kept me tossing and turning until five or after, when I managed to doze off for an hour or two.

By morning fear had become aversion. I had all along been a victim, but as I thought, of a passion that came out of the air. Now there seemed no casuistry in it, it was Shackleton who was the wily predator, setting snares for me. Panic seemed like a suitable reaction. I would have to call it off. Shackleton would never be fooled anyway, he would sense that I had changed my mind and I wanted to spare him the insult. It was a simple matter of calling with an excuse.

While I was looking for the number, Damaris blundered downstairs.

"What do you do for morning sickness? Anne's throwing her guts up."

"Tea and dry biscuits, I think. I read it in Dr Wimpole Replies. I'll go and see her. Is she still saying it's post-flu depression?"

"She's not saying much, actually. In fact she's scarcely breathing."

I ran upstairs. Anne was on her knees with her head over the lavatory. Strands of blonde hair were stuck to her cheeks with sick. She let me help her back into bed, and lay quietly with her head averted. She looked more consumptive than pregnant.

"Oh dear, I shouldn't have had those Bloody Marys," she sighed.

"Were you hoping to get rid of it?" She nodded. "That's foolish, Anne. Understandable, but foolish. There are more reliable methods these days."

"I couldn't do that. It's murder. I love children."

It did not seem like a suitable time to point out ambiguities in her attitude. "Then I suppose you must marry him. It won't be so bad. Sammy will put you on a pedestal and water you every day."

"But I'd rather live with you two."

"Oh." I had not thought of that, rather from an assumption that Anne was not given to formulating theories than because it was improbable. "Listen, I have to go out now, to make a phone call. We'll talk later, all right?"

"All right." She put up her hand to be squeezed. "Could I have 3B up here?"

"Of course. I'll put his bog in the bathroom."

Anne and 3B had gone for each other in a big way, rather to my chagrin.

Mrs Shackleton answered the phone. "I'm afraid Everard is in the bath just now, dear. Shall I get him to call you back?"

"I'm not on the phone. It doesn't matter."

"All right. Who shall I say called?"

"Diana."

"All right, Diana, I'll tell him. Goodbye."

The information that "Everard" was in the bath depressed me still further. Oh Lord, oh Lord – abluting himself for my pleasure. I pictured him in the tub, his mood probably insouciant, lightly touched with apprehension, the pressure of exams off, the prospect of adult freedom and achievement glimmering into the infinite distance beyond the immediate satisfaction of nobbling the English teacher. How could I tell him that he was, after all, too young, that, alas, our affair had not been written by Colette and that frankly I was chickening out. Perhaps if we met again in a few years, when he had moved up out of entangling social embarrassment? No, I could not say that. But then what? It struck me that I might be worrying unnecessarily. We might get to Haworth and back without so much as shaking hands. He was not the type to take me by storm if I showed disinterest. Or I could plead that old chestnut, the curse. On reflection this really seemed like the best course. It would leave his ego and my now paranoid sense of propriety intact.

Just to make certainty doubly sure, I did not put any prophylactics in my make-up purse.

Shackleton had parked in a lay-by and lolled against the car smoking. I had not known that he smoked, though he might have been disguising his nerves. The sight of him made me falter. He ought to have been posing for a Hilliard miniature. He wore tight black jeans and a black velour sweater over a cream shirt. He looked so elegant, so sensual, I would have liked to put him on a golden chain and fed him on sugared violets. The suspicion that I had always fought returned – that despite his youth and impudence and all the rest, he was one of Nature's élite and was entitled to special privileges.

"Hello, Miss."

"Hello, Shack."

"Was it you who called this morning? I don't know any Dianas."

"Yes, it was. I . . . I wanted to warn you I'd be late. Anne isn't well."

"Oh? Again? What's the matter with her? I hope it's not serious."

"We'll have to see. It's nothing to do with you, anyway."

He laughed. "Good. Shall we go in your car?"

"Okay."

With my hands firmly on the steering wheel and Shackleton toying with his ciggie, I began to enjoy myself. It had always been a pleasure to talk to him. His opinions were charmingly adolescent in some areas, which was not unhelpful in the circumstances. He believed in conspiracies to conceal the existence of extra-terrestrial phenomena, despised capitalism, international companies, organized religion and the police, believed firmly in the ubiquitous corruption of the latter, all government officials and the Education Committee, and thought that the C.I.A. and The System between them shared responsibility for the world's ills.

It was a fine day. Fulsome white clouds, their bellies fleeced with grey, billowed over the moors and the soot-blackened towns that straddled the hollows. The distraction of Shackleton could not sully the sense of being a pilgrim. The sight of the paths that Charlotte, Emily and Anne had trod, the landscapes they had loved, the air they had breathed, told me I was on consecrated ground. There could be no doubt that the spirits of the three sisters still walked these hills, drifting blindly, like the clouds. No hopeful supplicant approaching the temples of Delphi could have felt more humbly in the presence of immortals than I.

At least until we were on the outskirts of Haworth and the traffic started to build up.

"There must be something on, today," I said. "Surely all these people can't just be going to the Parsonage?"

"It's hard to say. Most of them don't look particularly literate, it's true. I suppose the foreign cars must be going there."

"I've never seen so much traffic. It's like a bank holiday. They ought to build a diversion so that these good people can go on their way."

Shackleton took off his sweater and rolled up his sleeves. The car was now at a standstill in a double line of traffic leading up the hill past the station and the railway museum. The sun broiled on bare skin and plastic seats. I began to sweat, and had to wriggle constantly to avoid becoming gummed to the seat. The smell of exhaust fumes was sickening.

"But where are all these good people going?" I knew I was sounding petulant. By now I realized that they were going to the Parsonage, but I hoped that if I protested hard enough it would turn out not to be true. It was hard to believe. Young children hung out of car windows, eating sweets, whining or screaming. Some of the male drivers sat naked to the waist. An ice-cream vendor was doing a brisk trade with the sweltering travellers.

"We'd better have an ice-cream, too. We've been here twenty minutes already, we won't get up the hill before lunch."

Shackleton got out and bought them. They were the softee variety, and tasted of diesel oil, and melted faster than the human mouth could suck. The ignominy of sticky fingers was something I could have done without.

"Are you really that keen to see the place?" said Shackleton after another twenty minutes.

"Aren't you?"

"Not really. I've never been particularly stuck on the Brontës. Their emotionalism was so unhealthy – fanatical. So obviously the product of sexual frustration. You should read some of the descriptions by Catherine of Siena of her so-called visions – pure sublimated orgasm, just like the Brontës."

"That's a very simplistic, post-Freudian cop-out, Shackleton. Plenty of people are sexually frustrated, but only one of them has produced *Wuthering Heights*. There's more to writing a novel than a quick conversion of lust into prose. Emily, particularly had a severe intellectual command of her material."

"Oh, really? 'Nelly, I *am* Heathcliff!' And all that rubbish about Heathcliff foaming at the mouth like a mad dog with passion. Well, of course, it could be I who is abnormal ..."

"But so what? I wouldn't mind being sexually frustrated if it meant I could write like that. Anyway, you're just at an age when passion seems unsophisticated. Don't forget they lived without central heating. You had to be more spirit than body to survive."

"As you wish."

There was something patronizing about his relinquishing the argument, but it was a topic I was glad to drop.

An hour and ten minutes later we had got as far as the queue for the car-park. The folly of the venture was now clear and we were both silent for long periods. Shackleton made light of it, obviously amused by my stoical determination to see the thing through.

After another three-quarters of an hour we got into the car-park and followed the crowd up through the Parsonage garden. A queue led away from the front door. We set out to find the end of it. It merged into a swilling mass of people, men, women, children, babies, dogs, candy-floss, ice-creams, cameras, sun hats, pink singed flesh, beer cans. We walked a little way down the steep high street. It shifted and wriggled with brightly-coloured tourists. The street was lined with shops selling Brontëana; Brontë tea-towels, Brontë ashtrays, Brontë pottery, Brontë postcards, Brontë knit-wear, Brontë sweets and biscuits, Brontë hotdogs, Brontë therm-ometers, Brontë cushions, Brontë pennants, Brontë soap, Brontë tea-caddies. It would not have surprised me to see a Brontë po; they were probably just sold out. We elbowed our way down the street. I was dazed. Would Heaven be like this too? My revulsion against the funfair/fish'n'chip/never-mind-why-you're-here-just-buy-the-souvenirs atmosphere was deep, but deeper was my shame for the dead sisters. How humiliated they would be to know that their hard-won fame and pitiful lives would give rise to this circus.

I stopped and waited for Shackleton to catch up. People buffeted and stepped on me, suggesting, according to their age and upbring-ing, various ways in which I could dispose of myself. I felt absurdly as though I were going to cry.

"Had enough?" said Shackleton, grinning.

"I'm glad they're dead. I'm glad they didn't see all this."

"For God's sake, it's not worth getting upset about. That's life, you know. You're the one who believes in free enterprise." He could not disguise his satisfaction that my temple had been turned into a den of thieves.

"Go to Hell. I'm going home."

I strode off back to the car, avoiding the Parsonage itself, which I could no longer bear to look at, quite prepared to drive off without him. His smugness was profoundly offensive. Perhaps there was something of self-indulgence in one's adulation of the Brontës, but their sufferings had been so real, their loneliness real, their love and bitterness and despair real. Shackleton's sneering dismissal of all that sprang from the same cruel ignorance as that of a child who tells its grandmother that it is glad Grandpa's dead because he smelled. No blame attaches to such innocent cruelty: it just makes one want to take the perpetrator by the throat and cause him pain, so that he will learn something.

But it took so long to manoeuvre the car out of the car park again that there was no danger of Shackleton's being left behind. He pretended not to notice that I was on the point of abandoning him.

We drove in silence until we were again on the open road. It was at least slightly quicker leaving than coming. I felt like playing up my offended sensibilities for all they were worth, and was pleased to note that Shackleton's nonchalant smile was freezing over. He offered several topics of conversation, but I snapped them all off and spat them out.

But as his discomfort increased I began to relent. He had probably had high hopes of the day: it had been planned for long enough. I was not comfortable myself to see him disadvantaged. Shackleton's brain was, I knew, sharper than my own, but my tongue had had more practice.

After a few miles I turned down a narrow lane and stopped on a grass verge that had been made by building a sharp angle into the stone wall. Shackleton showed no surprise, but calmly lit a cigarette. I was feeling pretty god-like by this time.

"Listen, Shackleton, I think the best thing would be just to forget about today. It was a mistake. A lovely idea – crossing boundaries and so forth, fearlessly extending the hand of friendship and so on – but it doesn't work. I can see that now. So . . . well, as I say – let's just go home and forget it."

He was looking into the middle distance, his elbow resting on the open window ledge. He blew a derisive column of smoke into the sunshine. "I'm hardly likely to forget such a glib epitaph. You really are a bitch, Miss Slade."

"I beg your pardon?"

"You heard."

My heart was pounding. I had expected him to say, "Okay, let's go", not treat me to a precise, damning analysis that could well be true. "If that's your opinion, young man, I'm surprised you took the trouble to show up. Perhaps when you're a bit older you won't be so ready to judge everybody only as they affect your convenience."

"For Christ's sake, will you stop throwing my age at me all the time! How old are you? Twenty-two? Twenty-three? You think that gives you the right to carry on like Catherine the Great? If you think it's so humiliating to get laid by an eighteen-year-old I'm surprised *you* bothered to turn up. Unless you thought it was your last chance."

"I didn't want to. I had changed my mind. That's why I phoned. But then I thought it would be unkind to stand you up. Believe it or not, I didn't want to hurt your feelings – such as they are."

"My feelings are confined to quite a small area, just now. The kindest thing you could have done would be to tell me you'd changed your mind and we could both have gone home, instead of going through with this farce."

"If I'd known your expectations were so specific, I would have done."

"Well what do you expect? I mean, there's such an enormous gulf between our mental and social development I could hardly hope for a real relationship. Laying you was all I aspired to."

"Aim a little higher next time. I keep forgetting – your brain may be developed, but the rest of you is at the same stage as 3B."

"Perhaps you should send me to Mr Dacre after all. Though I think you'd have the guts to do it yourself this time, wouldn't you?"

"Damn right, I would. There's nothing I'd like better than to wipe that smirk off your face, though I suspect it goes through to the bone."

"You know, it's simply amazing how you've managed to take the attitude that I've offered you insult after insult – starting with my age right down to my expression. But the truth is, until this morning you've been giving me an unmistakable come-on. That time in the music room you practically left puddles on the floor. Now for some reason you've changed your mind – out of respect for my age, apparently – and suddenly everything's turned around and I'm supposed to take it with a smile and work harder at getting old."

"Why not go the whole hog and accuse me of rape? That should make Brother William happy. You know fine well I didn't start anything."

"It's an academic question. You didn't exactly recoil in maidenly horror – until now, of course, when it actually comes down to it. Honestly, you're the last person I'd have thought was a cock-teaser. You're a complete phoney – you try to give the impression of being some sort of free spirit – above convention, or something, but in actual fact you're as much a prude as your precious Brontës. 'Oh no, I'd rather call you "Shackleton" – it's more erotic.' Erotic! You don't know what the word means. You're about as erotic as a T.V. dinner. You're a big disappointment, Miss Slade. A big disappointment."

I opened my mouth to reply, but nothing came out. Shackleton continued to glare out of the window. Something alarming was happening inside me, something the like of which I had last seen in the epic film *Krakatoa, East of Java*. It was akin to the panic I had felt when I ran out of 3B, only worse. Instead of striking me dumb and almost paralysed, this sensation seemed on the verge of bursting out in an embarrassingly physical manner. My heart was hitting itself compulsively against the floor of my stomach, and an unseen hand pumped my ribs and lungs in and out. All I could do was to try and keep those parts of my body that I could control as still as possible in the hope of containing the eruption. A heavy, hot weight sank into my breastbone and my vision began to blur. I listened in amazement as I let out a kind of sick gulp, then another. Then the gulps built up into formless yells as the spasms forced them out of my throat. I was terrified. I could hear myself screaming, but as if from a long way off: the noise seemed to flee before the next spasm, so that there was no release in screaming. But I could not stop, because of the terror of being trapped inside the four walls of a body that had gone berserk – it seemed I was possessed by a crazy animal maddened by the constrictions of its cage.

I do not know how long the convulsions lasted: I was aware of nothing but the fight between my body and this crude geyser of emotion that threatened to rip it apart.

But at last shapes began to come into focus again. I was being hit on the face, very hard. This suddenly struck me as hysterically funny – of course. I started to laugh, a mechanical, mad Mrs Rochester laugh. The tears soaked my face. Then I sagged forward over the steering wheel, shaking all over with laughter, then threw myself back in the seat. Shackleton was trying to hold me steady, but the constriction still maddened me and I fought him off. Then he got out of the car and came round to my side, pulled me out and propelled me along the road. Still I kept on laughing, but gradually with less violence. Shackleton put his arm round my shoulder and attached mine round his waist. He had to pull me, I was too weak to walk by myself. My head lolled against his shoulder, my laughter subsided into sporadic mutters of incoherent rubbish. We walked unsteadily along, careering in and out of the grassy ditch at the side of the road. I began to notice the hedgerow and the occasional row of terraced cottages with their iron gates and blank, black faces. Shackleton was talking to me, humouring me. At last my footsteps fell into step with his and we proceeded in a straight line. I was silent, reeling from what had happened. We still had our arms round each other, which was good because I had started to shiver. The shivers occasionally gathered into a little climactic sigh. My teeth chattered, and regularly snapped off minute scraps of tongue. But there was no doubt that I was re-installed in my own body. Despite the shivering I sensed an immense relief. I had been afraid I would scream myself to death. It was like being conscious when a terrible pain ebbs away, or waking up to find one has not, after all, been pushed off the Post Office Tower. I did not have the courage to look at Shackleton, but the feel of his slim waist in the circle of my arm was comfortably distracting, the gentle movement of the muscles and hips. He wore short boots under his black jeans. If I kept my eyes down it was not unlike taking a stroll with Wyatt Earp. I dreaded stopping, or arriving anywhere, and having to let him go and begin to sort out the confusion my hysterics had thrown us into. Neither of us said anything for what seemed like a couple of hours, but was probably twenty minutes. He was the first to speak.

"You must be worn out. We could sit under that tree and have a cigarette."

"Okay." There was no point in objecting. He was probably afraid we were lost. In any case we could not walk into an eternal sunset.

We sat side by side uncomfortably on the roots of the tree, hugging our knees like a couple of children.

"Have we come far? I suppose we left the car open."

"No. I brought the keys."

"What presence of mind! Are you a scout? Listen, Shackleton, I'm sorry. I don't know what happened. It scared me."

"Me too. It was frightening. I've never seen anyone go like that before. Does it happen often?"

"No, never. That was the first time. Don't talk as if it were an epileptic fit."

"Of course not. It was my fault, that's one reason why I was scared. I was terribly rude. I'm sorry. I didn't mean all those things. I don't know why I said them."

"Because they're true, probably. Some of them, anyway. And I hadn't given much thought to your feelings before that."

"Even so, it was quite unnecessary. I'm sorry. I always seem to be reducing you to tears."

"It makes life interesting. But there's no point in scrapping over the blame. It must have been building up ever since I started at that pen. All this just triggered it off."

"Was it so bad?"

"Worse. I had no idea what teaching would be like. The worst thing was knowing that I had got myself into it of my own free will. That made my head spin at times."

"Are you going to leave?"

"I don't know. Probably not. What else is there to do?"

"You could re-train as a chiropodist."

"Because there'll always be feet, you mean? It's possible. But so many women seem to be re-training as para-medics or para-social workers or para-somethings. I'd rather know the worst than second best disguised as something else. Women are in danger of becoming a race of half-breeds. Anyway, I suspect that most people's lives are pretty dull, man or woman."

"You're not ambitious."

"I suppose not. It seems a bit fruitless when jobs are so scarce. I suppose I could aim to be a Good Teacher, like Mr Marple."

"Don't you even want to get married?"

"I don't think so. I've never noticed that it generally improved the quality of one's life. It's funny, none of us wants to get married."

"That's a curious set-up you've got there, the three of you. Do you have sex together?"

"Mind your own business."

"Oh, come on!"

"Well, all right, no we don't. Would you like to think that we did?"

"Perhaps. You're all desirable in different ways. If you were ugly individually you'd be three times as ugly put together, but the conjunction of aesthetically pleasing flesh is acceptable in any combination."

"Well, I'll put it to them and you can bring a camera."

He laughed. "I'd bring more than my camera."

We fell silent again. It was late afternoon and the deepening sunlight was pulling shadows over the fields. I felt a nervous effervescence in the blood that signified only the presence of a mate. Every slight movement seemed to stir up a magnetic field. Ah well – why not? I certainly did not want to become the increasingly dried-up victim of middle-class hypocrisy that Shackleton had suggested. Here was a chance to leave the beaten track. After all, one only has one life, one youth, one body, one Everard Shackleton. I could live with the consequences more easily than with regret. A small bespectacled ghost drifted by, wagging a warning finger and murmuring that rules are not made for when one is feeling strong and pious, but for when one is feeling weak and tempted. But poor Charlotte, short, near-sighted governesses do only meet lovers in novels. Shackleton was right about the Brontës. All their moralizing could not disguise fascination with the darker side of life (i.e. sexual relations), the only thing I had experienced so far that convinced me I was alive. Thank goodness they had been so frustrated. If Charlotte had been alive today she would have gone to Keighley Comprehensive if there is one, got contact lenses, been at least three inches taller because of the orange juice and got herself laid in an empty railway carriage after a pop concert in Leeds. Perhaps her father would have gone into religious broadcasting and moved to London, where she would not have been honed by the Yorkshire gales at all, but perhaps by the T.V.-laden breezes of Worcester Park! The thought brought thought to a standstill.

I got to my feet. "Let's go for a walk."

Shackleton looked up at me and smiled. He took my hand as he got up and our bodies quietly and inevitably fused together. A car drove past. We drew apart.

"We can't stay here."

"Where then?"

"I don't know. Let's walk."

We walked, clamped together, stopping every ten yards to kiss.

At the top of the hill there was a plain, double-fronted cottage flush with the road. It was empty. We looked through the front windows. The rooms were bare, stained wallpaper, dusty boards, naked light bulbs. Some newspapers lay around on the floors and a tin mug and cigarette-ends took up the rest of the space. It was dismal, almost sinister. I had no wish to go in, and anyway all the windows and doors were locked. We walked round to the overgrown garden at the back. The grass was knee-high and at the end of the garden a few grotesque Brussels sprouts flourished in the choked cabbage patch. Under a plum tree was a tattered wigwam. It showed signs of recent use: the patch of grass in front of the opening was flattened, and there was an empty bottle of Dandelion and Burdock pop inside. The groundsheet was torn and filthy.

"Are there any rugs in the car?"

"Yes. But isn't it miles away?"

"Not really. I'll drive it up here."

Shackleton left and I squatted on the grass in front of the wigwam, watching the ants scuttle over my feet and trying to keep them out of my crutch. My mind was a pleasantly drugged blank, drugged by exhaustion, relief and surrender. I felt like Thumbelina wafted downstream on a lily leaf.

Shackleton was not away long. We spread the rugs inside and I lay down and waited while he tried to secure the flap of oilcloth across the entrance.

"Leave it," I said. "We'll be too hot otherwise." It was already too hot. The sun had been broiling on the wigwam all day, filling it with a cloying, foisty smell and a thick light that turned us to the colour of banana skins.

Shackleton knelt across me and we smiled. I was happy about the smelly wigwam. I had always liked snuggeries; this one reminded me of the gym store at school – the vapours of hot rubber and plastic, the seclusion with the nearest and dearest. But having Shackleton for a companion was somehow not like throwing over female for male partnership. There was something asexual about his appeal, so that adoring him was like adoring an idealized version of oneself. As I lay there passively and let him undo my clothes I did not bother to disguise my admiration; the beautifully proportioned leanness, the sensuous, asymmetrical lines of his face, the silky hair.

At that moment I felt I would have been quite happy to look at him, not to touch. But his warm hands on my skin brought me to life. It seemed that the hysterics had released more than the frustrations of teaching. Poor Shackleton, I did not give him a chance, but fell on him like a starving man on a juicy leg of lamb. Within seconds I was spinning in a new sensation, strung out on a steely thread of atoms dancing wildly in harmony. I was drunk with my capacity for ecstatic release and the immediate energy for more. I went on pounding away until my thighs ached and sheer physical exhaustion brought me gradually to a slumped finish. I fell on top of him and closed my eyes.

After a few moments something about the cool tension of Shackleton's body beneath my hot sweaty one gave me a twitch of unease. It occurred to me that when, what and if Shackleton had contributed had completely escaped my notice. Without a word or a glance he eased me politely off him, and we lay side by side looking at the hole in the top of the wigwam. The leaves of the plum tree were pushing their way through it, and their shadows played softly on the canvas. Our silence was not a comfortable, post-coital silence, it was a lid on embarrassing unpleasantness. I should have liked a token cuddle, an exchange of lukewarm compliments; even a smile would have been reassuring, but his unblinking gaze and the businesslike neatness of his crossed feet and hands clasped on the stomach spoke only reproach. He looked like the effigy of a peeved crusader. I shut my eyes and yawned.

At that he turned his head towards me.

"I'm sorry," he said, in an unpleasant tone, "I have the feeling I was in the way."

"Don't be like that. I enjoyed it."

"So I gather. I was only sorry I couldn't be of more use."

"Well, I was wondering if you –"

"Yes. About half an hour ago. Don't worry, you didn't notice a thing."

"No, I didn't I'm afraid. I needed it more than you did, that's all. Don't let's have a post-mortem."

"You certainly needed it. Though why you save it up for unworthy churls like myself I can't imagine. You'd get the same results with a broom handle."

"Shackleton, look I'm sorry. Why do you take it so personally? Because you must be the best at everything? It's never perfect the first time – we're not used to each other. It's like dancing."

"Yes, teacher."

"Oh well shut up, then, if you insist on throwing a tantrum. It's nobody's fault. You just have to learn to take things as they come."

"Oh-oh, it's cliché time. Don't you want to say a few words about the rough and the smooth, swings and roundabouts, fair weather and foul?"

"Look, smartarse, what do you want me to say? If you wanted to run the show you should have said so beforehand. These are the swinging seventies, do you still expect women to lie still and think of England?"

" 'Run the show', 'steer the ship'. Don't you ever make up your own words?"

"Yes. 'Goodbye'." I had started to pull on my clothes. He watched me and then began to dress himself. I got out of the wigwam as fast as decency would allow and finished dressing outside. Presently he came out too.

"I'll give you a lift back to your car, of course."

"I can walk."

"Suit yourself."

But he came, anyway. We drove in silence to where he had left his car and he got out without a word.

Driving on home, I was surprised at how calm I felt. The spell was broken, which was the original idea of course, but even so I was surprised that it worked. As I had suspected, the anticipation of making love to Shackleton had been more pleasurable than the thing itself. Like wriggling a loose tooth, there is a thrill when it comes away, but one's tongue relentlessly explores the gap for the old sensations. In a way I missed the Shackleton I had lusted after, but he had definitely disappeared. I could cope with having done it, despite the undignified scene that followed, and be glad that it was over and done with. My mind had been cleared of him; he was already diminishing to the dimensions of a historical incident.

I could not so easily forget his jibes about me and clichés. I could not say it wasn't true; one never really listens to oneself speak. That he meant to be hurtful out of injured pride allowed me to assume he had exaggerated. I was glad he had resorted to spitefulness: it restored the sense of his immaturity, which I was now anxious to keep in mind.

It was relief, after all, not to be able to discuss the affair with Damaris and Anne. Easier to forget it, rather than spread knowledge which might in the future be aired at inconvenient moments. Besides, our attention was fully occupied with the matter of Anne's pregnancy.

She was being horribly ill: food and nausea and sleep followed each other in four-hourly cycles. Damaris and I became demented trying to keep spoonfuls of food down her, thrilling to initial triumph and then, moments later when we were downstairs, the sound of retching in the loo. At our most frustrated we suspected Anne of annoying us on purpose, which was total nonsense. She would rather have died than give anyone a moment's trouble.

Damaris was even less patient than I was. She was a horse, constitutionally, herself and I could see that although she still cared for Anne a great deal, the mental gulf between them was a problem when they were too much alone together. I encouraged her to get on with the opera and took over most of the sickroom duty myself.

Concern for Anne in fact prevented a somewhat critical thought from surfacing, that I could well be pregnant myself. That is how one makes babies, after all. I did not know whether I was more shaken by the possibility itself, or by my completely forgetting about it until five days after the event. Never had I run such a risk – had I been that hysterical? I had been so obsessed with Shackleton as an instrument for administering Life in large chunks full on the sensibility that his ordinary physical properties were temporarily eclipsed. Now that this lust for abstraction no longer gave me an excuse to do something which I could not excuse in any other way, it was succeeded by jangling awareness of practicalities. I did not want a baby: I did not want to be sick twenty-four hours a day, lose my job and my figure, get rotten teeth and varicose veins and sleepless nights. The idea of reproducing Shackleton's genes was a crumb of comfort, but supposing instead it was a cross between Shackleton's mother and my cousin Harcourt? One had to admit that the potential for genius was much greater than its occurrence, and Shackleton had used up several generations potential in one go. I did not believe in abortion, and besides, all this was before they could be purchased at every kiosk. What would I do for money? The school would turn me out. Anne could marry Sammy, or at least claim support, but Shackleton was a write-off in either case. Claiming anything from him would anyway entail admitting the liaison, and I had done nothing but be glad no one knew about it ever since it happened. I should have to go on the parish. Damaris could not be expected to support me. Us.

The thought was appalling. "Us." Another whole new human being, independently operated, who would shortly grow as large or larger than I was, need everything I did, want to do everything I did and nothing that I said. In my imagination the offspring of that unremarkable coupling assumed monstrous proportions. And it would always be there; one could not go away for a single night without making all sorts of complicated arrangements for it. All bad enough if one wanted the damn thing in the first place, but for an unwanted child it was a hideous prospect, worse even for the child than for me. Who would want to be born into such a set-up? Or rather, absence of one. The threat of change suddenly put a high value on the way life was now.

I waited for my period as for the headsman's axe. Hitherto I had always been sceptical about the influence of emotions on bodily health. Unlike the dear Brontës, I was quite robust. But now anxiety shrivelled my stomach to nothing; the only things that tasted good were gin and tobacco. I could not sleep, nor concentrate, nor listen to what was said. I examined myself obsessively for signs of growing nipples, incipient oedema, falling hair, stretch marks, darkening of the navel line, permanent desire to wee, and found them all. I took hot baths and cold showers, ran up and down stairs, took a book on folk medicine out of the library and scanned it for mention of a homely morning-after (hopefully, week-after) contraceptive that might have survived in oral tradition.

By the time the deadline came and went I was convinced I was pregnant. All that remained was to buy the pram.

But Anne's condition was so much more graphic than mine that I simply did not have the nerve to make any more disastrous announcements. At least it could wait until the thing was certain, by which time Anne's future might be satisfactorily settled.

A couple of weeks passed. During that time we hardly went out. We functioned by routine, somewhat mindlessly, Damaris cheerfully penning octaves, Anne and I lost in our separate anxieties. The future, as such, receded by the minute. The weather was fine. We all looked forward to a next day that would be the exact repeat of the one before. Knowing that it could not be like that for ever made it a poignant expectation.

After two weeks Sammy reappeared. He had been camping again, a ritual with him apparently. He started calling on Anne every day, sometimes twice. We left them alone in the sitting-room at the back, Damaris retreating to her room, I often to a deckchair in the garden and an anxious half-hour with Evelyn Home, on the lookout for useful addresses. Sammy's sturdy, peasant voice could be heard in spates of urgent rhetoric, followed by long silences broken by encouraging interrogatives. In fact Anne hardly said anything. He always left her in tears. My anger at his pestering mounted daily. He was trying to wear her down, convince her that staying with us would never work. His nagging resolved any doubts I might have had on that score. Certainly there would be problems, especially if babies went on popping up at the present rate, but whoever said life would be easy? All my latent feminism gathered to a head. I re-read *The Female Eunuch* for moral support, and was particularly cheered by the new look for child-rearing. Why not be casual, philosophical about it, let things happen? If one refused to call a disaster a disaster then it stops being one. I made up my mind to speak to Sammy, to persuade him to leave us alone.

One Sunday afternoon the scene between him and Anne sounded particularly fraught. She started crying almost as soon as he arrived and he was actually shouting at her. That was it for me. The lout had to go, before he got round to persuading her with his gym shoe. I waited for him by the gate. He always left early on Sundays, to take his mother to Benediction.

When he came out of the house he looked distracted, and was red in the face. I caught him by the sleeve. He started, and pulled his arm away viciously.

"What do you want? I'm in a hurry."

"Too bad. It won't take long. I just think you should stop pestering Anne. She never wanted to go out with you in the first place – she only did to be polite, and I wouldn't be surprised if you got her pregnant deliberately because you knew that's the only way she'd ever agree to marry you. Just leave her alone. She's quite capable of marrying you to be polite, too, but she really wants to stay with us and the sooner you get that into your thick head the better."

Sammy's face had gone grey and glistening, the brows drawn, into a menacing crowbar. "You stupid bitch. Don't you know what's been going on? I thought you dykes told each other everything. Get out of my way, I've got things to do."

"I know she's pregnant. What else is there to know? What are you talking about?" A contraction of fear went through me. Why was Sammy so murderously angry? What dark secrets could Anne possibly have kept from us?

"Get out of my way." He pushed me aside and got into the car, roared up the engine, his large foot pumping the accelerator in sinister fashion.

"Don't come back!" I shouted, hating the high, female, ineffectual sound that came out with my dire threat.

"Don't worry!"

The car shot off down the lane. I stood and watched it, jabbering futile curses.

Anne was standing at the front door, her hand over her mouth and tears streaming down her face. She ran towards the gate and leaned over it to catch sight of the disappearing car.

"Didn't you stop him?" she wailed. "Oh no, no, we must stop him."

"Why Anne? What's the matter? What's going on?"

"He's going to kill him, I know he is. We must *do* something, Carlo – call the police – something! Oh quick, we must *do* something!"

I took Anne by the shoulders and shook her, panic rising. "Kill whom, for God's sake? What are you talking about?"

"Shackleton, of course."

"Shackleton? Why? Why on earth . . .?"

"Because it's his baby, not Sammy's. I was hoping you wouldn't have to know, but in the end I had to tell Sammy – he wouldn't leave me alone – and now he says he's going to kill him. Oh Carlo, we must *do* something!"

"Be quiet! Be quiet a minute!" I clapped my hands over my ears and held my breath. All my mind was saying was Shackleton, Shackleton, Shackleton, like a roll of drums.

"Please, Carlo, let's do something – let's call the police, he doesn't stand a chance against Sammy."

"A-all r-right. I'll g-get the c-car. W-wait here."

Damaris leaned out of an upstairs window. "What's all the noise about?"

"C-come w-with us, Dammo. W-we'll explain in the c-car."

She stared at us for a moment, then disappeared.

Somehow I got the car started, my nerves so shot to pieces that I could not find the right key, let alone the ignition. I jumped it in second, stalled the engine six times, and then shot out backwards through the closed gate, splintering it into a pile of palings in the road. At that point, however, it was chaff before the wind. Damaris and Anne scrambled in and we were off. I was glad to be driving: at least I could grip the steering wheel.

Anne sat in the back, crying freely. Damaris was beside me. "Will someone please tell me what's going on? I was on a very sticky octave."

"You t-tell her, Anne."

"No – you."

"All r-right. L-listen to this, then. S-Sammy's j-just found out that Sh-Shackleton is the father of Anne's k-kid so he's g-going to k-kill him he says of c-course I don't s-suppose he w-will b-but he might m-muck him up a b-bit."

"What!" Damaris jerked upright and looked aghast from me to Anne and back. "That can't be true. Not you too, Anne?"

"What do you mean?"

"Well – I mean – oh damn it, what's the use of pretending now? I thought I was the only one."

The car lurched off the road, over the pavement and back again.

I said, "You weren't. I was next." I wanted to laugh. It was so ludicrously right, somehow; it neatened up the edges of this catastrophic year. Why not Anne, too? He had had equal access, equal opportunity: why should Anne have got away with it?

Damaris was swelling with anger. "Stop the car! Stop the car!" she yelled, banging her fists on the dashboard.

I did so, throwing us all at the windscreen.

"What are we doing?" she said. "Why rescue him? Let Sammy smash his lovely face in, I feel like helping him! How could he, the bastard!"

Anne put a hand on Damaris' shoulder. "Oh no, Dammo, that's terrible. Please let's go on. It wasn't his fault entirely – at least not in my case. I couldn't help it, he's so beautiful. You can't let Sammy spoil his face, it isn't right. Please, please, we're wasting time."

Damaris ground her teeth. "He deserves it. Who does he think he is?"

"Anne's right, though, he shouldn't be maimed for life, it will reduce his earning capacity. Think of his nice parents – and the school. They can't afford any more scandal."

The revelations had cured my nerves. The whole saga of Shackleton and his insatiable curiosity now seemed so much like high farce that it could not be allowed to end in real violence, it was out of key. My loathing of brute force in the person of Sammy was paramount: we could deal with Shackleton later.

"You don't have to come with us, Dammo."

"Of course I'll come. You're right. I don't want Sammy to get in first. The rat! The absolute rat!" Damaris' rage was assuming Wagnerian proportions.

"Please let's get on," urged Anne, "he'll be there by now."

I started the car again. "Hell. Where are we going? Does anyone know where he lives?"

"Give me the telephone directory," said Damaris. We always kept one in the car, for locating cinemas and the like. "Just head for the school for now. I know it isn't far from here."

So, while I drove through the kindly summer Sunday afternoon, Damaris feverishly sought the Shackletons' address, and located it in the A-Z of Manchester. She gave me directions, but apart from that we were silent. Every time we stopped at a traffic light Anne would moan in desperation.

The silence got more tense as we neared Shackleton's house. Suppose we were too late? Could I stand seeing Shackleton's unforgettable face smashed to a pulp? Rage against Sammy, and simple fear of his physical strength, made me shake. I remembered the expression on his face as he got into his car, and the way his foot pumped with rhythmic menace. Perhaps the three of us together would not even be a match for Sammy. I felt sick. Judging by the ashen faces of Damaris and Anne, so did they.

The house was in a street of prettyish red-brick semis, growing extensions over the garage, attic studios and glassed-in porches. Roses, pyracanthas, square lawns and new tarmac were prominent.

The bay windows, with their stained glass lights, no doubt concealed a fair whack of Parker Knoll furniture and Sanderson prints. At such a time on Sunday afternoon, kettles would be boiling for afternoon tea after a leisurely washing-up of lunch, toddlers might be paddling in plastic pools, teenagers doing their homework to Radio One. In short, it was a street to pull the heartstrings of anyone sensitive to the good things in English domestic life. It did not seem quite like the nurturing ground for rare talent, but that only proved how resilient talent was to peace and plenty.

It did not take us long to find the right house. Sammy's stubby red Renault was carelessly parked. I drew up behind it, being careful to leave access to the drive in case the parents wanted to go for a spin. Anne was out of the car before I had turned the engine off. I could not help admiring her pluck; maternal instincts had obviously taken a curious turn. Pale and bedraggled as she was, there was a lust for action which was new.

Damaris' fighting mood seemed to have subsided a little. Anne went straight up to the front door, but Damaris and I dithered for a moment by the car.

"Don't hear the crunch of broken bones," said Damaris, shivering.

"Come on!" called Anne and beckoned us urgently. We hurried up the drive. Anne had gone inside; the door must have been open. Now we could hear Sammy's voice, bellowing. We stood in the hall, semi-paralysed. The decor was all glistening white paint and turquoise carpets. Mrs Shackleton was standing at the kitchen door with a tea-towel in her hands, looking dazed. Anne ran upstairs.

"What on earth is going on?" said Mrs Shackleton. "Mr Plummer's up there. There's a dreadful row. Are they all right?"

"It's nothing. Don't worry. How are you? I'm awfully sorry to disturb you on a Sunday afternoon like this. We've come to get Mr Plummer. Oh dear! What was that?!" We all jumped at the noise of the loud crash which shook the rubber plant beside the telephone. Anne's shrieks had joined Sammy's.

"Come on," said Damaris, embarrassed by, but biting on, the Special Branch image.

We rushed up the stairs. The three of them were in the front bedroom, Shackleton's, obviously. There was a piano, piles of books, and posters for East European drama festivals. Sammy had Shackleton by the shirt, which he had drawn into a kind of noose round the neck. He had jammed the body up against the fitted wardrobe and was systematically banging its head on the hard-board, at the same time shouting in breathy, uneven phrases. Shackleton made no resistance at all.

"Filthy – little – sneak," muttered Sammy, to the rhythmic clunk of Shackleton's head, "right – under – my – very – nose – you – mother – fucking – runt."

I felt sick, as much because of Sammy's language as anything else; it was a sinister indication of how moved he was.

"It wasn't," protested Shackleton, squirming pitifully and try-ing to prise Sammy's hands off his throat, "It wasn't then. You're being awfully irrational, Mr Plummer."

"No, it wasn't then," wailed Anne. "Please stop, Sammy – please!"

"I – don't – bloody – care – when – it – was – by – the – time – I've – finished – with – you it'll – be – the – last – bloody – time – get it?"

At this point he yanked Shackleton away from the cupboard and flung him against the bookcase. Books rained on top of him as he slid to the floor. Sammy pushed Anne off and she too fell, onto the bed. Sammy made to pick Shackleton off the floor again. Damaris and I looked at each other. Then I grabbed Sammy by the collar of his leisure shirt and Damaris attempted to twist his arm behind his back, which she might have done if she could only have got hold of it. It was then that Sammy noticed us.

"What the – ? Get off me, you creeps!"

"Leave him alone, Sammy. You'll kill him. It's none of your damned business, anyway."

"Get off!" Sammy detached us both in a single movement and we staggered across the room, knocking each other over. By this time Anne was on her feet again, pounding Sammy's back as he bent down to drag Shackleton to his feet. Damaris and I joined the fray. At one point he punched me in the eye, at another I got an excruciating kick from his radial-tyred plimsoll. As far as I could tell Sammy suffered no damage at all. The only sounds were Anne's fading pleas, grunts, pants, gasps and the thud of books and limbs and bedside lamps. The strength of the brute was unnatural: his muscles actually had real power, of a kind that I thought came in with The Age of Steam. My untried tendons were quite unable to cope. Within minutes I was quivering and helpless. Damaris stood up to it rather better, but then he got hold of her copious red hair and she really started to scream. Instinct was telling me to give up and get out of the range of those thrashing limbs, but we were at least keeping him off Shackleton, though not for much longer. The whole time Shackleton sat slumped below us, propped up against the bookcase, rubbing his head.

A firm hand gripped my wrist and detached it from Sammy's ear. A large, middle-aged man with a receding forehead and small moustache had Sammy's arm deftly twisted behind his back and was making ponderous soothing noises. Sammy struggled for a while, but, unbelievably, he too seemed to have tired at last, and gradually quietened down, spitting and cursing. Mrs Shackleton hovered near the door, still twisting the tea-towel.

"Okay, son, okay," said the man, steering Sammy out of the door, "that's enough now. Pick on someone your own size, Samson, who do you think you are, Joe bleeding Bugner? That's right, come along ..."

"All right, all right," said Sammy, "let me alone. I won't touch the little runt."

"We'll just make sure of that, sir, by seeing you off the premises. Come along, now."

"All right!"

The man directed Sammy down the stairs. There was something unmistakably fuzz-like about his handling of Sammy. I assumed he was off duty.

Mrs Shackleton watched them go, gazing at Sammy in awe. Then she went over to her son, who was still propped up against the bookcase.

"You all right, Everard? Whatever did you do to make that nice Mr Plummer so angry? I thought he was going to kill you. A good job your father wasn't home, he'd have had heart failure."

"Ask the Three Graces here, Mother. I'm not sure I know myself what it's all about."

Mrs Shackleton turned a respectful gaze on me. I blushed.

"Well, you see, Mr Plummer thought that Shackleton had done something that he didn't like – well, he'd been to the pub at lunchtime, I think he often does, and his brain was inflamed – of course it's partly the strain of the summer term – he's had so many tennis tournaments to arrange – it's enough to unhinge anybody."

"I see." She didn't. "But Miss, I still don't quite understand what you ladies are doing here."

"Ah! Well – Mr Plummer was with us when the ... er ... misunderstanding broke out."

"I see. Well, Everard, we'll talk later. I'd better go down and see what's happening. What a good thing Barry was at home."

"Yes. It's a good thing he's a policeman."

Damaris looked disapproving, but I did not need her to tell me I was being unsuitably flippant. It was an awkward situation. Morally, I suppose, we were dust beneath Mrs Shackleton's feet, but she would behave as though she owed us respect, and if it was going to get us out of painful confessions it seemed only human to take advantage of it.

"Would you like some tea? I think we're all a bit shocked."

"Thank you. A cup of tea would be very nice."

"I'll put a bit of a noggin in it, I think. My heart's fluttering like a bird."

With a final worried glance at her Everard, Mrs Shackleton left and closed the door. I slumped to the floor. Damaris took the chair from Shackleton's desk and sat astride it, resting her chin on her arms across the back, staring at Shackleton.

"You all right?" she said.

"Yes, thank you, Miss."

She sat up with a jerk. "You can cut that out, Wunderkind. I'll have you know I'm here against my better judgment."

"What judgment?" said Shackleton mildly.

"The bit that said we should have let Mr Plummer's nature take its course. It was Anne's idea to save your life, and as it's her kid we came along."

"Let's get this straight. What Mr Plummer was trying to say in his unique three-dimensional way is that I'm responsible for Anne's condition."

"Don't be timid with language all of a sudden, Shackleton. You got her pregnant, that's all."

Shackleton blushed. "I wasn't trying to spare my own feelings."

"Well we're all beyond the euphemism stage."

"Yes, all right. But listen, are you sure? I'm not trying to get out of it, but, Miss Slade, didn't you say it had nothing to do with me – that day we went to Haworth and you said she wasn't well?"

"Thanks for reminding me. We didn't know then. We found out at the same time as Mr Plummer. Of course we thought it was him. Good God, it never even occurred to me."

"I don't see why. I assumed you all told each other every-thing."

"You mean," said Damaris, "you thought we would all dash

home with the good news that we'd got laid by the Head Boy, as if we'd won something? Do you think it's something to be proud of?"

"If you were ashamed of it, why do it?"

"I was drunk."

"Oh come off it, Miss Fotheringay, don't play the outraged virgin. You may have been drunk, but anyone who can find prophylactics in the dark is in full possession of the faculties that count."

"Insolent prig," muttered Damaris, shuddering at the memory.

"And could you please pass the ciggies, they're just behind you."

Damaris threw them at him.

"But when did all this happen?" I asked.

"After Terry's party."

"She persuaded me to stay," said Shackleton.

Damaris opened her mouth and shut it again. "I refuse to discuss it."

Anne was still sitting curled up on a corner of the bed, plucking at the candlewick.

"There's no need, I've got witnesses," said Shackleton.

"Damaris, dear, why didn't you tell us? Warn us, I should say. All this might never have happened."

"Why didn't I? Why didn't you? Why didn't Anne? Because we were ashamed to, that's why."

"Thanks," said Shackleton, passing round the No. 6. "What a fuss about nothing. You make it sound as if you'd been licking the cat's bum in some secret ceremony. As I said, I assumed you told each other everything. That's what women do, isn't it?"

"Little Women, perhaps, but it's not what grammar-school teachers do when they get laid by one of the kids."

Shackleton shrugged. We sat in silence for a while. Then I said, "Well, let's get practical. The baby's yours. What are you going to do about it?"

"Whatever I can."

"Zilch."

"It's true I can't support it at the moment. But I'm prepared to admit responsibility." He spoke with a slight frisson of Queen and Country.

"That won't bring home the bacon."

"She doesn't want to ...?"

"No, she doesn't."

"Well, I'm glad. We should be working towards a society where people can mate in a natural way without being stigmatized for it."

"You're certainly doing your part."

"I'm sorry. I can't do anything else at the moment."

"Sammy won't marry her now, you know."

"I never wanted to marry Sammy," said Anne, in a small grey voice.

"Do you want to marry the magic carpet here?" I said, indicating Shackleton.

She shook her head.

"Anne doesn't have to marry anyone," said Damaris. "Carlo and I will look after her. I certainly don't intend to marry. Men are slobs. Even the intelligent ones fart and pick their noses."

"They're the worst," I said, nervously. Now was the obvious time to break the news about my condition, but Mrs Shackleton came in with the tea-tray. I went to the bathroom.

For some minutes I sat on the throne, my head bowed in my hands, trembling with delayed shock. The bruises began to hurt, and the muscles in my arms quivered. The suburban prettiness of the bathroom questioned the reality of what had happened next-door; turquoise tiles, applied by an amateur hand, turquoise low-flush suite, powder-pink mats and lavatory-seat cover, the wallpaper pink rosebuds on a white ground, a plaque over the bath requesting the user to leave it as they found it, in verse. A pleasant bathroom, obviously belonging to somebody's mother. It was only when I stood up and made to flush the toilet that I noticed the healthy gush of blood streaming down the turquoise porcelain. I laughed out loud. How could I previously have failed to give thanks every day that I was not pregnant? Another piece of luck. Perhaps life might be worth living after all. I stuffed my knickers with a thick wadge of toilet paper. On the landing I intercepted Mrs Shackleton and asked her for a tampon. She made a conspiratorial face and took me into her bedroom.

"Here you are, Miss. Take two."

"Oh no, one is enough, thank you."

"Would you like a Veganin?"

"No, thank you. I have to drive."

"Miss?"

"Yes?"

"Can't you tell me what's going on? I'm worried. I don't

understand why that Mr Plummer was so angry with Everard. What's he done? It must be something terrible. It's so unexpected. He's never been in trouble. Oh dear." She put her hands to her face. "I'm afraid of knowing. I feel queer. It's the shock, I expect. Or the Change, maybe. I don't understand that boy, Miss. He's grown right away from us."

I looked around the room for inspiration. There was a faded carpet with floral motif, more candlewick on the bed, and shiny beige curtains. The bedroom suite was the dumpy varnished oak that bludgeoned the room's attempt at fragility. On the dressing table, with its glassed-in crocheted runner, were bottles of Avon cosmetics, Edwardian glass knick-knacks and a photograph of Everard as a baby. The room breathed the low-aspiration, high-security domestic certainties of my own suburban home. I had chafed under those certainties, but now they seemed touching and worthy of protection. It was not that I thought Mrs Shackleton naïve. More than most mothers she would be able to face the disruption the truth about her son would bring. But her pain would be just as great. Why hurt her gratuitously? She was a good woman. Again I envied Shackleton.

"The point is, it isn't my secret. I can't betray confidences. Do you understand?"

"Not really, Miss, no."

"Well I can't explain, I'm afraid. But you don't have to worry. Everard's future will not be threatened. In fact I rather think he won't be affected at all. Please don't worry." I noticed with distress that it was still a joy to say his name, to have it in my mouth.

"Thank you for that, anyway, Miss." She sighed and glanced at herself in the wardrobe mirror. "We've never really got close to that boy. Blood is thicker than water, after all. Though that's nonsense, really. You never know what you're getting, even if it is your own, do you?"

"What do you mean, Mrs Shackleton?"

"About his being adopted. Didn't you know?"

"No."

"Yes. He knows too, of course. I used to be the almoner, you see, in the days when they were almoners, and one of my patients died. There was this little boy of two in the house with his grandfather – Lord knows where the father was, or if there was one, if you know what I mean. The mother was very young, scarcely out of school. I can remember her lying in bed staring at everyone as if she'd had a vision of Hell and nothing else was important. She wouldn't speak. Such a desolate look. And the house where the grandfather and the boy lived was desolate, too. It moved me very much, Miss, more than what you might call downright sordid things. So I offered to adopt the child and the grandfather was glad. He didn't know anything about children. He wasn't interested, just kept talking about his dead wife all the time. Terrible atmosphere for a child."

"Thank God the mother died. Thank God you were there to take him."

"Yes, I suppose so. But he's never really felt like ours." She sighed and smiled. "The trouble is, we can't take any of the credit for his brains, but we have to take the blame for it if he gets in trouble."

"No you don't. You certainly do not. Not in this case, anyway."

"It won't stop me worrying, though."

"No. Has Mr Plummer gone?"

"Yes. He promised to leave Everard alone. He was a bit shaken, I think."

"I should think so. He's normally quite law-abiding."

When I went back into Shackleton's bedroom the three of them were sipping tea, he being mother. He handed me a cup. I looked at him with a new detachment. How I would have loved to know what became of the memories of those first two years, what patterns of assumption might have been formed from observing his miserable grandfather and his demented young mother. Or had the years of "normal home" driven them so far into the unconscious that they were for ever at rest? I regretted that I would have no opportunity to ask him.

"Have we got anywhere?" I asked.

"Where would you like to go?" asked Shackleton.

"You're still feeling co-operative, then."

"Tell me what you would like me to say and I'll say it."

"Sorry."

"Sorry. Sorry? To you two? No way. To Anne, yes. But even so, you're not being very realistic. Did you expect me to carry a packet of rubbers around in school? If the brothers found them they'd probably throw me out, at least withdraw my common-room privileges. Anyway, you're all supposed to be liberated women, why leave it up to the man?"

"Please don't use that word in this context."

Shackleton smiled a crooked smile. "Still trying to jack up your ego on my lack of years, Miss Slade? You can't go on doing that for ever, you know."

"It isn't your lack of years that soothes my ego, Shackleton. It's your lack of sense of what you've done, of what you'll become if you go on picking up and discarding at your present rate. We've learnt from the experience, I think, but you don't seem to have. It's alarming in you. I thought you really did have a sense for the eternal verities."

"I'm too young, Miss Slade. One has to be nearer death, like you, for eternal verities."

"You're to be pitied, Shackleton."

"Oh, thank you, Miss. 'Pitied!' What balls. Why dress up simple facts in consumptive notions? Look at it from my point of view for a change. You were all single women new in town without sexual partners. I'm normal, from the neck down, anyway, of course I was interested. The girls I get to meet are mostly good little Catholics, or real scrubbers. It's possible, but hardly worth the trouble. So –" He shrugged. "I'm sorry if you weren't each the Only One, but I liked you all, really."

"Shut up!" shrieked Damaris. "You pass yourself round like a butter-dish and expect us to be grateful we were in the right place at the right time?"

"Okay, I understand that the group sex aspects of it are not flattering to you. But logically, you were all willing on an individual basis, so you have absolutely no grounds for complaint." He spoke like Brother Basil rejecting a petition for less rugger practice.

"But Shackleton," I said, "dignity is no outcome of logic. You could at least have shown more discretion – I mean, the entire female staff –"

"Not Mrs Prudhoe."

"Well, ring her up. Why should she be different?"

"Then you did know about Miss Cromwell. In that case I don't have any sympathy for you. You knew I was a monster from the start."

"Miss Cromwell?"

"Miss Cromwell?"

"Miss Cromwell?"

Even Anne had sat bolt upright. We stared at Shackleton, and at one another. The Mystery of the Ladies' Loo revealed. Her too. It was incredible. At this rate Shackleton would double the population of North Manchester in five years. I was beginning to get light-headed.

"Are you sure that's everyone, Shackleton? How about your mother?"

"That's cheap." He blushed. "Leave her out of this."

"No I won't, not if you insist on this pseudo-sophisticated artist's licence attitude and won't face facts. You've fathered two children – that we know of. Miss Cromwell seemed capable of dealing with the situation herself, but Anne is different. She's more vulnerable. It was crappy of you to take advantage of her. You could at least admit that."

Anne wriggled and looked distressed. "I don't want you to crusade on my behalf, Carlo. I would never have told Everard the baby was his if it hadn't been for Sammy making such a fuss. People never leave me alone. I told Everard he could come. It wasn't his fault."

"Come where?"

"To the house." She sighed and pulled a lock of tarnished hair, now seemingly more grey than blonde, that slanted across her forehead. "Remember when I came back from camping? And I was at home sick? Well, Everard called and asked if he could come round in the lunch hour. He had the car at school. I said he could and – well, we were alone ... it was inevitable, really."

"I am sorry about that," said Shackleton. "I'm afraid I rather assumed you were on the pill, because of Mr Plummer."

"I was, but somebody pinched them at camp."

"Oh. That was rotten luck."

"Yes, wasn't it," I said, "jolly rotten. Really awful, rotten luck." I was irritated by the realization that Anne had been the easiest pushover of all, was still a little awed in Shackleton's presence.

"You mean," said Damaris, finally shocked into lowering her voice, "You mean it was in our own house, Anne?"

"Yes. On the sofa, actually."

I remembered that day. I remembered standing with Terry Yeats watching Shackleton arrive in the Morris Traveller. That was the day Grass was creamed by Mr Dacre. The day Shackleton kissed me in the music room. It was with even more profound, cold fascination that I contemplated him now. Of one thing I was certain; no woman could have behaved with such blithe cupidity. Perhaps I was wrong, but it seemed to me that this gentlemanly, undiscriminating promiscuity almost indeed amounted to a kind of innocence that a woman could not share.

Damaris stood up. "I've had enough. I suggest we thank Mrs Shackleton for the tea and go home."

We all stood up.

"Listen," said Shackleton, in persistently enlightening mood, "I wish we could part on friendly terms. I'm sure in time you'll come to share my view. Could I call in some time during the holidays? I'd like to talk to you all, really."

"Send us long, literary letters," said Damaris, "that we can trade in for hard cash when you're famous."

"Okay. I'll expect you'll be famous too, Miss Fotheringay. I'm looking forward to hearing the opera."

"Perhaps you'll conduct it," said Damaris, coldly.

"Perhaps I will."

Damaris pushed past him and opened the door, sweeping a plastic bust of Wagner to the ground as she did so. We all followed her.

Mrs Shackleton and Barry, the policeman, were sitting on deck chairs in the garden. We resisted invitations to linger.

Shackleton accompanied us to the car. He stood on the pavement and watched as we drove down the road. His hands were in his pockets, the careless hair dipping over his eyes. The sight, as usual, affected the heartbeat. I felt a fit of the if-onlys coming on and sadly repressed them. The atmosphere in the car was heavy.

"Well, girls," I said, trying to inject a note of Joyce-Grenfell-like optimism into my voice, "that's that." Damaris and Anne said nothing. I knew them both to be taking private farewells of Shackleton in their own way. I knew, too, that he had spoilt us for other men. Following Damaris' lead we would deal in absolutes in future; garden varieties would not do.

"You know we really ought to start making decisions now." Still silence. Damaris sighed, her breath ruffling the pages of the telephone directory that lay on the dashboard. "Like whether we want to renew the lease on the cottage."

"Of course we do," said Damaris at last. She turned round to Anne. "You want to stay and have the baby with us, don't you?"

"Oh yes, please. I don't feel so bad now you both know everything."

"I wish I could say the same," said Damaris.

"It will be fun having a baby in the house. I hope it's a girl. It would be hard on a boy to be brought up by three women."

"I shall never marry," said Damaris.

"Nor shall I, probably."

"Well, if you two don't, I hope I won't."

"Men are so – *deprimierend*," said Damaris. "Life is so much more civilized without them. I mean, what can they give you that a woman can't, except sex?"

"Umm. There remains the slight problem of what to do for sex without them."

There was a pause. Then Damaris and I looked at each other and laughed.

"Sublimate," she said. "Sublimate and be free."

"Sex?"

"Yes. I could write an opera about it."

"About Shackleton."

"Yes. Why not? I'm fed up with carding machines, anyhow."